ERIC P. JOHNSON

Rings of the Santa Order

Contents

1

The Awakening

Tears pressed from the corners of his eyes, clamping down his eyelids so tightly that it dribbled a thin salty stream to his pillowcase. His ears flooded with the rushing sounds of a thousand violent rivers crashing over rugged river rocks as he felt his heartbeat quicken, thundering under his ribcage.

A deathly cold dark presence had crept into the room and pressed down heavily upon the sleeping Joseph, pinning him to his mattress under an unseen weight. With every pounding heartbeat, the unwelcome intruder drove out all feelings of happiness from the hauntingly still room.

Joseph's right middle finger burned like an ember fueled by bellows, and the majestic gold ring with curious markings and gems on his right hand was the source of the scorching pain. Frigid fingerlike projections emerged from the black mass and adhered securely to the round band, giving its wearer immortality.

Screeching and shrills permeated Joseph's room each time the dark figure tried to pry the ring from Joseph's possession. Yet, magically bound to the finger, the precious metal was loyal and unremovable unless willfully separated, with the understanding of surrendering to mortality's grasp.

Impossible, nobody can take the ring from me! The bewildered man's thoughts scrambled inside his head. The skin of his finger writhed in pain, stretching and tearing small fissures as the ring cut into his flesh and slowly began slipping over his knuckle.

Joseph clenched his right fist and grasped the ring with his opposite hand, gripping it firmly, refusing to relinquish it. Then, suddenly, from out of nowhere, a wadded-up cloth bag flew through the air at the attacker, followed by a small object that penetrated the dark figure and smashed against the wall before falling to the floor in a bent metallic mess. Instantly, the dark mass dispersed, leaving the room still and void of evil.

What in the world, or not of this world, just happened? He thought. Turning his head to the left, Joseph peered around the room, giving an inspection of the crime scene. All was in its place, nothing disturbed.

Joseph's sweat-soaked plaid pajama shirt adhered uncomfortably to his back and chest, and his thundering heartbeat began to slow and normalize as he lay motionless in his bed, processing his assault. Was this all a dream, or did this happen in actuality? He questioned further.

His confusion and anxiety had temporarily distracted him from the burning pain emanating from his right middle finger. With the ring securely fixed in its proper place, Joseph held his hand up in the air, using the curtain-filtered streetlight entering his room as his light source; he inspected his finger further. Darkened tissue under the ring extending to the knuckle was evident of charred flesh, even in the dimly lit bedroom.

So, this was real, after all. Confirming thoughts engulfed his mind and twisted his guts with inner nausea that only comes with the most adventurous roller coaster ride.

Sitting up, Joseph gathered the wadded-up cloth bag on his bed, then reaching down to the floor, retrieved a crumpled pair of half-moon reading spectacles.

Oh, you went and did it this time, didn't you? Gently, the shaken man began to reshape the brass-framed glasses carefully. There you are. Good as new. Joseph said in a soft voice. Grabbing the cloth bag at the foot of the bed, the husky fellow breathed a steamy vapor against the foggy lenses and gently polished the aged-looking glass. "You have been courageous and heroic tonight, and I am very grateful. He spoke to the antique spectacles and soft cloth bag with all the tenderness and deep respect of talking to a dear friend.

Joseph carefully placed the shiny eyewear in the pocket of his pajama shirt and rose to his feet. Making his way to his desk, he turned on his lamp for better lighting. Rolling his finger side to side to inspect the charred skin, he noticed the darkened areas began to lighten in color and heal magically before his eyes. Slowly, the rejuvenated skin appeared more natural, and within moments, all pain had completely subsided. The healing properties of immortality received through the ring restored his finger to perfect health.

It was just after 1 am, and Joseph's mind raced with thoughts, every ounce of sleep being chased away by the awakening. If this were a nightmare, it would have been the most realistic one ever experienced. He thought. There was no mistake about it, however. It had all happened just like the former investigative reporter had experienced it. This paranormal event would have been more confusing and unbelievable a few years ago. Now, things were very much different. Joseph reflected.

Joseph Amesbury was now living in a world of magic, genuine miracles, and the responsibility of bringing peace through his selfless acts. A man once admired by his press colleagues and the media as a top-notch reporter, Joseph had abruptly abandoned his illustrious career. Not having any family to be concerned about his disappearance, he now lived a life cloaked in secrecy under a new name. With the aid of magic, he crafted a new identity for himself. On official records, his name was now registered as Asher Moby Jupes.

For those who knew Joseph, his abrupt absence from the Daily Gazette was unusual for his character and heavily shrouded in mystery. Not only had the famed reporter been missing in action, but his beautiful secretary, Annabel Dixon, also abruptly resigned after his disappearance and refused to leave any forwarding address. Like Mr. Amesbury, Ms. Dixon was never heard of again, giving rise to several juicy rumors in the Gazette office that swirled around like a dust storm on a hot summer afternoon.

Sadly, after their disappearance, a few dishonest reporters at the Gazette seized the opportunity to take advantage of the missing couple's absence by crying foul play against the secretary, stirring the steamy pot of fiction. Those attention-seeking opportunistic reporters had hoped their scandalous articles in the paper would yield increased sales and lead to possible career promotions.

The short-term profit bump at the Gazette was successful and fueled other gossip drenched in malice, deceit, and guilt of unsubstantiated claims. Yet for others with a more romantic outlook on life, juicy conversations of a secret lover's rendezvous involving a handsome reporter and his stunning secretary running away were often enjoyed as a favorite pastime at the office drinking fountain. Regardless of the rumor, the stories surrounding Joseph and Annabel became the most widespread gossip in London.

Following the couple's disappearance, investigational reports revealed that Mr. Amesbury's desk drawers, his personal belongings, and unfinished articles he had been working on had been abandoned and undisturbed.

With no leads, signs of a struggle, or missing belongings apart from his favorite mocha fedora being unaccounted for, the famed reporter appeared to have vanished into thin air. Unable to close the unsolved case, detectives simply had no choice but to move his name to the Missing Person's Report. Unfortunately, in due time, the stories, gossip, and scandals surrounding Joseph and Annabel became forgotten, like the buried news articles of yesterday.

Asher stepped away from his desk a few paces, paused, and stood in the silent room. The low incandescent light radiating from the bulb of his desk lamp produced a rough silhouetted shadow on the aged gray-wood plank board wall in front of him. Squinting intently at the blurred outline of his belly, his face instantly relaxed, and his mouth gap widened, revealing his pristine white, perfect smile. It was Asher's most distinct feature and helped distract from the large belly spilling over his beltline.

What has happened to my physique? I'm not the Greek god I once was, Asher chuckled. His giggle was enough to make the shadowed outline of his tummy move like the waves rolling toward the shoreline. His animated shadow caught him off guard, provoking further laughter. Placing his hands on his hips, he pushed his pelvis forward, arching his back and shoulders backward far enough until the stretch produced audible pops with welcomed pressure relief to his lower back.

"Ah, that was a good one, wasn't it, Guinevere?" Asher questioned out loud in his empty, dimly lit room.

"You a Greek god?" A snickering voice came from the front pocket of his shirt."

Asher lowered his chin to his chest, "Alright now, no need to be so sassy, Guinevere. After all, I straightened up your frame and polished your lenses." Asher felt a slightly irritated thrash come from his pocket.

"And about time, too!" the voice thundered from his pocket. " I was feeling a little neglected and under-appreciated. I just sat in your pocket, waiting to be taken out. Next time you are in trouble, I might not come flying in to rescue you!"

Joseph gently pulled the glasses out of his pocket and rested them on his desk. Guinevere was brass framed, simply constructed, and had arms curled mildly at the ends. Beautifully engraved outer arms with curious shapes and text matched the engraving on Asher's ring, which was well fixed to his hand. The glasses appeared to be regular spectacles to the average person and did not have animated features, moving eyes, or even a mouth to explain her lippy expressions.

It was a mystery how a voice would emanate from the brass spectacles, with the only moving parts being the hinged arms. Magic was the only explanation, and given all the magic surrounding Asher, it wasn't hard to accept.

Mr. Jupes looked down at Guinevere and continued, "I want to ask you something. How did you and Mr. Baggins fly across the room?"

Mr. Baggins was the name Asher gave his trusty magical bag, not that it looked like a hobbit, but that it was magical, and he couldn't think of a better name for a bag.

The metal glasses vibrated slightly on the desk, then spun around and faced Asher.

"Well, if you must know," the smart-alecky voice countered, "In times of great need or peril, only having all of us together can we defeat such an evil entity."

Asher flashed a curious look back at his brass friend. "All of us? Are you saying I cannot defeat evil alone, but only if Mr. Baggins, you, and I are together?"

The glasses quivered, "Don't be so full of yourself and your magical abilities, Mr. Jupes. But yes, You, Mr. Baggins as you call him, myself, and the ring together form a powerful magic hard to defeat. Granted, you have your magical abilities to be admired, but great magical power can only be brought about by all of us together in one place with the same purpose."

Asher pulled the office chair from under his desk and sat down.

"This doesn't quite answer my question, though. How did you and Mr. Baggins suddenly appear out of thin air and fly across the room? I did not summon you."

Guinevere gave a slight vibration and responded softer, respectfully, "Divine powers intervened. Regardless of our location, we will reunite to give strength when such events happen."

The brass spectacles spun around, and she folded her arms closed. "I'm feeling tired now; put me back in your pocket so I can rest." Her sassy voice demanded before falling silent once again.

Asher tenderly lifted the glasses, walked to his closet door, and placed them in his sizeable red coat pocket with white furred cuffs. Walking away from his closet, he could have sworn he heard a muffled snore rumble behind him. Asher had grown to appreciate Guinevere despite her extreme sassiness and was profoundly grateful for her constant vigilant work watching over him. After all, Guinevere had protected Mr. Jupes so valiantly this evening.

Asher again approached his desk and gathered Mr. Baggins with the utmost respect. "Thank you, Mr. Baggins," he said warmly to his cloth-confidant. Folding the soft red Santa bag, he respectfully placed it on the golden silk pillow under his bed.

Mr. Baggins was an extraordinary bag that communicated with Santa through small inscribed parchment that would magically appear to provide instructions, give guidance, or deliver items to Santa upon request. Being crafted by magic, the indestructible velvet-like bag could stretch, shrink, or morph into the size appropriate for the need, though only if used for good, not for self-serving purposes. The plush container was crafted from the softest material ever imagined, incomparable to any fabric made or created on earth. It was reversible in color with intrinsically detailed embroidery work on the red side or solid plain black on the other.

During World War II, when Kristoff Christkindle used it, black was the choice of color to avoid attracting attention. Asher, on the other hand, preferred to keep the majestic ruby red rather than the dark ebon color used in the past.

Suddenly, a thundering knock at the front door rattled the aged door, quickening Asher's heartbeat. Who in his right mind is standing at my front door this early morning?" the alarmed, flushed-faced man questioned. Tiptoeing to the doorway, Asher smashed his ear against the door for an investigational listen.

BANG, BANG, BANG, the door violently shook in opposition, slamming against Asher's unsuspecting head pressed firmly against the heavy wood. The anxious doorstep visitor continued aggressively pounding the old oak door, flooding Asher with additional adrenaline. Asher, now standing, was rubbing his sore head with his shaking hand. "Who is it? Who is there?" Asher demanded. Straight away, the room fell silent and still.

2

The Great Forefathers of Christmas

A sher's pulsating headache failed to divert his attention from the profound silence that ensued after the relentless knocking on his door. *Who, in their right mind, would pound on my door?* He pondered. Crouching down, he cautiously peered through the ancient keyhole in an attempt to unravel the mystery. The makeshift spyhole disclosed the presence of someone standing beside his door, yet the minuscule opening restricted him to merely glimpsing the midsection of a substantial torso.

"I bear an urgent message," came the hushed response in a thick German accent from the other side of the door. Even concealed behind the sturdy wood barrier, Asher promptly recognized the voice of his predecessor, Kristoff Christkindle. Twisting the brass knob, Asher swung open the door, welcoming his friend with the most substantial bearhug the visitor had ever received. "Delighted to see you, Mr. Christkindle, though you do appear somewhat altered from my recollection. What brings you to my abode at this early hour?" The warm glow on his guest's countenance reciprocated and acknowledged the warm reception. "Yes, I've shed a few pounds, haven't I? May I come inside? And please, Asher, do call me Kristoff."

Closing the door behind him, Asher ushered Kristoff to the oversized stuffed leather chair in the entry and invited him to sit. "This must be of the utmost importance for you to seek me out in the dead of night," Asher remarked, sitting on the matching stuffed ottoman at Kristoff's feet. Kristoff placed the tips of his right thumb and index finger over each eyelid, gently massaging his weary eyes. "Yes, in the middle of the night."

Following Asher's selection as the next Santa, Kristoff, the former Santa, awoke to find Guinevere perched on his nose, trembling in frightful concern. The quivering of the magical creature on the bridge of his smeller roused the portly man, drawing his attention. Yet, Kristoff's focus shifted swiftly to the curious return of Guinevere after her allegiance had transferred to another. Before dwelling on this further, swirling green and red smoke vapors filled the brass spectacle's lenses, unveiling an unusual vision that shook the former Santa to his core. The vision depicted Asher's enchanted ring being forcibly removed, revealing a brief tenure as Santa and an unidentified assailant. More distressing to Kristoff than the brevity of Asher's service was the revelation that his successor would be attacked, the ring forcibly taken, suggesting the involvement of dark magic. Kristoff feared that he and Asher were already acquainted with this ominous vision.

The night Kristoff received the visitation from Guinevere, Asher was still a neophyte to the bestowed magic. As a newcomer to the Santa Order, he required time to comprehend the significance of such a revelation. Sensing the need for a more subtle jarring from a familiar magical entity, Kristoff decided to visit Asher unexpectedly.

"I attempted to arrive earlier in the evening, Asher. Two days ago, I suddenly felt compelled to visit you urgently. I sensed a connection to the vision I shared with you earlier, prompting me to leave Germany swiftly. No longer traveling by magic, I am at the mercy of modern transportation, disappointing in many ways." Asher grinned in agreement.

Kristoff surveyed the room and then returned his gaze to Asher. "This home in Maine is splendid. I've always admired cape-style houses with steep roofs and built-in dormers. Brilliant craftsmanship and architecture. Leaving London must have been challenging, I suspect." Asher nodded, "Indeed, leaving London was difficult. After some time and many patrons visiting our Christmas boutique, I encountered an old colleague, an investigational reporter. It wasn't intentional or investigational, just unfortunate luck. We dodged a potentially significant news story, but we wondered how long until someone would recognize us and alert the media. That event forced us to part ways from our beloved home in Europe." Asher gazed down, stroking his silky white beard.

Kristoff glanced at the majestic grandfather clock against the far wall, then back at Asher. "Apologies for disturbing you so early in the morning," he chuckled slightly. "I had the Taxi driver pass by your house before heading to my hotel to get an idea of where you live. I noticed your inside lights on and saw your shadow pass by one of the windows. I had the strangest feeling of stopping and checking on you, somehow related to that vision I warned you about. I also have new information that may shed light on the intruder in the vision and the attempt to take your ring. So here I am, Asher, checking on you."

Asher stood and paced the floor before speaking. "Your timing is impeccable," Asher said. "The vision you mentioned happened just before your arrival, but with some variation from the one you shared with me." Kristoff stared intently at Asher as he turned and paced the floor again. "What do you mean it wasn't the same as the vision I had seen?" Kristoff questioned. Stopping midway through his pace, Asher turned and faced Kristoff. "I don't believe it was a man you saw trying to remove my ring. It was not human-like, something of dark magic,

11

not a physical body but an authentic force of power. The whole thing felt like a horrible dream, the most frightful nightmare, and I wasn't sure I would ever wake up."

Asher recounted his alarming paranormal experience with Kristoff over the next hour, trying to lighten the mood with warm pumpkin spice rolls and chilled Yoo-hoo chocolate-flavored soda. Curiously, both men found that a cold Yoo-hoo could magically ease even the most stressful moments.

In the time following his relinquishment from the Santa role, Kristoff had transformed from a portly figure to that of a healthy, average 70-year-old male. His snow-white beard, once adorned with silky ringlets, succumbed to a close shave, revealing a younger face accentuated by a two-inch vertical scar on his right cheekbone. The only remaining facial hair was a slickened handlebar mustache resting below his nose and curling up precisely at the corner of his lips. "I must say, Kristoff, that mustache is truly admirable." Asher complimented. Kristoff pinched the curl of the handlebar whiskers and rolled them into a tight point, "I always fancied the look." Kristoff grinned, beaming with pride, "couldn't wait to have one myself."

The two men chuckled in agreement as they discussed the physiological transformation, and then Kristoff grew silent and reserved. "Asher, following the vision, I felt an unrelenting prompting to reflect on the night Gunter was shot. I distinctly remember Hanz being hauled away in a transport vehicle by the arresting Nazi soldiers. But I have always wondered what became of him." Kristoff's voice lowered, pausing briefly. "This is why I have been in Germany. I have been seeking out the answer this entire time." A look of concern shone in Asher's eyes as he stared intently at Kristoff. "Were you successful in your research?" Asher inquired. Kristoff nodded affirmatively. "Yes, it wasn't easy, given the many years since the war. I discovered that he escaped from the transport vehicle that night, making his way to a rendezvous point established by him and Gunter. Further intel reveals that he escaped to Argentina, hoping to help establish the 4th Reich."

Asher leaned forward with a puzzled look. "So why all the worry? Surely, he has passed away since then and is no longer a threat." Kristoff stood abruptly and, with a firm voice, sharply corrected Asher. "This is precisely why I am here tonight. However, I believe he may be alive through some form of dark magic. Before retreating to Argentina, he discovered a book lost to the Santa order for many years, thought to have been amongst Hitler's most guarded treasures. Hanz must have found its location and made off with it." Kristoff said. "So what is in this book, and why is it so guarded?" Asher questioned.

Kristoff tipped back his head and finished off the last of his Yoo-hoo. Resting the can on the table next to him, he leaned back in his chair and grinned at his friend. "Asher, pass me another pumpkin spice roll; we have some catching up to do."

The first rays of the early morning sun filtered through the short branches and narrow crowns of the towering coniferous trees lining the street in front of Asher's home. In a scene reminiscent of a masterpiece painted by a divine artist, the sunlight illuminated the dark gray bark, casting soft gray shadows on the mature balsam fir trees. Grouped rays of light traversed the front yard, reaching the heavy wooden door adorned with a firmly attached metal number seven. A sliver of morning light slipped through the skeleton keyhole of the antiqued brass hardware, creating the smallest circle of light on Asher's pant leg. "Would you look at that?" Asher exclaimed, pointing at the toasty spherical light. "Daylight came rather fast, didn't it?" Kristoff replied.

Several hours had passed since the two men engaged in an intense conversation, surrounded by the warmth of chocolate soda and delectable pumpkin spice rolls. Kristoff slid to the edge of his seat as the catch-up session neared its end. "I have truly enjoyed this early morning rendezvous, Asher, but my time has come to depart. And I almost forgot to share the message that brought me here in the first place. I want to inform you that the wicked Hanz successfully escaped Germany and headed to Argentina before the war's end. He rendezvoused with others seeking to establish what some have called a 4th Reich."

"If he did escape," Asher interrupted, "What happened to the book you spoke of earlier this evening?"

"We call it The Great Forefathers of Christmas," Kristoff explained. "It's a collection of journals dating back to the first Santa in the Sacred Order. The book reveals magical secrets, including those of your enchanted ring. Our secrets and wizardly abilities are detailed in it. However, the missing magical gem from the ring is of particular concern if discovered by someone not associated with the Magical Order and used for evil."

Kristoff paused for a moment, pensive, then continued, "Corbit Hayes, one of our Santa predecessors, was attacked during WWI. The gem was knocked loose, and it was the only damage the dark magic entity could do to the Master Santa ring. Something truly evil must have been involved in the attack.

What happened to the gem?" Asher asked.

"A second ring was created using the missing gem," Kristoff continued. "It yielded magical power, including seeing into the future.

Over time, the book and ring ended up in Hitler's possession, contributing to the development of advanced weaponry. Fortunately, the Nazis didn't discover all the abilities of the magic jewel."

"Can the lost gem influence or control the Master Santa ring?" Asher inquired.

"No," Kristoff replied. "All the gems are considered part of the Master ring, which can control all other jewels when reunited."

Asher closed his eyes, absorbing the information. "How did Hanz obtain the ring and book, considering they were Hitler's most guarded possessions?"

"After Gunter was killed, Hanz must have doubled back to Berlin, located the ring and book, and successfully transported them to Argentina. I fear Hanz's grandson, Savio, now seeks the Master ring for complete rule over the earth."

As Kristoff stood up, he revealed the fate of his immortality. "This will be the last time I meet with you. My time of mortality is finished. See, they get placed back into the magic bag." "His name is Mr. Baggins," Asher proudly declared. "Fitting name indeed," Kristoff agreed. "Remember what we have discussed tonight, and keep your eyes out for Savio. May you be guided in your divine mission." With those words, Kristoff stepped out the door and vanished.

3

Magic Magnolias

The events of the morning chased away Asher's fatigue. His mind raced, rehearsing his conversation with Kristoff earlier that morning. The events, the mysterious book, and the one-gem ring whorled in his mind. Sleepless nights were not unfamiliar to Asher. Many nights in the past, he had struggled to get in that last-minute article, or the stress of the journalism lifestyle kept him awake late into the night. But this was different. He was not under pressure for an article deadline; this was stress-induced insomnia. The troubling thought that someone might possess magical powers for evil purposes weighed heavily on him. What was this person able to do with this ring? Was there an endpoint to his desire to use magic for evil? Who is this person, after all, and how will I find him?

These questions lingered throughout the morning. Asher peered up at the desk clock. The glowing green at 10:32 stared him down, making his heart leap. "I can hardly believe it!" he exclaimed to an empty room. Asher had been awake all night. "Wait until I tell Annabell what happened?" he marveled.

Readying himself for the day, Joseph stepped out of the house and headed towards Annabel. A few paces down the street, Asher's elderly neighbor awkwardly backed her lunar silver Honda Civic down the driveway. The car would lunge forward and then back. The front wheels cranked hard to the left and slowly back to the right, almost to the breaking point. Under the hood, the power steering pump whined as if it was angry that it was getting such a workout.

The older sedan's driver's taillight had a new diagonal crack spidering outward from the lower left corner, leading to a quarter-sized hole in the red plastic. A white glowing lightbulb shone brightly and was easily visible through the fractured lens. Asher couldn't help but also notice two pencil-sized yellow paint rubs extending from the impact site of the broken lens towards the bumper, revealing further damage to the car. "Not again," sighed Asher, tallying it as the third incident in the last two months.

Upon reaching the corner of the driveway, Asher discovered the victim. A faded yellow mailbox post with silver scratches was now leaning towards the street, and large gouges in the trunk of her large waterlily tree confirmed his suspicions. The impact must have been significant; a light blanket of flowers had showered down from the bloomed branches, creating a circular pattern on the ground surrounding the trunk and mirroring the tree canopy above. Asher swooped down, gathered a few of the shell pink star-shaped flowers, and placed them carefully in his shirt pocket, thoughtful not to crush them. "I know just who to give you to," he said to the flowers.

Block after block and with a smile stretching from ear to ear, Asher pressed on towards THE YEAR-ROUND CHRISTMAS BOUTIQUE. The excited flower-gatherer did his best to distract himself from his ever-relentless thoughts of Annabel rehearsing in his head. It was no use, however, and before long, he found himself giving in to the excitement of seeing Annabel. He wasn't sure if his excitement was because of sharing the news of the previous night's event or simply that he would see Annabel.

Asher had always maintained a professional relationship with Annabel. He respected her highly and would not let inappropriate feelings find a place in his mind or heart. She was stunning, and all eyes were upon her when she entered a room. *Maybe that Kristoff fellow was right after all.* The thoughts invaded his mind again. *Perhaps she may have had her eyes on me all these years. Was I really that dense?* He criticized himself further. Distracted by a woman was all new territory for Asher. For the first time in recent memory, something besides work consumed his every thought.

Asher's late arrival at the store today was uncharacteristic for him. It would undoubtedly surprise his former secretary, who was now the co-owner and the reason behind the successful Christmas boutique. Always caught up in his work, responsibilities, and the Santa order, Asher had been oblivious to any signals, hints, or flirting coming his way. Sadly, so consumed by work, he never picked up on the idea that his loyal secretary may have more than work on her mind. If it had not been for Kristoff pointing it out earlier in the day, he might not have realized it alone for quite some time. Asher's ability to observe the minuscule details surrounding him had proven to be the downfall of any potential relationships or courting of women.

Before being called to the Santa order, he had been so caught up in solving mysteries as an investigational reporter that he was blinded to the most apparent detail staring him in the face. Women swooned after him, and his cluelessness regarding the fact made him even more attractive. Before long, Asher found himself in front of the Christmas Boutique store. He felt nervous this time about seeing Annabel. A freefall feeling inside his gut filled his belly, adding to his anxiety. His breath quickened; however, it felt shallow.

Gazing through the storefront glass window, Asher noted an elderly couple standing next to an artificial Christmas tree loaded with various ornaments for sale near the front of the store. A young woman with two small children in tow was seen flipping through the pages of Santa picture books near the rear of the store. The cashier's counter was vacant, and Asher could not see her walking the store sales floor. She must be in the back looking for something, he thought. Deciding the time was right, he sucked up his courage and made his way to the front door.

"Merry Christmas!" a recorded voice sounded out from a Rubik's cube-sized speaker behind the front door when Asher stepped through the threshold. Innumerable times, entering the store day after day, Asher no longer noticed the repetitious greetings welcoming customers to the store. "I'll be with you in a moment!" a soft, distant voice called out. "No rush; take your time," Asher replied in disguise. Annabel had been busy restocking shelves in the back of the store and could not see who had entered the boutique.

Asher tiptoed to the counter and stealthily rested three magnolias beside the register before concealing himself behind the adjacent bookshelf. Peering over various Christmas books and knick-knack souvenirs, Asher secured a direct line of vision to his unexpected gift recipient. Creaking floorboards rattled under her feet as his coworker approached the cashier counter. Asher's heart accelerated with every nearing footstep. Standing frozen, he could feel the urge to swallow deep in his throat as he waited in anticipation. "What is this, and how did you get here?" Annabel's tender voice questioned the innocent flowers lying in front of her.

Annabel gathered the delicate flowers and pressed them to her round button nose, squishing the silky petals against her warm skin. Drawing a slow, deep breath, she treasured the aroma that filled her nostrils. Unaware of his actions, Asher held his breath, mimicking her while he observed her coral-pink lips stretching across her face, dimpling her cheeks. "So you like them, eh?" Asher suggested from behind the display of souvenirs. Annabel's hand dropped to her chest, holding the delicate magnolia inside her closed hand. "Did you get me these magnolias? She asked. "Did you know that these are my favorite flowers?" Asher grinned. "I think I have known for quite some time. I remember you sharing this with me in the past. You told me that as a young girl, you gathered fallen flower blossoms from the ground and placed them in a shallow water bowl in your room. The perfume-like fragrance would last for days." Annabell blushed. "So you were listening to me after all.

Do you remember anything else I shared in that conversation?" Asher's neck felt uncomfortably warm. "I uh…. It's well…um," Asher struggled to form a comprehensible sentence. "Let me help you." Annabel interrupted. "As a young girl, my family visited the U.S. on vacation during the spring. The vacation home that we stayed in had the most beautiful Waterlilly. I would lay under the tree and stare at the flowers flickering in the wind. I dreamed that someday a boy would bring me a bouquet of Magnolias, and by the gesture, I would know he was the right one for me. Asher felt his neck grow warmer and radiate up the sides of his face.

"Yes, I remember you sharing this as well. I actually have more in my pocket." His words welcomely broke the brief silent pause in the conversation. Plucking out two additional flowers from his shirt pocket, he placed them delicately in Annabel's hand, closing her fingers over them with his other hand. "Go place them in water," Asher said. Annabell's face glowed, matching the pink flowers lying on the counter. Asher did not immediately retract his hand after giving her the magnolias from his pocket, and Annabell took notice. His resting hand on hers felt warm and calming. She had been longing for this moment for years.

For Asher, It felt natural to have his hand touch hers in this new way. He did not want to let this moment end; it felt like something was right about it, like his hand was supposed to be there; something was familiar about it, though he had never held her hand before. It was a feeling of knowing someone forever after meeting them for the first time. It was hard to explain but factual.

Asher looked longly into Annabel's eyes. "Can we go to dinner tonight?" Annabel lifted her closed fist to the tip of her nose and breathed long. Trying her best not to reveal her excitement, she held her hand before her mouth, blocking the giddy smile stretching across her face. Trying to hide her emotions was useless because her wide smile pulled the corners of her lips so tightly, revealing the porcelain white teeth behind her hand.

"Yes, dinner would be smashing." She said, resting her hand on the countertop once again. *I can't believe this is really happening.* Annabel thought. *Asher...asking me on a date!* Her thoughts continued. Excited by the prospect of an actual date with Asher, Annabel could hardly contain her excitement. *This is so ridiculous,* she thought. *I am a grown woman, yet I feel like a little girl on a playground who was just informed that the cute boy in her math class has a crush on her.* As quick as the rush of emotions came, the awkward silence filled the room, and nothing came to her mind to say to Asher other than to agree to a dinner date.

Come on, Ananbel, get it together. Her mind swirled with thoughts. Suddenly, she formulated a small but coherent sentence, "How about 6:30 at Angelos Pizza?" she questioned. "I was just thinking the same place, Annabel. Great minds think alike," Asher grinned. Annabel's mouth felt dry as if she had just crammed several saltine crackers that soaked up every trace of moisture in her mouth. Her tongue felt like a wad of cotton gauze stuck between her cheeks, yet the palms of her hands felt wet and a little slimy, soaking the magnolia petals inside.

Anxious to not look nervous to Asher and wanting to keep the conversation flowing, she accidentally blurted out, "Ok, I'll kiss you there." Annabel's stomach twisted, and her cheeks flushed warm. All audible sounds in the store ceased for what felt to her like an eternity.

"I meant… I uh," she struggled to find the right words, "I'll meet you there!" she shouted, flailing her hand in front of her and knocking over a tall stack of souvenir mini-wreaths to the floor that had been stacked perfectly on the counter.

In a flash, Asher squatted down, collected the mess of mini-wreaths, and placed them back on the counter in an organized tower. "Yes, let's meet at 6:30," Asher said as he turned and headed for the door. Behind his back, Annabel's glowing face now matched the bright red stocking hanging from a display case to her left.

How in the world did that just slip out of my mouth? She questioned. *That was so embarrassing! But then again, perhaps he didn't even hear my slip-up. After all, he didn't even react when I said it.* The embarrassed Annabel replayed the event in her mind as she watched Asher walk away. Looking over his shoulder, Asher shouted back over his shoulder to Annabel, "Ok, I'll kiss ya there at 6:30," as the door gently clicked shut after him.

4

The Clarion Call

The afternoon hours slipped by, and Asher found himself back in his closet, changing out of yet another shirt. "Nope, not this one either!" he grumbled, tossing the dark green polo onto the growing pile of rejected shirts on his bed. He had spent the last 45 minutes sorting through his wardrobe, trying on shirt after shirt, only to find himself dissatisfied with how each one looked. He had never cared so much about his outfit before, but now, for some reason, it felt crucial to look his best.

He pushed hangers aside, shoving shirts to the back of the closet until his hand brushed against a black short-sleeve button-up with a tiny embroidered gray snowflake on the pocket. "This is perfect," he murmured, a smile tugging at the corners of his mouth. "Annabel got me this for my birthday last year. And after all, black is slimming." He spoke to the empty room as if someone had been listening, feeling a tiny spark of satisfaction at the find.

It was 6:05, just enough time for Asher to walk to Angelo's Pizza and meet Annabel on time. He was slightly nervous to see Annabel after her little word slip earlier in the day but, at the same time, excited to see where it would lead. I sure hope I don't mess things up. I need a miracle to help me land a second date with her. After all, that gal is way out of my league. He told himself.

Before heading out, Asher dashed back to the bathroom mirror, brushed his hair back with his fingers, and sprayed one last burst of hairspray to hold them up. Sprinkling on a few drops of his favorite cologne, he headed for the door, determined to have a wonderful evening with Annabel.

Asher had only made it three paces when a red streaking mass flew across the room out of nowhere, crashlanding in front of his feet. Startled by what happened, Asher bent over, retrieved Mr. Baggins, and placed him on the tall, narrow table by the entry door. Instantly, the bag wiggled and twisted, and a small parchment floated upward before fluttering down like an autumn leaf detaching from a maple tree branch. Asher groped at the paper several times before successfully snatching it from the air and proceeded to read with curiosity. Urgently awaits a young girl of eight in a county far from here. With nothing to eat and feeling her parents' defeat, she wished for your help this eve. This was not the first time the clarion call came to Asher to come to the rescue. His calling as Santa was not limited to the Christmas season. His responsibilities had no calendar or timeframe, and he always fulfilled his duties when beckoned by divine request.

Glancing at the timepiece on his wrist, Asher knew he had to be quick. "You better not be late for Annabel! This is your one shot at a remarkable woman, and you best not screw it up as you have for the past many years!" Came the snarky instructions from Guinevere, now vibrating irritably in his snowflake-embroidered shirt pocket. "I understand, Guinevere, but it will only take a minute. Remember, I'm Santa, and I can do magical things." The metal glasses shook again in his pocket. "Typical response. It's a wonder she stays around." The sassy glasses grumbled once again before falling silently still.

Asher zeroed in on his watch once again. "I can do this. I can make it happen." He convinced himself, and with the snap of his fingers, his Santa robes instantly replaced his dinner date attire. "See, that was fast and easy, Guinevere." Asher collected Mr. Baggins and pulled the inside red material outward, allowing the black material back inside. Now, you match my majestic ruby-red clothes; all I need now is to find the portal to get me to that family in need. Yanking the brass-handled glasses from his shirt, Asher plopped the spectacles on his nose. Instantly, red and green vapors swirled in the lenses. "Ah, there you are." He said, stepping several steps to his right, then disappeared out of sight.

The tug at his navel was intense as always, the moment his body was pulled deep into the time travel portal. It was like stepping out of a plane and entering a freefall before pulling a ripcord. The unusual thing was that his body did not flail, and the air felt still and unmoving. Asher always struggled to keep his eyes open during the freefall part of the travel portal, but this time was different. For a brief second, he could crack his eyes open just enough to glimpse his surroundings. If he hadn't known better, he would say he was staring at a TV screen while someone was racing through the channels as quickly as they could push the button on the remote. Different events, places, and people are continuously streaked by in colorful flashes of light.

It took everything he had to keep his eye open, and before he knew it, his eyelids snapped shut, leaving him in darkness with the same freefall feeling. Asher was familiar with using these portals to travel great distances, but he could never quite get used to the intense pressure in the gut. Lucky for him, it only lasted a few brief seconds.

In a flash, Asher found himself on a dirt road in the early evening with scattered street lights broadcasting a dim light intermittently in all directions. Inspecting his surroundings, Asher promptly knew he was in a foreign country, and by the looks of the architecture, it was possibly Mexico or even somewhere in South America. Red-bricked buildings pressed against one another in various stages of completion. Most buildings were single-level houses mixed with two-storied ones, creating an uneven skyline. Dark refrigerator-sized water tanks rested on rooftops, and long exposed rusty sticks of rebar towered skyward, awaiting further construction. Buildings in various colors and shades could be seen as far as the eye could behold.

The street was quiet and lonely. A few dogs could be heard barking in the distance, but no human activity was on the street. The neighborhood felt oppressed by poverty, and Asher started understanding his purpose at this wish visit. Asher had been clutching Mr. Baggins when suddenly the velvet bag began floating upward, pulling Asher forward with purpose towards a darkened, unfinished building across the street. "Walking in a foreign country clothed in a red Santa suit and being led by a magical bag is bound to get looks, Mr. Baggins," said Asher, But it was useless; the bag continued tugging and yanking Asher like a leashed hound pulling his owner towards its intended target. Step after step, approaching the rundown house, Asher felt an uneasiness growing inside him, like someone was spying on his every move from the shadows where he had just been standing moments before.

His focus was momentarily interrupted when a gust of wind outside the house he was heading to caught his eye. "You see that, Mr. Baggins? That's a history lock being created just at the corner of that house. Small dusty swirls of wind began spinning over the dirt walkway leading into the house. Two 12-inch high dirt tornadoes formed, sucking up pieces of broken twigs, dry leaves, and tiny pebbles into its windy belly. "There must be some intense emotions in that house," Asher said. "It takes a great deal of emotion to form a History lock. I first saw one of these while interviewing Kristoff as a reporter."

"It was like I had time-traveled." Asher continued addressing Mr. Baggins, "One moment, I was in London walking to an interview; the next moment, I was walking through post-bombing rubble covering the street in London back in WWII. A few steps later, it all disappeared."

It is rare to see a history lock form, and this was only the second time Asher had witnessed one being created. His first time seeing one form was shortly after becoming Santa when he noticed a childless couple adopt an orphaned child. He was invisible to the adopting parents and everyone in the tear-filled room. Still, the raw emotions impacted all in attendance, causing even Asher to be brought to tears over the tender moment of a five-year-old girl being given the gift of parents and creating a new family.

Unseen to others that day but evident to Asher were the two dusty-looking swirls of air moving into the adoption office, locking that moment into a history lock. Asher did not realize until today that these history locks resembled the events, places, and people he had streaked by while traveling through the portal earlier.

"Alright, Mr. Baggins, let's go knock on the door. We are in the right place and needed. Mr. Baggins slowly floated back down and tucked himself into the wide, glossy black belt encompassing Asher's rounded midsection. Reaching forward, Asher rapped on the paint-cracked door softly. Surprisingly, he could not detect anyone inside or hear any voices, even though the windows were wide open, allowing the cooler evening air to enter. Asher leaned closer to the door, hoping to enhance his audible detection, but the silence was all that came. Crack… a broken twig snapped under the foot of the unseen onlooker still observing from the shadows across the street from him. It was now crystal clear that someone was indeed spying on Asher.

The aged metal door in front of Asher cracked open with just enough of a gap to see two brown eyes about chest high peaking out. Staring back at them, Asher watched the pair of eyes widen, sending thin black eyebrows upward into soft arches that complimented the olive-shaped orbits. "Santa viniste!" a small, excited voice cried out behind the door. "Si estoy aquí María." Asher replied tenderly.

27

The little girl's eyebrows arched even higher with the acknowledgment accompanying her name. Asher cherished the gift of speaking all languages and was simply amazed that talking to others in a foreign language always sounded like his native English. In contrast, everyone in the conversation heard him speak in their native tongue.

By degrees and inch by inch, the flaky painted door widened until standing before Asher was a malnourished girl of about eight. Her bony shoulders were squared, and thin arms dangled at her side, poking through the armholes of her tattered but clean nightgown.

Stepping back to allow Asher to enter, Sofia's smile stretched across her face, exposing her innocent smile with two vacant spaces where baby teeth recently resided. "Will you go get your mother and father for me?" Her little head bobbed up and down, then she dashed away and out of sight, leaving the door slightly open.

Through the opened door, Asher could hear voices approaching from the back of the house, questioning the girl about a visitor at the late hour. The front door drew inward slowly, and a couple stood before Asher, young in years but aged from a hardened life.

"Santa, this is mi mamá Catalina and mi padre Mateo." the beaming-eyed Sofia said. Catalina was as thin as a reed but far from weak, and the rounded shoulders under her shirt were evidence of strenuous manual labor. Her slender nose accentuated her hollowed cheeks, and her light brown eyes peered forward, demanding attention as if pleading for help. Catalina did not speak but looked over at her husband, who stood, mouth gapped open, staring at the chubby white-bearded man cloaked in red.

Sofia reached up and pushed her dad's mouth closed. "See Papá, it's really him." Mateo's slender frame was firm and unmoving, and if he had wanted to run, it would have been useless. Seeing a man dressed as Santa standing in his doorway on a random night was enough to startle the man stiff. Mateo rubbed his deep-set eyes several times and squinted at Asher. Pushing back his charcoal-black hair, he looked over to Catalina, who was shrugging her shoulders back at him.

"¿Puedo pasar?' Asher inquired. Mateo waved his arm, welcoming Asher into his home. As Asher stepped inside, he took note of the small yet impeccably clean living space. All walls bore the warmth of red brick, held together by exposed cement, except for the far wall, which was smoothly plastered and painted a light shade of pink. A slightly crooked family picture hung on that wall, slightly tilting to the left. The dining table, crafted from reclaimed plywood, rested on stacks of bricks, and mismatched plastic yard chairs encircled it. An old Coke bottle with aging flowers, now replaced by a crystal vase, made up the centerpiece.

"Thank you for allowing me into your beautiful home,' Asher complimented in perfect Spanish. Catalina's face lit up warmly. 'I know you must find this hard to believe, but it is true. Divine magic is given to mortals to create miracles in times of need, and I was summoned here tonight by Sofia.'

"Asher walked to the far wall, straightened the crooked family portrait, and reached into his magic bag. Pulling a crystal vase from Mr. Baggins, he placed it on the table where the Coke bottle had once rested. 'Look!' Catalina exclaimed, pointing at her table. Sophia giggled, her eyes staring up at Santa. Shoving his hand into the bag again, Asher retrieved a colorful bouquet and delicately placed it into the container. 'It needs something more,' he said, tapping his bearded chin. Waving his hand over the flowers and snapping his fingers, water filled the vase to the brim. 'That will do just fine,' Asher said, feeling somewhat satisfied.

"Asher eyed the kitchen, mainly noticing empty shelves, a small bag of dried beans in the corner, a slightly wilted tomato, two jalapenos, and a small onion on a plate by the sink completed the quick survey. 'Mateo, Catalina, it would be an honor if you would allow me to put a few extra items on your shelves.'

"Mateo dropped his face into his hands. 'It has been challenging to provide for my family. Catalina works hard and does what she can, but I have struggled to find work. Sometimes, we have little to eat. I'm at a loss for what to do.' Mateo grabbed a hanky and swiped at his nose.

"'What type of work are you familiar with? What have you done in the past?' Mateo looked up, 'I have done just about everything. I have driven delivery trucks, worked in construction, and sold street merchandise.' Mateo looked blankly down at the floor. 'Sometimes I just wish I could do better for my family—a helping hand up. I have nowhere to turn.' Asher stood listening and stroking his beard. 'Yes, indeed, it would be nice to receive an instant financial increase, given the situation. It would put food on your table and in your cupboard, so to speak. However, an old saying comes to mind: If you give a man a fish, you feed him for a day. If you teach a man to fish, you will feed him for a lifetime. Mateo locked eyes with Asher, 'What does that mean for me?'

"Asher waved his hand in a semicircle motion. Nothing magically appeared in the room, but the family could hear someone running away from the house through the open window. 'Was that a dog running away?' Catalina asked. Sofia and her parents darted to the window to investigate. A new white delivery van with a door decal that read Mateo's was parked in the street next to their home with an enormous red bow attached to the windshield.

"All the legal paperwork has been taken care of, the tank is full of gasoline, and your first delivery route will be found in the glove box. You start at seven tomorrow morning. Mateo, you know deliveries; you have been taught this in previous jobs. Now go and feed your family for a lifetime.' Asher said with delight. Thrusting his hands on either side of his red-robed torso, Mateo squeezed Asher in the biggest hug he may have received.

Asher turned to the entry room and, with the same semi-circular motion, waved his arm in the air and snapped his fingers. A gust of wind swirled around the family and through the house so intensely that it forced their eyes shut until it abruptly ceased. Peering through the cracks in her eyelids, Catalina could make out a new living room set, a small wooden table with four matching chairs, and the beautiful bouquet that Asher had left previously. Her Kitchen had been transformed and would be the envy of every home—new appliances and cupboards filled with dry goods completed the remodel.

"Catalina, you can now feed your family properly." In the blink of an eye, Catalina joined Mateo, who had never stopped hugging Asher. "Gracias Papa Noel gracias," Came the grateful words from the tear-soaked parents.

Asher looked towards Sofia, who was petting the soft couch fabric in her tiny hand. Walking to her, Asher sat on the new sofa and invited her to sit with him. "Your wish for your parents brought me here tonight. It was your belief and selflessness that helped summon me."

A smile stretched across her face as she gazed towards her parents. "This night would not be complete without giving you your unspoken wish." For a third time, Asher waved his arm and snapped his finger. Sofia giggled and cheered when she looked down and found herself wearing the most exquisite white princess dress with gold glitter details, blue ribbons, pink flowers, and rhinestones in the middle.

Asher pulled back his long red sleeve slightly and peeked at his wristwatch. "This is where I must leave you. I have an urgent matter waiting for me back home." Just as he finished speaking, a frustrated grumble echoed outside the window, followed by a loud "Ahhrrr!"

Everyone dashed to the window, arriving just in time to see a man roughly pulling himself off the ground, dusting off his backside. "So it appears we had someone listening in on a conversation they hadn't been invited to. Isn't that correct, Savio?" Mateo called out in an elevated voice to his next-door neighbor.

The dusty man turned to face the four staring through the window. Savio was a man in his forties with thinning hair and a nose crooked from past fights. His thick eyebrows nearly connected over his nose, giving him a permanently intense expression. A dimpled chin and a firm jawline lent him a military-like boldness. He was dressed entirely in black—a t-shirt, pants, and shoes devoid of any brand logos. The only color on him was an antique-looking ring, its center gem held tightly by a crudely made but smooth gold band.

Looking down at the ground he had just picked himself up from, Savio grumbled, "I just saw someone dressed as Santa enter your house and got curious. I wanted a second look."

"Well, your curiosity tonight has made you a witness to the truth behind the legend of Santa," Asher said, removing his white glove and extending his hand toward the embarrassed but intrigued eavesdropper. Come closer, Savio. Let me greet you formally."

Savio hesitated only momentarily before thrusting his arm forward, gripping Santa's hand with a firm shake. His eyes widened as he noticed Asher's thick fingers and, more importantly, the ring that adorned one of them. "What a magnificent ring you have, Santa." The majestic piece of jewelry commanded Savio's attention, his curiosity fully piqued.

Instead of letting go, Savio yanked Asher's hand closer to his eyes for a more detailed inspection. "A pity, Santa—one of the gems appears to have fallen out. Curiously, I have a gem in my old ring that looks very similar." Savio smirked, the glint in his eyes betraying his thoughts. "What a coincidence, don't you think?"

Asher quickly retracted his hand, slipping it back into his silky snow-white glove. "Sorry to cut our introduction short, Savio, but I must be on my way. Good evening to you." He began to dash away, calling over his shoulder, "It was nice meeting you, though. I hope you can understand that things tend to get busy for me."

Before Savio could respond, Asher disappeared, ducking out of sight between two darkened buildings, leaving Savio standing alone, his mind racing with the implications of their encounter.

"Yes, Santa," Savio replied, his eyes narrowing with a hint of defiance. "I understand… more than you know…"

5

A Table for Two

S tanding inside his home entryway, Asher faced the front door, his stomach spinning from the nauseating Argentina portal trip. "That was super odd. The way that young man stared at my ring, you would have thought he recognized it," the bewildered Asher thought.

Mr. Baggins wiggled his way out from under the large black belt, pressing against the side of Asher's belly. "That was a tighter fit than usual!" the velvet bag muttered, floating across the room before resting on a small square pillow stacked on the sofa. Asher scrunched his face, "It wasn't that tight, Mr. Baggins. But now that you mention it, I have noticed my midsection widening somewhat."

Asher flashed a look at his profile in the hallway mirror. "I can't understand why Annabel would be interested in a guy that looks like this," he said, holding his stomach with both hands, resembling a mother expecting a baby. "Annabel, Oh no!" Hastily inspecting his watch, Asher melted—7:14 pm. "I screwed up again. Guinevere was right; knowing those sassy glasses, she may never let me live this down," he complained. "I lost track of time helping that little family, and that Savio guy didn't help matters either. Annabel must be furious!"

Asher raised his hand and snapped, emanating tiny brilliant green and white sparks between the thick pads of his fingers. Instantly, the long, flowing coat sleeves began crawling up his arms and stopped just above the elbows. His bright red suit coat appeared to be wicking up dark coloring, like a paper towel soaking up spilled ink, and continued until the entire material became solidly black.

Suddenly, a tiny embroidered gray snowflake on the shirt pocket reemerged as if an invisible magic needle was artistically sewing the white thread. Asher's glossy black boots had instantly changed into his comfortable matte black loafers, and it happened so quickly that it was undetected by any on-looking eyes. Still, the bottom of his feet tickled slightly, making him aware of the completed wardrobe change back to his previous evening date night attire.

"If only I could time travel and make things right," Asher thought. It would not be of any use, however. He knew all too well that time travel is not permitted magic for selfish purposes. Risking its use, even for such a need, could have everlasting consequences.

Asher raced out of his house so fast he forgot to lock up and sprinted to the pizza parlor, passing several storefronts and onlookers who couldn't help but stare at the jiggly man ambulating at such speeds. Even a toddler indulging in her ice cream cone momentarily stopped licking the frozen treat long enough to glimpse such a spectacle. His worried mind and the rushing wind in his ears somehow blocked out the honking horns and puttering exhaust of cars zipping past him up and down the road.

Before long, Asher approached the pizza parlor and saw the long line of customers wrapping around the front of the building to the neighboring store. A thick aroma of oven-baked pizza hung in the air, welcoming the patrons and, in some ways, could be considered cruel torture for the empty-bellied sidewalk loiterers. At least twenty or so hungry individuals crammed in line were growing impatient, anticipating the moment their teeth would sink into the savory baked dough. Angelo's Pizza was always busy and proudly served up a variety of masterpiece pies.

For both Annabel and Asher, the Angelo's Special was their favorite. The thick cheese, Italian sausage, Roma tomato, and mushrooms were somehow packed in tightly with a light tomato sauce that didn't overpower the complimentary flavors. Just the right amount of spinach added a greenery touch to the deep dish's buttery crust, encasing the delectable entree.

Asher sped past the ever-growing line of customers and burst through the parlor's front doors. The tables were packed, and no open chairs or tables were available—all but one.

Asher made his way to the lonely table to find a folded paper napkin with an ink note hurriedly scribbled on it. "She waited a long time, Asher," a deep, familiar voice from the small kitchen window clamored. "Did she say anything?" Asher asked. Angelo rubbed his flour-dusted mustache, "She didn't say a word. Didn't have to. Her eyes told the sad story. She left a note on the table and marched out. I believe the note might be for you, Asher. L'hai fatto di nuovo, Asher. You did it again," the large Pizzaiolo murmured as he disappeared from the kitchen window.

Asher snatched the neatly folded paper napkin from the table and opened it carefully, treating it like a new book being opened for the first time. Asher's heart sank as he read the note left by Annabel. *"This time it really hurt!"* was all it said, but he knew he had messed up again. What would it take to make things right with her?

The balancing act of caring for others and those who meant the most to him proved too tricky. He was trying to fulfill his Santa responsibilities, but the casualties were too close to the homefront this time. He messed things up, and Annabel paid the price. She was not alone in her pain, however. Asher hung his head low, wishing he could make things right. *Will she ever give me another chance?* He thought, extinguishing the dancing flame of the table candle with his fingers.

I should never have taken Annabel for granted. She has done everything for me and supported me all the way. I would be gobsmacked if she stayed around now. I wouldn't blame her, not even a second, if she walked away from me for good. His quiet moment of introspection found him zoning off for some time, staring blankly at the floor. "Head home and sleep this one off, Asher," said Angelo, poking his massive head through the rectangular kitchen window. "No use in trying to apologize at this time. The lady needs a little time alone to vent. Your apologies would go unheard. Give her some space, but you should let her know your error." Asher shrugged, "When did you become such an expert in relationship advice?" Asher asked. "Forty-two years of marriage and apologies make a man a little more aware. Not an expert, Asher, only aware."

Asher nodded and smiled for the first time since entering the pizza parlor. "I will follow your lead, Angelo." Picking up the pen from the table, Asher flipped the napkin over and jotted his "awareness" message, as Angelo suggested. ANNABEL, I REALLY MESSED UP!....

Asher refolded the napkin, then, with his best efforts, drew a cartoon of himself inside a large dog house on the outside of the soft paper, then tucked the note inside his front pocket. Turning for the door, Asher glanced back one last time at Angelo to see him sticking his enormous hand through the kitchen window in the classic thumbs-up position with the reassurance of his pizza-twirling friend.

The clattering tailpipe of a car reverberated through the street, seizing Asher's attention. Behind the wheel, a man in his 30s with dark, curly hair drove slowly, attentively scanning the sidewalks for potential taxi passengers. With Annabel's place just a short distance away, Asher opted for a leisurely walk, dismissing the need for transportation. He delved his hand into his pockets, continuing his stroll down the sidewalk.

Suddenly, with a swift whoosh, a radiant red mass ascended from behind Asher, brushing past his right ear and hovering in front of his face. "Mr. Baggins, what brings you here?"

In response, Asher swiftly extended his hand, firmly seizing the plush Santa bag and concealing it from view. In that fleeting moment, the upward motion of his hand inadvertently caught the attention of the eager chauffeur, who promptly applied the brakes and pulled up beside Asher. "Need a taxi, do ya?" inquired the man with a thick Chicago accent. Asher shook his head, "No, it was a mistake, sorry."

Just then, Mr. Baggins slipped out of Asher's grasp, winding himself around the rear passenger door handle, contorting into an accordion-like shape, attempting to pull the door open. Reacting swiftly, Asher reached up, securing both Mr. Baggins and the door handle, successfully opening the door. "I guess I will take that ride after all," Asher declared as he settled into the back seat, closing the door behind him.

"OK, a quick change of mind. I get it. Happens to me all the time." The driver said as he pulled away from the curb. "The name is Anthony, and who do I have the pleasure of driving tonight?" Asher began shoving Mr. Baggins into his pants pocket, "Asher, you are driving Asher tonight." Anthony craned his head around and took in a side glance at Asher. "Where we takin ya, Asher?" "1204 Packard Street, apartment five." Asher blurted out, still fighting with Mr. Baggins. "That's like two minutes away, you know," Anthony said sarcastically, staring at Asher through the rearview mirror.

"Yes, I know. I suddenly felt the need to take a cab ride, and you happened to show up at the right time." The Taxi driver nodded, pressing the accelerator down a little firmer. "Sounds good." Mr. Baggins had given up the struggle and was now relaxed, folded up nicely in Asher's pocket. "So, what is your story, Anthony? If I am correct in my assumption, you may be from Illinois. "Darn right. Born and raised in Chicago. GO CUBBIES!" The slender man said, pounding his chest with his fist. Asher made eye contact through the mirror hanging from the windshield. "So what brings you here, if you don't mind me asking?" Anthony shrugged. I don't mind at all; you can ask me anything you want. Came here in hopes of a better-paying job.

I never finished school, you see, just did any job I could find. Once the twins arrived, things got really tight financially for us, if you know what I mean. We moved here to be closer to my wife's parents and have some help with the kiddos. In fact, when you waved me down, I was just on my way to the dinner to pick her up from work."

Asher thumped his pocket, letting Mr. Baggins know he believed he knew why he was in the taxi. "How do you like working in the taxi business?" Anthony flashed a look again at Asher, "It's just another job, but if I hustle and stay out late, I can make enough to get by. If it weren't for wife working, we would be up the creek in a hurry." The driver fell silent, reflecting on his financial burdens.

Asher tapped the driver on the shoulder and then pointed at a six-apartment cream-colored building with dark green shutters. "It's right there, just on the right.' Anthony pulled the rattling car to the curb and placed the vehicle in park.

"Sorry to have made you late picking up your wife. More than most, I know that a gal should not be kept waiting." Anthony chuckled. "Ah, it'll be ok. A few more minutes on the clock for both of us can surely help. Tryin to tuck away a few extra dollars for Christmas. Kids are eleven years old, and things aint exactly cheap. Been promising one of those Xbox game thingies for a while now. It might just be the year I can finally make it happen," Anthony said.

Asher smiled. "I believe you are right, Anthony; this will be the year for them to get it. Asher's eyes met Anthony's in the rearview mirror. "What do I owe ya for the ride?" Anthony returned a smile, "Nothing, it's on the house. Payin' it forward kinda-thing."

Asher stepped out of the car and poked his head through the open front passenger window. "You are a good father and husband, Anthony. Your ship will come in, I have no doubt. Just keep after it, and don't lose hope. Thanks for the ride." Asher said warmly. "Pleasures bin all mine, sir," Anthony said, dropping the car into drive.

"WAIT!" Asher shouted. Anthony stepped hard on the brake pedal, instantly stopping the car. Asher pulled Mr. Baggins from his pocket and approached the door. "I have something for you." Reaching into his magic bag, Asher retrieved an Xbox console with two wireless controllers, a few kid-friendly games, and a small card attached to the bow. "I know your kids will love this," Asher said, handing it through the window.

"How, what, I uh…. You jumped in my car empty-handed. Where did you get this? How did you get this?" The confused driver questioned. "Merry Christmas, Anthony," Asher said with a twinkle in his eye. Oh, by the way, you can call me Santa." Anthony looked at the package and laughed, not noticing the inscription on the affixed card. "Santa, ha, ha, That is a good one! I don't know how you did it, but seriously, thank you." He said, clearing his throat, then sped away to pick up his wife.

It wouldn't be until later that night when he read the inscription that he would believe Asher was, in fact, Santa, To: Tyler and Tommy. The tag was made out to his twins, though their names were never disclosed during the conversation. Asher turned and headed up the steps to Annabel's doorway with a heavy pit in his stomach, knowing he would soon face a very uncomfortable conversation. Looking back one last time, he watched Anthony's tail lights disappear in the distance

6

Outside Looking in

Asher's footsteps were heavier than usual tonight. It was as if he'd waded through a swamp of gooey mud, each step dragging him down with an invisible weight. The impending conversation with Annabel felt like an elephant on his chest, turning his dark boots into leaden burdens. With taxing steps leading up to the front door, he struggled to find the right words, only to watch them fade away as quickly as he thought of them, and immediately, he was back clamoring for a logical reason for not meeting Annabel for dinner earlier that evening.

Asher paused at the door, raised his trembling finger to the bell, and pressed the button sheepishly. The chime reverberated off the walls and the tile floors, signaling his presence, and an alert flashed on Annabel's phone. Staring down, Annabel glared at the video of Asher standing at her door. Leaning in closer, with his finger still lingering on the button. Asher questioned *Is that a mini camera lens?"* Scrutinizing the doorbell, Asher noticed the reflection on the convex glass, turning his nose into a caricature and elongating his forehead with a comical exaggeration. Inward and outward like a chicken pecking the ground, Asher was entranced by the funhouse mirror effect and found amusement in his distorted image.

"Having fun?" The sudden question jolted him, embarrassment settling over him like a leaden cloak. "I uh..It was that I..uh," Asher struggled to form a coherent sentence, still leaning forward into the curved glass reflection. Turning towards his inquisitor, who stood with folded arms, he straightened, cleared his throat, and tried again. "I…uh, I don't know," A slender index finger pressed against his lips, pausing him in his words. "Shhhh. Not another word."

Annabel stared at Asher, the silence stretching into an eternity. She stood silent, cheeks flaming, and her face turned a shade of red that could make a cherry envious. Then, in a sudden burst, she threw her arms up, burying her face in her hands.

Caught off guard, Asher remained frozen, unsure what to say or do. He watched her shoulders teater forward and back in unison with her head in a bobbing motion. Her shaking increased steadily until her body appeared to be quivering to the point of bursting. Annabel inhaled deeply before erupting into the loudest laugh he had ever heard, followed by a snort and additional gasps and giggling. Asher watched her with a mix of bemusement and wonder, unsure if he should run for his life or join in on the hysterics. Quickly assessing the situation, Asher snorted hard, mimicking her, before bellowing a hearty hee-haw laugh that could refresh the driest of eyes with a flood of tears. The porch echoed with their contagious laughter, both collapsing to the floor in amusement. Annabel clutched her stomach, and Asher's eyes filled with jovial tears that rolled down his cheek.

The giddy couple shared another round of laughter, letting the joy linger in the air before stillness settled again. Annabel sat upright, followed by Asher, who gazed longingly into her eyes. Leaning over, Annabel delicately placed her hand on Asher's, causing a warm flush to color his face."It's tough to stay mad at you for long. You have this knack for banishing anger effortlessly. Her face adorned a half-formed smile as she spoke.

"Annabel, I wanted to…" Asher began, but her index finger gently silenced him again. "Shhh… don't spoil the moment. Let me finish," she whispered, and his smile widened, exposing a few teeth.

"Yes, I was upset about you not meeting me at Angelos this evening, but more than anger, I felt hurt. Sharing you with the world is not easy. Your genuine dedication to being Santa is admirable, but I often feel like I come in second place. It's not a pleasant feeling at all." Asher's gaze dropped to the floor, and Annabel fell silent, comforting him by stroking the back of his hand.

Turning his hand over, Asher interlaced his fingers with Annabel's. "No one has cared for me as deeply as you have. You've been my constant through thick and thin all these years. Reading your note and not sitting with you for our dinner date tonight made me realize I couldn't go on without you." Annabel's eyes met his, her pupils unusually prominent.

Their locked gaze was broken as Asher found himself captivated by her soft, full, pink lips. Slowly, as if drawn by an unseen force, his head inched closer until he could feel her warm breath on his face. In anticipation, Asher closed his eyes, expecting their lips to meet in a tender kiss.

"Got your Pizza!" a voice disrupted the magical moment. Reacting, Annabel jerked her head to see who approached, her notably warm lips barely brushing against Asher's in a disappointing air kiss. Both exclaimed in disappointing unison, "Pizza?" followed by Asher asking about the sender and expressing his frustration, "Such bad timing!"

The delivery driver, a college-aged young man with unkept dirt-blonde hair, explained, "Yeah, I've heard that before. "The order is from Angelos Pizza, and the man said it's on the house and meant for the sweet lady at this address. I'm guessing he was talking about you, ma'am. That man was nice and a good tipper. Oh, and he scribbled a little message for you on the box." Annabel grinned, taking the steamy box and inspecting the note: "Please forgive Asher; he's just a rookie, after all." It was well known in certain circles that Asher's dating experience qualified him for extreme rookie status.

"Don't want to overstay my welcome a second longer. The young man said, then turned and headed back to his car. A few yards away, the young food delivery driver shouted over his shoulder, "Enjoy the hot pie!" Annabel couldn't resist a smile. "Oh, that dear Angelo. He's honestly the best," she declared, her nose instinctively hovering over the pizza box, absorbing the tempting aroma. Asher, beside her, nodded in agreement, his eyes widening with anticipation as he popped open the lid. The surrounding air was instantly filled with savory vapors, weaving an irresistible spell. "I agree," Asher chimed in, his excitement palpable. "Let's dig in!" And with that, they descended into a shared moment of culinary bliss, savoring not just the flavors of Angelo's masterpiece but the warmth of their shared connection.

"Annabel, I never intended for the evening to unfold as it did, and I deeply regret leaving you in that situation. When Mr. Baggins urgently called for my assistance, I thought I could make a quick visit and still be on time for our dinner date. In my mind, I believed that addressing his request promptly would free me to give you the undivided attention you deserve. Ignoring him would only lead to persistent interruptions or distract my focus later in the evening. I intended to balance my responsibilities and prioritize you."

Annabel gently placed her half-eaten slice of pizza on the box and wiped her mouth with a napkin. "Asher, I understand your commitment to your divine calling as Santa, and I know there will be times when you need to fulfill your responsibilities. While I respect your aversion to technology, I wonder if reconsidering using a cell phone might help.

A quick call, a brief text, or even voice-to-text through a smartwatch could prevent a repeat of tonight's events."

Reaching over to Asher's hand, she softly stroked it once again. "Communication is key, and technology can be a valuable ally. I believe it can enhance your ability to balance your duties and our time together. I'm here to support you, even with the technological side of things."

Asher's gaze shifted upward, his heart melting under the warmth of Annabel's convincing smile. "This calling as Santa has brought many changes into my life, and I realize embracing technology is one more change that can make things better," he admitted. "Yes," he exclaimed, "whatever it takes to make things right, and if it means avoiding hurting you again, I am all in."

Annabel flashed another reassuring smile. "I'm here to help with all technological questions," she teased, waving her phone in her hand.

The tension that had lingered dissipated as quickly as it had appeared. It was as if the challenging evening had never happened. "So, what was the urgent mission you were sent on?" Annabel inquired, shifting the focus to a lighter note, emphasizing the bond that had weathered the storm of the night.

Asher recounted the entire event to her as it had unfolded. The room fell into absolute silence, immersing themselves in the magnitude of the revelation. "So, who do you think that man was outside the window? What did you say his name was?" Annabel asked, her voice carrying a note of curiosity fused with an undercurrent of concern. Asher's face took on a corpselike pallor. " His name startled me when he first disclosed it, but his reaction to my ring and the missing gem confirmed my suspicions," he admitted, his words weighted with an unspoken fear.

"When Kristoff, the former Santa, visited me, he spoke of one of the gems missing from the ring that dark magic had removed," Asher continued, his voice dropping to a hushed tone. "A new ring had been forged, and the missing gem inserted. The ring possesses magical properties, the most notable being the ability to see into the future." He paused, the room now thick with an unsettling tension. "Kristoff told me that the person currently coveting the ring is desperate to acquire the master ring from me."

Annabel took another bite of her pizza slice, her expression thoughtful. Suddenly, a flickering white streetlight three houses away seized her attention. Squinting her eyes for a better view, she instantly discerned that the light source wasn't a mere streetlight but a hovering white orb with intense green sparks tumbling around like captured lightning bugs. Annabel rubbed her eyes, half expecting an illusion. Nudging Asher's ribs, she exclaimed, "Do you see what I'm seeing?"

Asher swiveled his head just in time to witness the enchanted orb elongating, extending upward and outward, forming appendages. The lower half took on the semblance of legs strolling down the sidewalk, the middle section truncated, and two pendulum-swinging portions formed into what looked like arms. Asher focused on the now-formed head, observing as features materialized—orbits, a nose, and pursed lips appeared. The shadowy figure advanced with unwavering intensity, its course unfaltering. Annabel and Asher stood frozen, fixated on the transformed figure approaching. A passing car's headlights briefly illuminated the determined figure. Asher gasped, "It's Savio!"

Asher leaped to his feet and grasped the front door's doorknob, giving it a quick turn, and flung the door open. Savio noticed them retreating and quickening his pace. Asher looked back over his shoulder and could see Savio sprinting towards them.

"Annabel, let's get inside!" Not wasting a second, Annabel dashed inside, securing the door behind her, then made her way to the living room and flicked off the light. "Good idea," Asher complimented her. "Darkening the room will give us a visual advantage to see him. "Did you say that was Savio?" Annabel questioned, joining Asher at the window. "Yes, I'm almost positive it was. Let's just keep out of view."

Asher replied. Like a well-practiced dance couple, the two lowered themselves until just the top of their heads and eyes were visible over the lower window sill.

The night air thickened with an unspoken tension as Savio paced the sidewalk, scrutinizing Annabel's house. His head twisted back and forth as if seeking an entry point that eluded normal perception. A muttered dialogue ensued, with Savio seemingly conversing with an unseen presence.

"Can we get out through the back?" Asher's voice revealed a hint of desperation. Annabel's response echoed doomily, dispelling any hopes of escape. "No, there is no exit out back; it's a completely enclosed patio. The only way is through the front. We are trapped!"

"Annabel, you are shaking," Asher observed, genuine concern in his voice. "That's not me, Asher. I'm not even touching you." The inexplicable distance between them heightened the eerie ambiance. "There it is again," Asher's left upper thigh quivered. A sudden realization struck him, and he fumbled into his pant pocket. "Guinevere!" he exclaimed, the sassy glasses making a grand entrance.

"Well, don't just stand there admiring my beauty; put me on, hurry!" Guinevere's sarcastic tone cut through the tension. With a mixture of excitement and urgency, Asher smashed Guinevere onto his face. Red and green vapors swirled within the ocular lenses. "There it is!" Asher pointed excitedly at the far wall in the living room. Annabel, still bewildered, questioned, "There, what is?"

"Just hang on to me," Asher instructed, grabbing Annabel's arm as they made their way to the living room.

With each step, a surreal storm enveloped them. Swirling wind and tornadic sounds filled the room, yet nothing in the house moved. Annabel felt an odd force pulling at her, and Asher's reassurance barely blunted her anxiety. "We are escaping by using a magic portal. It will feel weird for you, but you will be fine." Asher harbored doubts about transporting passengers through a portal, but it was their only option.

As the arm-in-arm couple advanced toward the portal, the room's atmosphere grew charged with magic. Asher sensed the familiar tug at his stomach, but this time, it felt different. A struggle ensued as if they were falling through the portal but being held back by an invisible force. Instinctively, Asher jerked hard on Annabel's arm, and the two tumbled into the portal, disappearing from the house.

They reappeared in a crumpled heap on the sidewalk outside Annabel's home. Helping her to her feet, she recognized the familiar surroundings. "Why did we come here?" she asked, bewildered. "I saw a single portal and aimed for it. This is where it took us," Asher replied, uncertainty clouding his expression.

Hiding behind Mrs. Morton's rose bushes, the duo observed Savio's intrusion into Annabel's house. Each room lit up as he meticulously searched, leaving a trail of mystery as he passed through each corridor. Still in the dark, Annabel whispered, "What is he looking for?" Asher remained silent, his eyes fixed on Savio. Looking down at his finger, he pointed at Savio's target—" The Master ring!"

"I know it feels like we should call the police because someone is intruding in your home," Asher responded, his uncertainty apparent. "But honestly, I'm not even sure who or what kind of magic we're dealing with here. After all, he appeared as an orb, and I imagine he can disappear as quickly as he shows up."

"I'm not sure if they will find him, but okay, yes, let's do it. Let's call!"

Annabel pulled the phone from her pocket; its screen's blue glow reflected on her nose and cheeks. "See, Asher, another reason to get a cell phone," she remarked playfully.

Asher flashed a look of agreement back at her, coupled with a smile. Annabel began pressing the numbers, but before she could press send following the 9-1-1, the lights in her home instantly blacked out. A bright green flash and a loud snap followed, reverberating off the side of the house behind Annabel and Asher.

An ominous silence settled, leaving everything hauntingly still and heavy. "I think he's gone," Annabel declared.

"The question is, where did he go? I assume Savio returned to Argentina, but I cannot be certain. The frightening thing is that he's onto me and us," Asher admitted, dropping his head slightly, a defeated expression on his face.

"Who could have imagined a world where Santa is real? More than that, who could have imagined that Santa would need to protect his magic?" Asher frustratedly blurted out.

Annabel reached over, placed her hand under Asher's chin, and lifted his head upward. "Look at me, Asher."

"There has always been antagonism to virtuous, noble, or moral things in the world. Without evil, we would never be able to see the good, delightful, and pleasant things around us. All things need opposition for appreciation, though it can be a genuine struggle from time to time. If things were not hard, how could we grow or expect to learn and progress in this life?" Annabel's words penetrated deep and softened Asher's heart.

"You always have a way of talking me down, Annabel," Asher said, squaring his shoulders.

"If you ever begin to doubt your duty," Annabel continued, "Remember that this assignment to be Santa is a divine call to help others in need, and your efforts will bless innumerable people. Like an apple sliced, you can count the seeds. But you can never count or predict the apples that may come from planting one apple seed."

Asher's face reflected appreciation for her counsel. "This is becoming quite the adventure, isn't it Annabel?" "One thing is certain: we must be observant and not let down our guard," Annabel replied. "This Savio character is not one to be trusted, and it is now evident that he has malicious intent." Asher nodded his head in agreement. "We are safe for the moment, Annabel." Let's get inside and inspect your house."

7

A Dark Secret

Thunder rumbled ominously behind him, and the air crackled with sulfur, the flash of light fading as quickly as it had appeared. "So annoying, that guy is! ¿Cómo puede ser? How did he get away?" Savio muttered in disgust. Carlos, sitting by the front door, jumped at Savio's call and hurried over, though his gait resembled a hobble rather than a run. An old ankle injury had never fully healed, twisting his knee and hip. He lived in constant pain that often kept him awake at night.

"You're moving so slow, Carlos," Savio said impatiently. "Hurry up already. Where's my drink?" Carlos, 5'6" and in his late twenties, with a freckled face reminiscent of the moon, looked down at Savio's feet and offered him a gourd bottle with a metal straw protruding like a flagpole.

"Sorry, sir. Here's your mate. I chopped and ground the yerba mate leaves this morning."

Savio snatched the drink from him and pushed him aside. "I don't know why I keep you around, Carlos. You're as useful to me as a used shoe. But you do make a good mate. A little more chopped leaves next time. Don't screw it up again."

"Yes, Master. I'll do better next time," Carlos replied, avoiding Savio's gaze as he turned to leave. Like a buffalo with its head bowed under years of servitude, Carlos bore the heavy burden of his past. Born in Balvanera, a rough neighborhood in Buenos Aires, he learned to navigate the city by day while avoiding its dark alleys at night. Growing up, he often found himself involved in shady dealings, and when that failed, he resorted to theft. The turning point came in his late teens when a rival gang beat him, breaking his ankle and nearly killing him. Savio recognized his vulnerability and devised a plan, appearing to offer help to the injured teen before cleverly manipulating him into servitude, using threats of dark magic to keep Carlos in line.

When World War II began, Savio's grandfather acquired an upper-class house and embarked on a secret journey, trafficking stolen gold and valuables from innocent Jews. Those ill-gotten gains funded a lavish lifestyle, hidden behind a secret identity crafted after his escape from Germany when the war ended.

The house was anything but modest, featuring tiled floors, high ceilings with arches, and columns fit for a king. A collection of artwork adorned the entryway walls, including a prominently displayed gilded frame of Hanz in his Nazi uniform. Savio inherited the house from his grandfather after his parents died under suspicious circumstances, leaving him an only child with no one to share the inheritance. The house became his domain, serving as the headquarters for Savio and his crew, their activities financed by a life of crime.

"Felipe! Where's Felipe?" a voice echoed through the hall. "In his office, sir," Carlos replied from across the room. "Of course he is," Savio muttered as he headed toward the back of the house. Felipe joined their group not long after Savio took Carlos under his wing. Their meeting occurred during a conversation over Fernet, an aromatic bitter spirit mixed with Coca-Cola. That drunken discussion turned into an impromptu job interview for a mastermind crime plotter, where Savio learned about Felipe's checkered past and technical skills.

As Savio entered Felipe's office, he found Carlos sitting with his face inches from a pizza box-sized monitor, hammering away at the keyboard without looking up. The office was a chaotic mess, with papers scattered across the floor, haphazardly stacked books on shelves, and empty energy drink cans everywhere. City maps thumbtacked to the walls were crisscrossed with yarn in multiple colors, intersecting at various points. Handwritten notes beside the thumbtacks read: 12:03 PM, 4:47 AM, 1:18 AM... GOOD LOOT!

"Detailed to the minute, I see," Savio remarked, tracing the yarn with his finger. Felipe finally looked up and noticed Savio studying the map. "That's right, Savio. I've been monitoring these spots. The marked times indicate the windows to get in, grab the loot, and get out undetected." A sly grin spread across Felipe's face. "Looks like this will set us up for the rest of the year." Savio returned the smile. "You're the mastermind behind the heists and have never failed to deliver. With your skills and this ring, we're pretty safe and sound."

Savio walked over to the cluttered desk and shoved a stack of books off the chair, sending them crashing to the floor. "Maybe you can mastermind a way to keep this room less cluttered," he suggested, but Felipe remained silent, focused on his typing. Savio pulled the chair up to the desk and sat, feeling uncomfortable under Felipe's unyielding gaze. "Now that I have your attention, I need your help again." Felipe continued to stare at him. "Couldn't get the ring, eh? You want me to track down that Asher guy again, right?" Savio nodded. "Exactly. I haven't mastered traveling with the ring yet. When I appeared, I ended up down the street from the location you gave me instead of inside the house as I planned. That distance ruined the surprise attack, and they got away."

Felipe turned his chair to the right to face Savio. "So the address I gave you was correct?"

"Yes," Savio replied. "Those tracker tiles you provided were key. When I encountered the Santa character and spotted his ring, I managed to slip one of the tiles into his pocket during our conversation about it. Without those, I would have been lost trying to find him again."

Savio clasped his hands together. "Teamwork and technology."

Felipe resumed his focus on the computer, his expression thoughtful. "The only problem we're facing is the intermittent connection. Technology can be finicky. I'm not sure if it's a flaw in the tracker or interference. Maybe his ring is causing it," Felipe speculated.

"Where is he now?" Savio inquired, watching Felipe click the mouse and type furiously.

"It's glitchy," Felipe said, frowning. "I can't tell if this is his last known location or if he's still there. The signal is weak and coming from across the street, but I can't confirm anything."

Savio studied the unstable signal, tapping his finger on the desk. "Until I understand this ring and where I am, it's not safe to return yet," he said. "And besides, Felipe, we lost the element of surprise. That fat guy knows someone with magic is after him. He'll be looking for me. We need a strategy to catch him off guard."

Savio took a sip from his mate, savoring the last drops as he emptied the container. Felipe scowled at the gurgling noise from the empty gourd bottle. "Carlos, get me another mate!" he called out, glancing at the gourd before returning his attention to the screen. "Make that two, Carlos. I'll have one too!" Felipe's voice echoed through the room.

"Just one more heist, and we won't need Carlos anymore," Savio said, his voice filled with pride and confidence. "He's too slow, and he's going to get us caught. This last heist will set us up for life."

Felipe glanced at him. "So, how do you plan to get rid of him?"

"The same way I got rid of his parents all those years ago," Savio replied with a wicked grin. "He'll just disappear."

Savio and Felipe treated Carlos like a servant, offering him no respect or reciprocity. Feeling trapped with very few options and a deep fear of the police, Carlos complied with their demands, knowing Felipe would threaten to report him if he didn't. Being confused by his circumstances, Carlos continued to play the role of a butler, doing whatever they asked.

"I'll be right there," Carlos called from down the hall. "Someday, I won't, though," he muttered to himself. As he approached the kitchen, he grabbed two more gourd bottles, poured the crushed yerba mate into each, tilted one gourd at a 45-degree angle, and added a little hot water. He paused, inserted the metal straw, then added more water. As the yerba mate absorbed the liquid, foam began to form. Topping it off with more hot water, he said, "Perfect," feeling a slight sense of pride in his precise preparation.

Carlos was a perfectionist in many aspects. His need for precision was ingrained in him, cultivated with purpose. He couldn't tell if it was a skill he had developed over time or if it was inherited from his parents, whose shadowy past loomed large over his chaotic childhood.

As a child, love was a rare commodity in his home, and affection felt like a distant dream. Verbal abuse was commonplace, leaving Carlos longing for a real connection. He suspected his parents were involved in illegal activities, perhaps even mafia connections. Then, one day, they vanished without a trace, leaving only questions behind. Carlos was forced to fend for himself on the harsh streets, marking the end of his childhood on his eleventh birthday.

Approaching Felipe's office quietly, Carlos held the gourd bottles with pride. When he reached the slightly ajar door, snippets of conversation caught his attention. "We have to be careful and do our best so Carlos doesn't find out our plans after the last heist," Savio whispered to Felipe, provoking Carlos's curiosity.

Carlos usually ignored the details of Savio's conversations with Felipe, but the secrecy and whispers surrounding this one made him curious. Why the secrecy? Why was he being excluded from their plans? These questions swirled in his mind as he hesitated, frozen just beyond the door. Holding his breath, he inched closer to the doorway, pressing against the wall to catch every word.

"Yes, it has to be a secret. If he finds out, it will all be over," Felipe continued. "I can't keep risking my life or going to prison just to take care of that jerk." The weight of his fear was thick and palpable.

Carlos flinched at Savio's dismissive tone regarding him. He had always accepted his role as a servant, resigned to a life of subservience. But now, standing outside the door, he felt the sting of betrayal. "Why would they do this to me and leave me out of their plans? I trusted them all these years," Carlos whispered, his voice heavy with rejection.

"Listen, Savio," Felipe said, lowering his voice. "He's loyal, though, and there's something to be said about that. After all, we can still use his help a little longer. He will be useful in this last heist."

Savios's laughter echoed harshly behind the door. "Useful? That pathetic kid? He's not worth the time we're spending discussing him!" A moment of silence followed, and Carlos's heart raced. Savio continued, his voice low and threatening. "If he finds out our secret, it'll ruin everything. He needs to stay in the dark, just like before."

Savio slumped on his empty drink once again."Carlos, where are the mates?" His annoyed voice rang out down the hallway. "What's taking so long?"

Carlos took a deep breath, and his hands shook as he grabbed the gourds again. Then, with a heavy heart and a sense of fate, he walked back to the office, feeling like an animal being led to the slaughter

8

Back Home

D o you think it is safe to go inside?" Annabel's voice quivered
with uncertainty. "Well, it is your house, and I am fairly
certain Savio left," Asher reassured her. With a cautious
hand, he twisted the front door knob and gave the door a slight nudge,
allowing it to creak open ever so slightly.

Pressing his ear against the crack, he strained to catch any hint of
movement beyond. "Do you hear anything?" Annabel's inquiry hung
heavy in the air.

"It's silent," Asher whispered back, his voice barely audible. With a
gentle push, he widened the gap, peering into the room. "It looks clear.
Let's go inside." With a shared nod of determination, they stepped over
the threshold, bracing themselves for whatever awaited them within.

With every step, they tread cautiously through the familiar halls of
Annabel's house, their senses heightened and nerves on edge. "Grab
what you need for a few days. We can stay back at the Christmas
boutique until we can sort things out. I don't think it's wise to stay
here," Asher suggested, his voice tinged with urgency.

"I agree," Annabel replied, her expression reflecting a mixture of concern and determination.

But as Asher attempted to clarify his suggestion, his words stumbled over each other in a jumbled mess. "What did you mean, 'we can stay back at the store'?" Annabel's playful tease hung in the air, causing Asher's cheeks to flush with embarrassment. "No, I, it's, uh..." He faltered, his attempt to salvage the situation falling short.

"Settle down, Asher," Annabel giggled, her warm laughter breaking through the tension like a ray of sunlight. "I'm just kidding, and I knew what you meant. I just wanted to fluster you." Relief flooded over Asher, and he couldn't help but join in on the laughter, grateful for the chance to ease the awkwardness that had settled between them.

"Well, we do have a guest room back at the boutique, and I can stay in the office. Sleeping in an office feels very normal to me after all the years I put in back at the Gazette." Asher suggested. Annabel grabbed a suitcase from the entry closet and began rolling it toward her room. "Do you think that your house is not safe either?" Asher shook his head. "No, I think Savio knows my house location as well as yours. He acted fast from the time he encountered me in Argentina. In only a few hours, he pinpointed my following location and now knows about you. My hunch is that he knows my house location as well. It's like he was tracking me, but how?

"I'll be right back. I'm going to pack a few things. It won't take long," Annabel declared, her determination palpable as she dragged her suitcase behind her and disappeared into the depths of her room.

As Annabel vanished from sight, a familiar muffled voice and a tingling sensation in his pocket caught Asher's attention. Guinevere, ever the cheeky companion, was requesting he put on his spectacles. Hastily grabbing the metal frame, he slid them onto the bridge of his nose, ready for whatever revelation awaited him.

"Here is the answer to your question; now pay attention!" Guinevere's voice echoed in his mind as the lenses shimmered with green and red vaporous clouds. This time, an image of a grandfather clock materialized, its hands spinning counterclockwise towards the center lens. Seconds later, Asher found himself transported back to Argentina, reliving the moment he first encountered Savio that fateful evening.

"Pay close attention to his sleight of hand work, especially his left hand." Guinevere's prompt cut through the haze of memories, urging Asher to focus on the crucial details hidden within the shadows of the past.

Focusing intently on Savio's left hand, Asher observed with a mix of fascination and apprehension as Savio deftly reached up, his movements fluid and practiced. With unparalleled skill, he dropped something into the outer pocket of the Santa coat, his actions executed with such precision that even a seasoned Vegas magician would have been left in awe. It was a seamless maneuver, executed with the finesse of a master craftsman.

"So that's how he did it. He must have dropped some sort of tracker into my coat pocket," Asher concluded, his mind racing with the implications of Savio's cunning tactic.

"Well, now that you've figured that out, kindly put me back where you found me," Guinevere's voice sounded resigned, a hint of melancholy coloring her words.

With a sense of gratitude for the assistance, Asher slid the glasses off his nose, folding the arms closed before gently placing them in his pocket once more. Instantly, the weight of Guinevere's presence disappeared, leaving his pocket empty once again, a silent reminder of the enigmatic ally he carried with him in the form of a humble pair of spectacles.

"If the tracker's inside my Santa coat, the only location he will have known is my house. But how did he find out about Annabel's house? He must be working with someone," Asher concluded, the pieces of the puzzle slowly slotting into place in his mind.

"That's the only way this could be explained. There must've been some digging going on from the time I returned to my house. I bet he's tracking me through my phone now," Asher muttered, his frustration mounting with each revelation.

With a decisive gesture, Asher reached into his back pocket, his fingers curling around the familiar weight of his phone. Without a moment's hesitation, he flung it to the floor, watching as it shattered into a myriad of pieces. "I've always hated this type of technology. I never should have allowed tracking my location on my smartphone," Asher lamented, the echo of his regret reverberating through the silent room.

Annabel darted out of her room and found Asher standing over his shattered phone; confusion etched on her face. "What on earth happened here?" she questioned, her brow furrowing with concern.

"We've been compromised and tracked. Quick, give me your phone," Asher demanded urgently. Annabel handed over her phone to Asher, a hint of amusement in her voice. "You know our phone contract is not up yet, right?" she joked.

"It is now!" Asher declared, his frustration boiling over as he brought his boot crashing down on the device, rendering it unusable in a single swift motion.

"Well, if anything, he knows my last location. Let's get a move on and get back to the boutique," Annabel suggested, her practical nature taking charge as she grabbed her suitcase and headed for the door.

"Wait, if he knows our phone records, he's going to know about my time at the Christmas boutique. We can never go back to that store, either. What's just happened to our lives?" Annabel exclaimed, the weight of their predicament sinking in as they faced the harsh reality of their situation.

"As long as evil hunts the good, we will be on the run, and our lives will be frequently disrupted," Asher acknowledged solemnly. "We need to find a place we can go for safety—somewhere that has no phone records of us or tracking. I will also need to recover the tracking device from my Santa coat before we go to our next location."

With determination, Asher and Annabel embarked on the daunting task of seeking refuge from the shadows that pursued them. Their resolve was unyielding as they faced the uncertain road ahead. We are heading for safety.

With a determined flick of his wrist, Asher closed his eyes and snapped his fingers. In an instant, he was enveloped in the majestic red Santa suit, the very same one he had worn in Argentina. With a sense of purpose, he reached into his pocket and retrieved a small tracking device no larger than a postage stamp. Tossing it onto the pile of broken phone fragments, he crushed it under the heel of his boot, obliterating any trace of surveillance.

"By all accounts, I would say we are safe, for now," Asher assured Annabel, a hint of relief coloring his words. "We will still need to start anew," he continued. "I will not be going back to my place for my things. When we find a secure place, we will make arrangements to have the boutique permanently closed."

"Where are we headed to?" Annabel inquired, her voice tinged with curiosity and apprehension.

"Grab my arm and hang on for the ride. We are heading for safety," Asher declared with unwavering determination, extending his arm to Annabel as they prepared to embark on their journey.

Asher reached into his Santa coat and gently retrieved Guinevere, awakening her from her slumber. Placing the spectacles on the bridge of his nose once more, he felt a surge of familiarity and comfort wash over him. "There's one," Asher announced, his voice tinged with determination as he grasped Annabel's hand, leading her toward the traveling portal.

Their destination lay in the heart of the kitchen, near the sink, where the portal awaited their arrival. As they approached, a familiar tugging sensation at their navels pulled them inexorably inward. With a resounding thunderclap, the two travelers vanished into the swirling vortex, their suitcases clutched tightly in their hands.

As Annabelle's surroundings materialized around her, she found herself standing in a slightly darkened room that bore the distinct atmosphere of an attic. The structure exuded an air of age and neglect, with dust clinging to every surface and cobwebs gathering in the peak corners.

A long table once painted a vibrant green, now stood faded and weathered, its legs showing signs of peeling paint. Across the room, a small kitchenette occupied one corner while a rough couch lined the eastern wall. Two open doorways revealed glimpses of a bathroom and a bedroom, both furnished with modest pieces that hinted at a simple existence.

The old coffee table in front of the couch bore the marks of time, with several stains marring its surface. Despite its evident lack of recent use, the room remained in relatively decent shape, a testament to the care it had received in years past. For Annabelle, the sight of this forgotten space sparked a mix of curiosity and apprehension, leaving her to ponder the mysteries that lay hidden within its walls.

Soft chimes from outside the window shattered the silence, their delicate melody resonating through the room. Annabelle's heart skipped a beat at the unmistakable sound of eighteenth-century airs emanating from the renowned Whitechapel Bell Foundry.

"Are we back home?" Annabelle asked, her voice tinged with excitement. "Was that the soft chimes coming from the Fortnum & Mason clock?" She dashed to the window, eager to catch a glimpse of London's familiar sights.

"Indeed it is, Annabelle. And yes, we are back home. Back in London, on Piccadilly Street," Asher confirmed with a smile, his eyes reflecting Annabelle's infectious joy.

"I can't believe it's true. I can't believe we made it back. Oh, how I missed the sounds and views of London. This will always be home for me. So, where are we exactly?" Annabelle inquired eagerly, her gaze fixed on the darkened streets below.

"I actually own this flat," Asher revealed, a hint of pride in his voice. "I always use it as a place of refuge when I need time away from the hustle and bustle. I've kept it quiet from everyone, and after becoming Santa, I felt it best to keep it quiet in case, for some reason, I would need to find refuge. Turns out I was right."

He paused, reflecting on the careful measures he had taken to maintain the secrecy and security of his sanctuary. "I've kept up with all necessary payments on the place, and I have someone looking after it. About once a month, the apartment gets inspected," he explained his words a testament to the foresight and resilience he had cultivated in his newfound role as Santa.

Asher glanced at his watch, a reliable companion that always revealed the correct time and date. "It looks like it's 4 AM. Not much is going on in the streets at this hour. Let's spend the next few days laying low while we sort things out, Annabelle," he suggested, his tone laced with a sense of determination.

"You can have that room all to yourself. I'll stay here on the couch. In the closet, there are some of my old clothes that I'll need to gather," Asher continued, his mind already racing with plans and considerations. "There's a lot to be considered and a lot that needs to be planned. We can have food delivered here in a few hours, just in time for breakfast. Firstly, I'm excited to have some good bangers and mash delivered from right down the street."

With a warm smile, he extended a hand to Annabelle. "Come, let's get you unpacked. Welcome home, Annabelle."

9

Seize the Moment

Several days had slipped by since they had settled into the cozy flat on Piccadilly Street. For Asher, the transition was seamless; his basic needs were already met within the familiar confines of the apartment, having spent occasional nights there in the past. However, for Annabelle, it marked the beginning of a new chapter as she carefully unpacked her suitcase and began to rebuild her life from the ground up.

With the tracking device eliminated, Asher's confidence swelled, and the lingering specter of danger began to fade into the background. The sense of security that enveloped them now was more palpable, casting a newfound sense of peace over their sanctuary amidst the bustling streets of London. As the days passed in the peaceful confines of the Piccadilly flat, Asher found himself with ample time to reflect on the events that had unfolded with Savio. The realization that someone was actively pursuing him stirred a sense of unease deep within him, casting a shadow over the recent tranquility of their temporary refuge.

Asher couldn't shake the unsettling notion that Savio might be connected to the sinister entity that had attempted to forcibly remove his ring on that fateful night when Kristoff had visited his house. The possibility that Savio was after his ring, with its potent connection to his identity as Santa, filled him with a growing sense of dread.

The revelation that Savio possessed dark magic only heightened Asher's apprehension, leaving him grappling with the unsettling reality of their adversary's capabilities. As he delved deeper into his thoughts, Asher resolved to remain vigilant, knowing that the threat posed by Savio loomed ominously on the horizon, ready to strike at any moment.

"How does he have magic? I didn't realize that dark magic could exist," Asher pondered, his thoughts swirling in a whirlwind of confusion and concern. The revelation of Savio's dark powers had caught him off guard, leaving him grappling with the unsettling implications of their adversary's abilities.

"But what does he want with my ring if that is his intent? How could someone know about my ring and Santa's magic?" Asher's mind raced with questions, each one leading to more uncertainty and fear. The mystery of Savio's motives and the extent of his knowledge weighed heavily on him, keeping him awake late into the night as he sought answers in the darkness of his thoughts.

Bong bing bong, the soft melody of the Fortnum & Mason clock chimed once again, breaking the silence of the night. Asher glanced at his watch, noting the late hour—12:15 am. His thoughts had consumed him for the past three hours, leaving him restless and unable to find solace in sleep.

"Having a hard time sleeping as well, eh?" Annabel's voice broke through the stillness, her footsteps echoing softly as she approached the couch where Asher sat, lost in thought. Taking up a temporary seat on the coffee table, she looked at him with concern etched in her features.

Asher sat upright, offering her a gentle smile. "Here, please sit on the couch; it's a little softer than that old wood table," he suggested, gesturing towards the inviting cushions beside him. Annabel nodded gratefully, grabbing a square couch pillow and tossing it to the side to make room for her to sit.

"So, what troubles you, Annabel? What is keeping you awake?" Asher inquired, his voice filled with genuine concern as he leaned forward, eager to offer her a listening ear.

Annabel sighed, leaning back against the couch and resting her head on the cushion as she stared up at the ceiling. "I love being here in London, back home. But even though we are back, I feel out of sorts. My mind keeps replaying Savio appearing at my home. I'm worried that I will suddenly run into him again on the streets, even here in London," she confessed, her words laden with apprehension and uncertainty.

Asher nodded in agreement, his expression mirroring Annabel's concerns. "Yes, this is what is keeping me up as well. I keep wondering if there is any way he could find us here. If he is able to dig up information about your house or mine, it will be under Asher Jupes. But the flat we are staying in was purchased using my real name, Joseph Amesbury. So, as far as tracking our location by investigative means goes, I think we are safe," he reassured Annabel, his voice calm and steady.

"I still wonder about where he gets his magic and how he was straightway focused on a strange man wearing a Santa suit in Argentina. His instant obsession with my ring is what bothers me the most," Asher confessed, his fingers absently rolling the ring around on his finger as he pondered the significance of Savio's unsettling fixation.

"How are you adjusting to us here in London, Annabel? I worry about you. I have disrupted your life from the moment I let you in on my secret. I was so foolish to do so. I feel you would have been better off not going with me, resuming your life as it was. I am sorry to have dragged you into this mess," Asher confessed, his voice tinged with remorse as he hung his head low, his gaze fixed on the wooden floor beneath his feet.

"Dragged me into this? Is that what you think?" Annabel's response was swift and forceful, her words carrying an undercurrent of frustration. "You know, Asher, I wasn't forced to go with you, remember? I went with you willingly. I had no reason to stay. Sure, I had a life here in London; friends that I could count on with one hand came and went. I never knew my grandparents, and I've basically had no family since the time my parents were taken from me by that drunk driver."

Annabel's voice softened, reflecting a depth of emotion as she continued. "So, to say I would have been better off without you is pure rubbish. I went with you because you are all I have, all I know, and who I love," she declared, her words carrying a weight of sincerity and unwavering devotion.

As Annabel's heartfelt confession washed over him, Asher felt a rush of warmth flood his cheeks, his heart skipping a beat at the realization of her feelings. "Did she just say she loves me?" Asher thought, his mind reeling with the sudden shift in focus from their troubles to the depth of their connection. In that moment, everything else faded away—the worries about Savio, the mysteries of magic, the tumult of their recent adventures—all replaced by the overwhelming certainty of their mutual affection.

Before he knew it, Asher found himself drawn closer to Annabel, their proximity suddenly charged with a palpable tension. Her leg brushed against his, igniting a spark of electricity that coursed through his veins, leaving him breathless and trembling with anticipation. As he struggled to find the right words to express the depth of his emotions, Asher's thoughts drifted back to that fateful night when they had shared a moment of quiet intimacy outside her house.

"This reminds me of the night we sat together in front of your house, right before the pizza showed up from Angelo's," Asher confessed, his voice filled with a mixture of longing and regret. With each word, his heart pounded harder in his chest, urging him to seize the moment and lay bare his true feelings.

"Only if I could have that moment back to do all over; I would have kissed you before that delivery guy showed up," he admitted, his voice trembling with vulnerability as he bared his soul to her. Annabel's smile widened at his words, her eyes sparkling with warmth and affection.

"Well then, seize the moment, Asher," she urged, her voice soft and encouraging, as if granting him permission to finally embrace the love that had been simmering between them for so long. As their eyes met and their hearts beat as one, Asher knew that he would never let this chance slip away.

Leaning in with a gentle determination, Asher closed the distance between them, his heart pounding in anticipation as their lips finally met in a tender, heartfelt kiss. In that fleeting moment of connection, time seemed to stand still, the world around them fading into insignificance as they surrendered to the overwhelming rush of emotion coursing between them.

It was a kiss that transcended words, a silent proclamation of their love and longing, more poignant and passionate than any scene Hollywood could ever script. With each tender caress, they poured their souls into the embrace, savoring the sweet taste of love and the promise of a future filled with endless possibilities. When they finally broke apart, Asher knew with unwavering certainty that this moment would be etched in his heart forever—a testament to the power of love and the magic of seizing the moment.

"Wow, I'm glad we seized that moment!" Asher declared, a smile tugging at the corners of his lips as he basked in the warmth of their shared affection.

"Me too," Annabel giggled in response, her heart rate stabilizing with each calming breath. "Well, at least this time, the pizza guy didn't interrupt," Asher chimed in with a chuckle of his own, the memory of their interrupted moment adding a touch of humor to the air.

But as their laughter subsided, Annabel's thoughts turned to the future, her gaze searching Asher's for answers. "Not to be a killjoy of the moment, but my thoughts keep swirling around in my mind. What is next for us?" she asked, her voice tinged with a hint of uncertainty.

Asher pivoted to face Annabel fully, his brow furrowing in thoughtful contemplation. "You mean, like a relationship?" he questioned, his tone tentative yet hopeful. Annabel's laughter bubbled up again at his response. "Not exactly. What is next for us here in London?" she clarified, her eyes bright with curiosity.

Realizing his misunderstanding, Asher nodded. "Oh, yeah, right, I thought that's what you meant," he admitted with a sheepish shrug, brushing off his embarrassment with a smile. "I keep trying to uncover this mystery about Savio," Asher said, changing the topic. "But every time I come up with a plan or an idea to look into it, a thought comes to mind to wait and be patient, that the answers will come. This is so hard for me to do, to sit back and be patient. You know me, the investigational reporter," he said with a wry smile.

"That must be truly difficult for you. I know you like to solve the unsolvable," Annabel said, her voice laced with empathy as she reached out to squeeze his hand in reassurance. "One thing I've come to know about you after all these years ...KNOCK, KNOCK, KNOCK.

Annabel flashed a look in Asher's direction, her eyes wide with alarm as a shot of adrenaline flooded her body. "Who would be knocking on the door in the middle of the night?" Annabel whispered. "Who even knows that we are here?" She added. Asher rose slowly from his seat, every movement deliberate and calculated to avoid making a sound. Casting a silent glance at Annabel, he pressed his finger to his lips, mouthing the words: DON'T SAY A WORD.

Cautiously, Asher approached the door, his senses on high alert as he strained to listen for any telltale signs of danger. As he neared the threshold, his gemmed ring began to vibrate faintly, the gold band growing warm against his skin with each passing second.

With a steadying breath, Asher pressed his eye to the peephole, his heart pounding in his chest. But the years had not been kind to the round glass, which had clouded and obscured its surface. All he could discern was a slender shadow of a man with slightly bowed legs standing three feet away from the door and swaying mysteriously from side to side.

"Who's there? Who's there?" Asher demanded his voice firm and commanding. The shadowed figure stopped swaying immediately, frozen in its steps, as if caught off guard by Asher's authoritative tone. Meanwhile, the vibration in Asher's ring intensified the moment the figure ceased its movement. Drawing the ring closer to his face, Asher watched in astonishment as the gems began to faintly glow with brilliant colors, their hues shifting and swirling in a mesmerizing display.

As the gems grew brighter with each passing moment, Asher's sense of unease deepened. Sensing the urgency of the situation, he motioned for Annabel to make her way to the bedroom, his voice hushed with urgency. "Hide yourself in the closet," he whispered. "I don't know who is behind that door or what. But whatever it is, I believe there is some sort of magic about them. It's as if my ring can detect it." Asher said, squeezing his ring.

Just then, the two heard the door handle jiggle, sending a shiver down their spines. "Quick, into the closet, hide yourself!" Asher urged, his heart racing as he prepared for the unknown threat looming on the other side of the door.

Grabbing the only weapon within reach—a table lamp for blunt force—Asher approached the door once again, his senses on high alert. He could hear the distinct sound of something metallic sliding into the keyhole, followed by the ominous click of the deadbolt being turned. Asher braced himself as the door slowly creaked open, revealing the mysterious intruder lurking in the darkness.

10

A Late-night Visitor

A sher held the lamp aloft, ready to strike with maximum force, the electric cord swinging back and forth with a rhythmic sway. As the front door inched open, a pair of skinny bowlegs emerged through the threshold, casting a shadowy silhouette in the dim light of the flat.

Despite the urge to unleash a preemptive strike, Asher hesitated, a strange sense of safety washing over him in the presence of the mysterious figure. And then, in a moment of realization, a name escaped his lips, whispered with a mixture of disbelief and yet recognition.

"Eckerd? Eckerd, is that you?" Asher inquired, his voice laden with uncertainty. Could it truly be Kristoff's friend standing before him, or was this merely a trick of the light, a figment of his imagination created by the chaos of the moment?

With a toothy grin, the figure stepped further into the room, revealing dirty, round-framed spectacles on the bridge of the man's large, hooked nose. His long, sparsely white beard flowed in various directions yet concealed the wrinkles on his weathered face. His crooked teeth offered a contagious smile, adding to the mysterious charm that seemed to emanate from him. His features became more evident in the dim light. "Why didn't you let me in?" he asked, his voice hinting at mischief.

Asher raised his eyebrows, taken aback by the unexpected question. "Let you in? I thought you were here to kill me," he admitted, with a note of suspicion.

"Kill ya? Well, where is the sense in doin' that, eh?" the skinny old man jeered, his tone marked with amusement as he shuffled closer, his presence filling the room with mystery and intrigue.

As Asher replaced the lamp and plugged it in, the dim light cast a warm glow over the bowlegged man, revealing his features in greater detail. It was indeed the very man who had welcomed Asher—previously known as Joseph Amesbury—to the Gelato shop. Asher's face reflected the recognition, a mix of surprise and realization flooding over him.

"Yes, it's you," Asher murmured, his voice colored with disbelief. It was the same man who had stood next to Kristoff on that fateful night, the night Joseph had been summoned to interview a man claiming to be Santa, a man who desired to reveal his secrets to the world.

Asher's memory of that first encounter flooded back, clear and unmistakable. He remembered the skepticism and intrigue that had filled the air that day and the moments that made him a believer in magic. And now, here stood the very man who had played a pivotal role in that momentous encounter—a man whose true intentions remained mysterious.

"Please, sit down," Asher gestured towards the couch. "Annabel, it's safe. Come on out here; I have someone you need to meet," he called out, his voice filled with excitement.

"Oh, I beg your pardon. I did not realize you were entertaining company at this late hour," Eckerd remarked, his thick German accent just as distinctive as Asher remembered.

"Oh, it's not exactly like that. It's a bit of a long story," Asher replied, his words feeling heavier than usual as he attempted to explain the situation.

As Annabel stepped into the living room, she observed the unexpected guest seated on the couch. Eckerd rose to his feet and extended his bony hand towards her. "It's a pleasure to meet you, ma'am," a scratchy, high-pitched voice greeted her warmly, his breath ruffling the long whiskers as he spoke. "The pleasure is mine, sir," Annabel said with a slight giggle, the man's wiggling whiskers catching her off guard. "I am so sorry; I didn't mean to giggle," Annabell said, covering her mouth with her opposite hand. "I take no offense to the matter schöne frau" Eckerd said, gently. Besides, my beard is my best feature and brings smiles to anyone who dares to look upon it.

"Please, have a seat," Annabel urged, ushering him to sit down again. Asher walked to the dining area, grabbed a chair, placed it next to Eckard, and sat down. Annabel settled onto the couch, forming a semicircle with the trio. "I am surprised to see you. I was very shocked," Asher revealed. "I would have expected Kristoff to show up at a late-night random visit, but I was a little astonished to see you there," he shared.

Eckerd leaned back on the couch, crossed his right leg over his left, and rested his ankle over his bony knee. "I am sad to report that Kristoff will not return but happy to share that he has crossed over and has been reunited with family once again in a state of peace and rest," Eckerd explained. A sense of sadness washed over Asher's face.

"So, what about you, Eckerd? How are you still here with us? I thought you had crossed over as well," Asher declared.

Eckerd reached up and stroked his beard, gently tugging on his whiskers. "Well, now, that is the funny part," Eckerd said with a sheepish, toothy grin. "Kristoff only told you that to keep me a secret." Asher locked eyes with Eckerd. "Why would he do that? Why would he want to keep you a secret?" Asher further questioned.

"I believe he wanted to protect me from any harm, but I mostly think he has a good sense of humor and needed you to grow into your responsibility of being Santa. It would have been easy for you to come to me with questions anytime they arose, right?" Asher nodded, "Yes, that is true. But it's been difficult and a little painful learning at times," he admitted.

Eckerd glanced in Annabel's direction and then back to Asher. "You see!" he said, his voice bright with enthusiasm. "You are learning already. There is no growth without pain, just as there is no pain without growth."

"He is wise in his words, Asher," Annabel confessed, smiling at her new couch companion. "I really like this gal, Asher. So, you are the lovely Annabel then, eh? Kristoff told me a bit about you. He was right about you. You are one sharp lady. I also believe he was right when he told me Asher needs to open his eyes a bit more and stop stalling. A gal can't wait forever, you know," he added, his tone light-hearted yet pointed.

Annabel felt a blush, the warmth spreading up to the tips of her cheekbones. Asher repositioned himself in his wooden chair and tugged at his shirt collar. "So you were saying that Kristoff wanted you to stay behind?" Asher redirected the conversation, seeking to steer away from the playful banter and onto a more serious topic.

"No, Kristoff didn't request that I stay behind. It was my own choice. You see, when Kristoff had a vision of someone attempting to take the ring from you, he felt compelled to stay and safeguard both you and the ring. He's truly selfless, with a heart of gold, and he wanted to ensure that the work continued uninterrupted. He'd already given so much for so long. I felt it was my turn to step up, to let him find peace, to cross over, and finally rest for a while. I'll return to my family soon, but for now, it was important that someone shared the knowledge he had uncovered when the time was right."

"When the time was right?" Asher questioned.

"Yes, when the time was right," Eckerd repeated. "And that time is today, in the middle of the night?" Asher pressed jokingly.

"Well, yes, as in the day, but the middle of the night was just my sense of humor coming through. Besides, once I deliver this information, I will also cross over to join with my family and Kristoff on the other side. So, I wanted to get an early start," Eckerd said, his face beaming.

"The night that Kristoff had seen someone try to remove your ring, he noted it was by dark magic. He also had told you that it was someone you knew would try and remove it. After he had returned home from sharing that information with you, Kristoff was much more pensive. Much more quiet. He spent several days pacing the house, writing down notes only to scribble them out and toss the paper in the trash. Then, one afternoon, I heard him shout aloud that he figured out a small but important fact."

"What did he find out?" Annabel interrupted, clearly consumed by the story.

Eckerd whipped his head in Annabel's direction, "Well, Kristoff had discovered that the night something tried to remove the ring was not an only one-time event."

Asher reached up and scratched his scalp. "What do you mean, Eckerd?"

"Oh, my English still fails me," Eckerd grumbled. "Let me try again. When Kristoff mentioned someone you knew would try to take the ring, the vision wasn't clear. He assumed it was someone familiar attempting to snatch the ring off your finger the night he visited you. Unfortunately, Kristoff arrived late and barely thwarted the attempt. When he returned home, he was puzzled over why he'd been shown the vision only to arrive after the attack. It didn't make sense. After days of pondering, Kristoff realized the warning wasn't about that specific attack but about a future event, another attempt by someone you know to take the ring. He concluded that there must be more than one individual after it. He also believed this new attack would occur shortly after today, hence my early midnight visit.

"So let me see if I understand what you are telling us. That scary night when dark magic attacked me, I was not attacked by someone I knew. You are saying there are two people after this ring and that the next attack against me will be by someone I know?" Asher quizzed further.

"Precisely," Eckerd said, nodding his head.

Asher leaned back in his chair and sighed. "I thought I had it figured out, and we are safe. If this vision or prophecy is correct, I placed us right in the path of another attacker."

"Do you know who or what they look like?" Eckerd shook his head. "No, it was not shown to Kristoff in enough detail. But he was certain it was someone you already knew."

"We must be vigilant and keep our eyes peeled, Asher," Annabel's voice was heavily painted with concern.

"We will be on the lookout, that is for sure," Asher replied. "Eckerd, did you know that someone named Savio appeared by magic the other day and entered Annabel's house? We suspect he was after me, or at least my ring," Asher's voice trailed off.

"No, I wasn't aware," Eckerd confessed, his tone carrying a hint of surprise. "This is news to me. I haven't been able to keep tabs on you or your movements. Kristoff simply instructed me to meet you at this location on this specific day." Leaning forward on the edge of the couch, he continued, "This is quite intriguing. Other magic at play... I suppose I never really considered it. I witnessed Kristoff's abilities firsthand once he embraced his role, but the notion of magic working against good is indeed alarming. Do you have any leads or suspicions?"

"In fact, I do have some information," Asher began, his voice carrying a sense of gravity. "The night Kristoff visited me, he spoke of a book called 'The Great Forefathers of Christmas.' It contains a collection of journals dating back to the first Santa in the Sacred Order. According to Kristoff, this book holds magical secrets, including those pertaining to my ring.

It delves into the secrets of Santa and wizardly abilities. Moreover, Kristoff mentioned something troubling: discovering a missing magical gem from my ring. This gem was found by someone unaffiliated with the Magical Order and was being used for nefarious purposes."

Standing up, Asher walked to the kitchen and retrieved a chilled glass bottle with a yellow label. "Would anyone care for a Yoo-hoo?" he asked politely, his gesture a brief interlude in the conversation.

"Yes, please. Kristoff and I used to enjoy these on late nights," Eckerd replied, his voice glowed with nostalgia.

"And you, Annabel? Would you like a late-night chocolate treat?" Asher inquired, turning his attention to her.

"Sure, if it's not too much trouble," Annabel replied graciously.

"No trouble at all," Asher assured her, grabbing two additional bottles as he returned to the living room. Eckerd twisted open the bottle cap, took a swig, and smiled. "Ah... just like old times," he remarked, a sense of familiarity flooding over him.

"I've developed a habit of drinking these when I need to think or when I'm under stress. They seem to do the trick for me," Asher explained, resettling himself in the conversation. "As I was saying, the book and the ring... I can't shake the feeling that there might be a connection to when some Nazis fled to Argentina. Kristoff mentioned his suspicion that Hanz took the book and the ring when he escaped Germany. I can't help but think that both items are somehow linked to Savio. I just haven't pieced that part together yet. It would certainly explain how Savio possesses magic and knows the truth behind Santa, confirming his existence rather than mere folklore," Asher continued, taking another sip of Yoo-hoo as he contemplated the tangled web of connections.

The trio spent the remainder of the night immersed in conversation, finishing a few more bottles of the beloved brown liquid. Eckerd entertained them with tales of past events and harrowing war stories, his enthusiasm infusing each story with life. As they reminisced, laughter mingled with the beverage's rich chocolate aroma, creating a nostalgic atmosphere that lingered long into the morning light.

"Would you look at that?" Eckerd exclaimed, pointing to the first rays of sunlight painting the streets of London. "We've spent the entire night chatting. Sorry if I've overstayed my welcome," he apologized, his voice hoarse from the hours of conversation.

"Goodness, no, Eckerd. You could never overstay your welcome," Annabel reassured him warmly. "Thank you, schöne frau. I'll never forget you and this night with the two of you," Eckerd expressed gratefully. With a gentle motion, he removed the immortality ring that Kristoff had given him during the war. Instantly, Mr. Baggins materialized out of thin air, perching himself on the table in front of Eckerd and assuming a posture akin to bowing to royalty. "Oh, there you are, ol' wonder sack," Eckerd greeted respectfully as he placed the ring inside.

"Asher. Annabel, my time has ended for me here in mortality." Eckerd's voice tinged with melancholy. "I want you both to know this is not the end." He continued, "Just as I will be reunited with Kristoff and my loved ones, so will you, in time, be reunited with your family and those who will pass before you. How silly to think that this life is all that there is. Life is eternal, and we live beyond the grasp of the mortal world. Always remember, we live to die, and we die to live. It's not complicated; it's straightforward in its form. Philosophy and science have complicated the simple, pure truth. One of the most important things we can do in mortality is to love those around us and look for ways to lift those who are heavily burdened.

Wiping a tear from his eye, Eckerd stepped back from Asher and Annabel. With a wink of his eye and a gentle wave of his hand, his body began to fade from view until he was no longer visible, leaving behind memories of a night filled with camaraderie and shared stories.

11

Angels Among Us

The next several days passed like a brief dream for Annabel and Asher. They continued their day-to-day routines but with a heavy awareness that they were being watched, knowing that more than one person coveted the ring. For Annabel, anxiety crept in, her mind filled with thoughts of potential attacks lurking around every corner. While she found comfort in not possessing the ring, the fear of being used as a bargaining chip gnawed at her. "Would she become a pawn in someone else's pursuit of the ring?" She thought.

Asher did his best to calm her fears, urging her to focus on preparation rather than dwelling on uncertain futures. "If you are prepared," Asher reassured her, "you will not need to fear." Together, they spent evenings brainstorming codewords, devising escape plans, and strategizing ways to alert others if an attack were to occur in public places. Their efforts aimed to empower them with a sense of readiness and control in the face of looming threats.

"I can't believe it's been six weeks since Eckerd bid us farewell, and here we are in November," Asher remarked, savoring the last bite of his bangers and mash that morning. Annabel nodded in agreement, focusing on stirring her Greek yogurt adorned with fresh berries and crunchy granola.

"The way Eckerd showed up in the middle of the night, I thought an attack was imminent," Annabel recalled. "He mentioned that after the day he visited, someone else would attempt to seize the ring," she recounted.

"I felt the same," Asher admitted. "Visions aren't always crystal clear in their details, though. The only certainty about visions is that what's seen will inevitably come to pass unless events leading up to the vision can alter the outcome."

"Do you think we've somehow altered the outcome of someone attacking you days after Eckerd's visit?" Annabel questioned, her hope evident in her voice.

"Hard to say," Asher replied thoughtfully. "I can't think of anything we've done that might have changed that. But then again, our absence from the bustling streets of London might have made a difference," he speculated. "Sometimes, even the smallest moments of inactivity can alter the course of the future. The way I see it, even small hinges can swing enormous doors," he added, his words offering some much-needed comfort.

"I guess time will tell. At least we've prepared the best we can," Annabel remarked, finding reassurance in their shared readiness for whatever may come. The two had begun to clear the table when Mr. Baggins floated as gracefully as an autumn leaf out of thin air, descending until he softly landed on the dining table where Asher had been sitting just moments before.

"Well, good morning to you, my faithful friend. What brings you this way so early in the morning?" Asher addressed the red velvet bag with a warm smile. In response, the bag gave a quick shiver, and its opening swayed back and forth in a welcoming nod as if acknowledging Asher's greeting. The bag shivered once again when suddenly a small piece of parchment emitted upward from the bag, sending the paper soaring above the table. Then, it floated down gently, resting on Asher's awaiting opened hand.

Pulling the paper taut, Asher read the note aloud. "Haste is required in this moment of need. Life precious will be spared if you're up to the deed. Listen closely to the words that fill your mind, and preserve life ever after in the nick of time." Guinevere thrashed wildly inside Asher's pocket as the last words passed over his lips.

"What do you think that parchment meant, Asher?" questioned Annabel.

"I'm not exactly sure, but I had better get a move on if I'm going to save a life," Asher said, his tone urgent. Reaching into his pocket, Asher retrieved his brass spectacles and placed them on the bridge of his nose. Through the vaporous green and red smoke shown in Guinevere's lenses, Asher stepped into the portal and disappeared, leaving a sense of anticipation and uncertainty behind.

The next thing Asher knew, he was standing at the edge of a grassy area with scattered ash trees and rolling hills dotted the horizon with various hazel and oak trees. A dirt trail winding through the area weaved through the vibrant greenery and disappeared in the distance. Large puffy clouds filled the sky, floating effortlessly towards lands in the distance, and the crisp air hinted that Asher was indeed in Ireland. Memories of his time as a reporter flooded back to him, and he couldn't help but feel a pang of nostalgia for the bustling streets of Dublin, which he had visited while working on an assignment several years ago.

Asher wondered if he was all alone. There was no sign of a passerby, hikers, or any bicycles thundering by, though footprints and tire marks in the loose dirt suggested this was a place of frequent recreational use. Asher felt a stiff wind rise in the portal behind him, shoving him toward the giant oak tree blocking the landscape beyond.

It was at that moment when all was still that a faint cry for help reached his ears. Asher sucked in a deep breath of air and held his breath, hoping to eliminate any sound, even the sound of his breath. As the cry for help pierced the silence, Asher's heart quickened with a mix of urgency and determination. Without hesitation, he pressed forward, his steps guided by the unseen force that seemed to beckon him toward the source of distress.

"Help me, help me, help me! Someone help me! Oh heavens above, help me save my boy." The terrifying words reached Asher's mind and ears with perfect clarity. Just on the other side of the oak tree, the words filled his mind as if some unseen force was leading him, yet no voice was discerned. Asher was positive he was being told what to do, but appearing as his thoughts.

As the urgent plea for help echoed in Asher's mind, a surge of adrenaline coursed through his veins, his heart racing in overdrive. With a sense of purpose driving him forward, he moved swiftly around the oak tree, his senses heightened and his focus unwavering.

There, just beyond the tree, he spotted a distraught woman kneeling beside a young boy, her anguished cries blending with the urgent thoughts that flooded Asher's mind. Without hesitation, he knelt beside them and assessed the situation. At this moment, Asher suddenly realized he could not see his leg, arm, or hands. He could feel them but could not see himself. *Am I invisible?* he questioned, waving his unseen hand in front of his face, confirming his suspicions.

The boy lay still, cradled in his mother's arms. His blood-soaked pantleg began to darken the soil beneath him. His breathing was shallow, and his pulse weak. A few feet away, his bicycle was in a crumpled mess, and various-sized shards of green glass from a broken whiskey bottle littered the dirt path.

Asher's mind raced as he absorbed the information flooding his thoughts, each word urging him to take decisive action. *The boy is hemorrhaging. Apply firm pressure to the wound.* The instructions filled his mind. Asher leaned close to the mother's ear and instructed her to press firmly on the bleeding wound.

The woman twisted her head to the right and left, trying to find the source of the disembodied voice. "Press firmly on the bleeding wound!" Asher repeated, his voice full of intensity. The woman flashed a squinted look in Asher's direction. "She must have heard me." he resolved. Not hesitating further, the trembling mother pressed her hand gently and cautiously on the wound. The young boy groaned, lifting his gaze in Asher's direction, only to lie back, motionless once again. As she pressed down on her son's leg, the woman watched with a mixture of hope and desperation, her prayers silently echoing the urgency in Asher's mind.

Her pressure on the wound is not sufficient. Once again, the words echoed in Asher's mind. Instinctively, Asher placed his hand upon hers and began to apply additional pressure. The woman looked once again at where Asher was kneeling. Can she feel my hand? He wondered. Asher placed his opposite hand on the woman's shoulder, hoping to provide comfort. She glanced briefly at her shoulder, then back to her son.

The strong woman rocked her son gently in the cold, quiet, grassy field. Asher's eyes filled with tears of compassion as he witnessed a mother's love for her son in such a time of tragedy and grief. An image of an old oil painting he had seen as a child hanging in a church resurfaced in his memory. The artist's hand had carefully depicted a woman, an honored mother, loved and revered, staring up helplessly at her dying son nailed to a wooden cross. A small rectangular brass plate with engraved letters read, "He died that we may live again," completed the artful piece. Asher knew in his heart that regardless of the situation's outcome, this family could be together again because, in truth, Christ died so that we may live again.

Tears of concern soaked the pleading mother's eyes as she spoke a silent prayer, her words too soft for Asher to discern. Then, suddenly, she began to sing the sweetest Irish lullaby Asher had ever heard. Perhaps it was the gravity of the situation or the mother's pure love, but the Ballyeamon cradle song lullaby sank deep into Asher's heart.

The Faithful mother continued the lullaby in its entirety, only to restart once again. It was a sobering sight for Asher, who was observing a loving mother's compassion in its purest form. Moments later, a couple riding mountain bikes together appeared around the trees. Witnessing the mother and child in distress, the benevolent passersby hastened their pedaling to offer assistance. "Are you alright, ma'am?" one of them called out, swiftly abandoning his bike at the roadside. "Please, we need help," the frantic mother implored. "Bridget, hurry!" he called to his wife, who was approaching them along the path, still pedaling.

"My son is badly hurt; the bleeding has slowed with pressure, but he's lost a lot of blood," the woman explained, her trembling finger pointing to the blood-stained mud. "What's your name?" the cyclist asked, trying to provide a calming distraction. "I'm Orla, and this is my son Liam." "I'm relieved we found you, Orla. I'm Declan, and my wife Bridget is on her way," he assured her. "Luckily, she's a staff nurse at the hospital and can help." Orla's eyes widened with gratitude at the mention of Bridget's profession. "Thank heavens," she murmured, a glimmer of hope emerging amidst the chaos. "Please, we need all the help we can get."

"Have you called for help?" the winded Bridget asked.

"No," Orla shook her head. "Something always happens when you don't have a phone. I left in such a hurry this morning that I forgot it."

"What happened to Liam?" Bridget continued.

"Liam was excited to ride his bike and was going fast around that bend of trees. I think he must have lost control and crashed, landing on an old discarded glass bottle. He was crying up a real fit when I got to him. He has been sort of in and out since," Orla said, staring down at her closed-eyed son.

"I've rang 112, and an ambulance is on its way," Declan said, stuffing his cell phone back into his pocket. "I know it looks like a lot of blood, given his soaked pants and soil, but I believe your quick thinking to apply pressure has saved your son's life. The pressure has stopped the bleeding. I don't think your lad lost consciousness from lack of blood. I wonder if he passed out from the sight of the blood." Bridgett wondered.

"I think your guardian angel must have been looking after you. Declan said, opening his backpack and retrieving a small first aid kit. "My wife always insists that I bring it. Turns out she was right." He said, handing the medical kit to Brigett. Opening the small box, Bridgett retrieved several thick gauze pads and shoved them under Orla's hand, instructing her to apply additional pressure. Orla looked up at Bridgett, her lips turning upward slightly at the corners of her mouth. "I was praying for a miracle, an angel to help me, and here you both are."

"I believe that there are angels among us in so many forms. Some we can see, and some we may not," Declan smiled as he knelt and helped hold additional pressure. Feeling the extra pressure, Asher stepped back and observed. Orla's eyes darted from Declan to Bridget. "It's curious you say that. I know it sounds strange, but I think I heard a voice telling me to apply pressure to Liam's wound. I heard it more than once. Then, more curious, I could feel someone's hand on my shoulder, but nothing was there when I looked." I know it sounds unbelievable, but I felt guided by some unseen person."

"Mum, It was Santy." Liam's delicate voice interrupted her. "Liam, are you ok? How's your pain? It hurts Mum. "Help is on its way. These kind angels called the ambulance. It should be here any moment." She reassured her son. "Mum, It was Santy," Liam repeated. "Santy? What are you talking about Liam?" Orla asked. The man touching your shoulder and pressing my leg. When I opened my eyes, I saw Daidí na

Nollag. You know, Santy. But he was sort of seethrough. He had one hand on your shoulder and the other on my leg." Declan looked down at Liam and smiled, "Like I said, there are angels among us. Some we can see, and others we may not."

In an atmosphere steeped in reverence, the ambient sounds around Asher gradually dulled into distant whispers. A potent tug at his navel signaled his return journey through the portal. "You've done well," resonated the voice within his mind. "The boy will endure." With those comforting words lingering in his consciousness, the portal sealed shut, transporting Asher back to London.

12

The Perfect Gown

Asher stood facing Annabel, his expression a mix of amusement and wonder. In the streets below, the soft chimes of the Fortnum & Mason clock rang out as if in harmony with the miraculous event that had just unfolded. "What happened? Did you actually save someone from death?" Annabel's questions came as quickly as a flash of lightning. "It was miraculous in so many ways. I have started to understand the profound meaning of angels." Asher said, his voice filled with a sense of awe as he sat down on the couch. Annabel joined him; her anticipation was palpable as she waited on bated breath for the detailed report.

"To be perfectly honest, I have long wondered about angels, divine intervention, helpers for a good cause, if you will. After what just happened, I'm starting to think that angels can come in the simple form of good people following an impression to help someone in need. Sometimes, people stand in need of assistance, and sometimes, people just need someone to smile at them, say hello, or even acknowledge them. Being an earthly angel doesn't take much; it's just a desire to do good for others." Annabel grabbed her water bottle from the coffee table and took a swig. "So what about the ones you can't see?" she asked. Asher stood, walked a few steps, and then returned to Annabel. "This is the miracle or the divine help we cannot explain. I believe we get help from those we cannot see but truly exist and are guided by divine instruction."

Asher spent the next half hour recounting the event to Annable. "So, who was the angel then?" Annabel probed. "I believe all three of us were angels, dispatched to answer a prayer and provide aid. I was sent to offer assistance in a perilous moment until earthly angels could arrive. I may have been sent to teach me that there is more to this world than meets the eye. I hold that there is a supreme God, a father of the spirits that define us, and that this Father loves us more than we fathom and even more than we can comprehend." Asher settled back onto the couch, his gaze fixed on the window.

Annabel slid towards the edge of the couch cushion and took another sip of her water. "So, have you seen God?" Her voice was heavy with curiosity. "Oh, I am sorry, I should not have asked you that. That is very personal and private. Forget I asked." The flushed Annebel muttered. Asher pivoted on the couch, his knee comfortably resting against hers. Reaching out, he grabbed her hand and delicately held it in his. "I appreciate your respect for a topic considered private or sacred. You truly are a remarkable woman." Annabel's cheeks flamed again. "To be honest, no, I have never seen God. My conversations with Him are just like yours, by prayer. He hears our prayers and answers them in a way that is best for us and our growth, and He sees a bigger eternal picture than we can see. He hears you too, you know." Asher's words made Annabel beam

"So what does God look like, you ask? I believe we've already glimpsed Him," Asher asserted confidently. Annabel's gaze lifted, a flicker of confusion passing through her eyes. "Allow me to elaborate," Asher continued, gently stroking his beard.

"Annabel, Often, we observe the traits of our family members' children, marveling at their looks and personalities. It's not until we meet the parents that we grasp the origin of these attributes. In this context, one could liken it to Santa Claus explaining how we don't need to visualize God's appearance, as God's essence is manifested in the diverse qualities of those around each individual, reflecting a facet of the divine from laughter to bravery, kindness to divine. Whether it's eloquence, entertainment, or other unique abilities, these are all glimpses of the Father's handiwork. When we eventually reunite with our Father in heaven, we'll realize that we've always known Him, for His presence has been woven into the tapestry of humanity. Every encounter on Earth, every reflection of His attributes, serves as a familiar guide leading us back to Him." Annabel nodded in agreement.

"When you put it like that," she began, a soft smile playing on her lips, "I can also reflect and realize: I've seen God in every step of my life."

Asher stood and walked over to the window. Picadilly Street was busy as usual despite the street being cold and damp. "Christmas is coming, Santa," Annabel said, wrapping her arm around Asher in a playful hug. A warm smile stretched across his face. "Speaking of Christmas, are we still on for next week's visit to Hyde Park Winter Wonderland?" Asher asked. "We most certainly are. I was able to pull some magic of my own once again and have you scheduled opening night to visit with all the little ones at Santa's Grotto. Everything is arranged, and they have packed your bag of gifts for the children, who have been good this year." Annabel gleamed.

Asher let out a hearty, full-bellied laugh, feeling refreshed after emerging from the portal. "I adored seeing the little ones last year," he reminisced, his eyes alight with fond memories, "watching their eyes light up as they received their gifts. But you know, the highlight of those special visits was seeing Mr. Baggins getting involved." He paused, a warm smile spreading across his face. "I'll never forget little seven-year-old Agatha. While other kids clamored for the latest toys or coveted cell phones, she had a different request. With her broken shoes and cold, wet feet on the way to school, she only wanted a new pair of shoes to keep her warm and dry." Asher's voice softened, emotion tugging at his words. "I'll never forget the tears that welled in my eyes, nor the warmth that flooded my heart when Mr. Baggins pulled out those new shoes, along with socks and the Harry Potter book she'd been asking her mum for."

"Why don't you come with me this time?" Asher suggested eagerly, closing the distance between himself and Annabel with renewed determination. "What would I do there?" Annabel questioned, her shoulders lifting in a shrug. "You'll be Mrs. Claus; just imagine greeting the little ones alongside me, handing out gifts, and reveling in their infectious smiles. After all, you were doing something similar at the Christmas boutique back in the US."Asher remanded her with a gleam in his eye. As Annabel turned to head back towards her room, Asher couldn't help but feel a surge of anticipation. However, before she reached the door, she spun around, sporting the biggest smile he had seen in quite a while. "I'm in; I'll do it!" she exclaimed joyfully.

"This is actually very exciting," Annabel continued, her excitement palpable. "The Mrs. Claus suit I wore in the Christmas Boutique was getting a bit worn. I was thinking it was time for an update, a new one." Her voice hinted at the impending shopping excursion. "Well, let me grab my wallet, and we'll find you a new suit."

Stepping outside, the brisk November air and the slight drizzle served as a reminder that winter was on its way. "It's good to get outside, don't you think?" Asher remarked, deftly navigating around a large puddle on the damaged sidewalk. "Oh gosh, yes, I needed to get out," Annabel exclaimed a sense of liberation in her voice. "I've been getting a slight cabin fever, staying hidden up there for so long. Anytime we can get out, it's heaven to me. So where do you think we should go to find the perfect Mrs Clause dress?" Annabel asked.

"A few stores are already gearing up for Christmas, and there's one shop in particular named Ann's Relics and Gowns that sells incredibly unique handmade costumes," Asher remarked, a reminiscent twinkle in his eye. "I stopped in there once for that work Halloween social party, if you remember. I wasn't too keen on the idea, but the pressure from the top at the Gazette made it abundantly clear that attendance was highly encouraged. Needless to say, that fancy Robin Hood costume came from that store. It was so humiliating, but I got quite a few looks from some of the ladies that night," he shared, chuckling as they continued their walk. Annabel couldn't help but join in on the laughter. "Oh yes," she said, poking him in the ribs playfully, "seeing you in those forest green tights was definitely a sight to remember."

The two continued their back and for teasing, passing by many shops and weaving themselves through the busy London streets. Soon, the two found their way into Ann's Relics and Gowns, standing face to face with numerous costumes. "I will browse the store a little and see if I can find the Christmas costumes section. Asher said, walking toward the back of the store."Sounds good. I think I will go to the sales counter and enquire about a sales associate, Annable replied.

"May I help you?" an attractive blond woman with warm chestnut eyes and a sun-bronzed face asked. "Oh, absolutely," Annabel replied, a hint of excitement in her voice. I am looking for something unique. I'm looking for a Mrs. Clause suit that is unlike any other. One that looks authentic yet inviting and elegant."

"We received a new shipment of Christmas wardrobes yesterday, but I have yet to have an opportunity to get them on the hangers; they are still in a box in the back. If you can give me a few minutes, I will get them." In the meantime, we have a few over by that rack, just over there," she said, pointing towards the front door she had just walked through. "Oh, thank you. I did not even notice those when I walked in." Annabel said sheepishly. The eye-catching sales clerk giggled, then turned and headed towards the back of the shop.

Just out of sight and feeling safe and unseen, Asher whispered softly into his overcoat, "Mr. Baggins, I need your help." Suddenly, the inside of his coat began thrashing around as if someone had caught a fish and was trying to hide it under their clothes.

"Settle down, Mr. Bagg,"s," Asher pleaded. "You are going to get us discovered!" He said, tapping the velvet bag. "I need your help. We need a Mrs Claus suit for Annabel. I knew this store had some excellent costumes, but now that I have seen them, I don't feel they are elegant enough for someone as beautiful as Annabel." Asher had previously considered making one magically back home but knew they both needed to get out and clear their minds a little. "If you create something perfect for her, I will put it somewhere in the store where she can find it, and then I will buy it for her. We can think of it as donating and supporting small businesses in London."

Mr. Baggins nodded in agreement before settling down. Asher glanced into his coat and found a neatly folded, brilliant scarlet gown where Mr. Baggins had been just moments before. "Thank you, Mr. Baggins," Asher murmured gratefully into his overcoat as he slipped through the doorway marked 'EMPLOYEES ONLY.'

Entering the merchandise supply area made Asher feel uneasy as if he were violating a significant rule and law enforcement might apprehend him at any moment. While he knew entering such an area wasn't a serious offense, he couldn't shake the feeling that he was trespassing. Despite his rationality, he couldn't help but scan the room nervously for any sign of employees."

"I think we're alone," Asher murmured into the empty space where Mr. Baggins had once stood. Stepping closer to the stacked boxes lining the wall, he methodically inspected each one, searching for the elusive Christmas costumes. "Star Wars, clown costumes, dark dresses for witches... no, not that one either," he muttered, pushing aside a box filled with princess dresses adorned with delicate embellishments.

With anticipation, Asher popped open a sizeable charcoal-colored box and found an inventory list resting atop a mound of red fabric. "Elf costume x 3 size medium, Child reindeer one-piece x 4, Santa suit XL x 4, Mrs. Claus x 3," he recited under his breath, his eyes scanning the list with determination. "Ah ha! Here you are," he exclaimed softly, carefully tucking the folded scarlet red suit from inside his jacket beneath the packing list. "That will suffice," he decided, closing the box with a sense of satisfaction.

Just as Asher slipped back through the employee door, he heard the faint echo of footsteps approaching—undoubtedly belonging to the attractive sales clerk. Swiftly retreating into the shadows, he pretended to browse the nearby rack of costumes, his heart racing with the thrill of his covert mission. With his practiced nonchalance, Asher waited for the clerk to pass before making his way back to Annabel at the front desk.

"So, any luck?" Asher nudged Annabel's shoulder gently. Annabel nodded towards the front door. "The lady mentioned they've got a few costumes on the rack, but she also hinted that they received some new ones the other day, maybe even some fresh gowns. They're not out on the floor yet, but she's going to grab them from the back," she explained, a hopeful gleam in her eyes.

"Awesome! That's great news," Asher grinned, feeling a surge of excitement. "I had a feeling there might be some hidden gems waiting for us."

Annabel arched an eyebrow teasingly. "Oh? And why's that, Asher?" she teased, a playful smile tugging at her lips.

Asher shrugged, a mischievous glint in his eye. "Just a hunch that there might be something really special tucked away in the back," he replied cryptically, heading towards the door and the rack of Christmas costumes. "I'll be around if you need me," he called over his shoulder, flashing a quick wink before disappearing into the rows of costumes.

A few moments later, the clerk returned, cradling the sizable charcoal gray box that Asher had uncovered in the back. "I found this box of Christmas costumes. Let's take a look together," she said, setting the box down on the counter. With eagerness, they pried the lid open, and the clerk's eyes widened as she carefully lifted out the gown left by Asher.

"Wow, just look at this one! I don't recall seeing it in the catalog, but I'm thrilled it made its way into my box," she exclaimed, draping the gown over the counter for all to admire.

Annabel couldn't help but share in the excitement, her eyes tracing the lines of the crushed velvet scarlet gown edged with luxurious white fur and adorned with intricate gold embroidery at the collar, hemline, and cuffs. "Incredible," she breathed, her fingers hovering over the soft fabric. And look, it comes with a velvet capelet and matching hat," the saleswoman added, her eyes sparkling with delight as she pointed out the accessories. "This one will fetch a price of around three hundred pounds."

"This is perfect, and it's just my size," Annabel exclaimed, inspecting the label. "A.J. Designs, size medium, made with love from angels above." With a smile, she and the clerk walked over to the full-length mirror on the wall. Annabel slipped on the outer jacket and capelet, twirling in circles and covering her head with the hat, admiring the elegant gown.

"You look dazzling," the clerk complimented the radiant Mrs. Claus.

"Hey, Asher, come look!" Annabel called out across the store.

As Asher approached, he couldn't tear his gaze away from Annabel. Her beauty, the magnificent gown, and the natural glow that radiated from her were captivating. "Wow, absolutely stunning," Asher stammered, fumbling for the right words.

"Why thank you, kind gentleman," Annabel replied warmly, twisting in front of the mirror to admire the gown from all angles.

"So, should I wrap it up then?" the clerk asked from behind. Asher felt a sudden rush of panic, his heart pounding in his chest and his face growing warm. Could it be? There's no way, he tried to convince himself, but the voice was unmistakable, familiar. Maybe she won't recognize me. After all, I'm white-haired and heavier now.

"Sir, would you like me to ring up the sale?" the slender blond behind him inquired. Asher felt a lump forming in his throat, but he swallowed hard to clear it. Slowly turning to face the woman, his eyes met hers, locking in a familiar stare. Her eyes looked a bit older now, with a few thin creases at the corners indicating the passage of years. But those chestnut eyes were unmistakable, confirming his suspicions.

"I, uh," the woman stopped mid-sentence, her voice tinged with uncertainty. Asher felt warmth flood his body, discomfort creeping over him. "Is that you, Joseph Amesbury?"

Asher cleared his throat. "Hi Emily, it's been a while, hasn't it?" Annabel shot a surprised glance in Asher's direction, her mouth slightly agape. "I imagine I look a little different than the last time you saw me, right?"

"As handsome as always. The silver hair is striking and makes you look more distinguished," Emily said, stepping forward and running her fingers through his hair.

"So, how do you know Joseph?" Annabel interjected, her eyes widening.

"Joseph and I dated in the past," Emily replied, though her gaze remained fixed on Asher. "He must have mentioned me to you, didn't he? We were very exclusive. You might have thought we were married; we spent so much time together."

"No, I don't recall him mentioning an Emily," Annabel said, her smile forced. "I think I might have remembered that," she added sarcastically.

"Well, I'm sure I was bound to come up in conversation sooner or later," Emily said, gently grabbing Asher's hand, which felt all too familiar. "Did you call him Asher? I could have sworn you did."

"It's complicated," Asher blurted out. "Perhaps we can tell you about it when we have more time."

"Fair enough. Just out of curiosity, are you two a couple then?" Emily asked, still holding Asher's hand.

"It's complicated, too," Asher interjected before Annabel could respond. Furrowing her brows, Annabel took hold of Asher's arm. "Let's pay for our things; we'll be going now," she said, ushering Asher back toward the front of the store.

13

Fiesta de la Tradición

"W hat's that uproar outside?" Savio bellowed from his recliner, his curiosity piqued. Carlos, who was organizing their tools for their next robbery, was startled. "Seems like a grand celebration in the streets. It's been the talk of the town about the November 10th celebrations," Carlos hollered back, placing his tool bag on the table.

"What could they possibly be celebrating? Life is not that exciting," Savio grumbled, his voice tinged with disgust. On the other hand, Carlos was captivated by the scene unfolding outside. He made his way to the front window and peered out. The local neighbors had transformed the streets into a vibrant tapestry of colors and sounds. The well-anticipated Fiesta de la Tradición, also known as Argentina Tradition Day, was in full swing.

Down the street, Carlos could see several men on horseback, their straw hats waving enthusiastically in the air, greeting the neighbors with a classic gaucho yee-ha. Boys and girls lined the streets, their makeshift horses crafted from old brooms and mops, their laughter echoing through the air. The stark contrast between Carlos' fascination and Savio's disdain for the celebration was palpable, reflecting their contrasting personalities and outlooks on life.

This year's celebration promised to be bigger and more exciting than ever. Citizens wanted to bring the traditional San Antonio de Areco festivals to their community, including parades, artistic events, and demonstrations commemorating the birth of writer and journalist José Hernández in 1834. Hernández had penned *El Gaucho Martín Fierro*, considered the pinnacle of gaucho literature in Argentina.

"It sounds like they are really into it this year!" Carlos said, his excitement evident.

Savio's disdain for the celebration outside was palpable, his voice dripping with venom as he lashed out at Carlos. 'It's clear you would like to join them, Carlos. They're your type of people. Perhaps you should be back on the streets with these fools. Maybe you would be better off with them than with us. Are you finished packing for the heist?' His words hung in the air, heavy with hostility. The tension in the room was thick, a silent battle of wills that threatened to erupt at any moment.

Stepping away from the window, Carlos headed back down the hall and out of sight. "Such a worthless person," Savio grumbled. "Still, I need him around just a little longer. I'll just have to tolerate him until then," he mused. Leaving the comfort of his recliner, he made his way to the front door, pulled it open just enough, and screamed, "¡Tranquilizarse!" at the top of his lungs. The cheers and laughter abruptly stopped, and a few children cringed at the sound of his voice. Savio slammed the front door and headed to Felipe's office to review tonight's plans.

Carlos had been impeccable at his assignments. He may disagree with the type of work he had been involved with, but Savio and Felipe were all he knew. They were not family, and for that matter, he could hardly call them a friend. But what they were to him was company, and having company was better than being alone. "It could be worse; other people have it much worse than I do." He would comfort himself. Looking for the positive, even in the face of evil, kept Carlos going even in the most challenging days. His internal struggle, torn between loyalty and his own moral compass, was a constant battle.

"I will triple-check the list, Sir," Carlos replied. "Lock pick, small mirror, screwdrivers, pliers, narrow blade scissors, slim jim, crowbar," Carlos read the list out loud to prove he was diligent and as a way of talking over Savio to drown out his voice. "Small file... won't forget that again. He continued. Last week, a small error occurred in their string of thefts. A small file was left out of the bag by accident. Though not needed during that heist, it was an error indeed. This seemingly insignificant mistake could have serious consequences. It was not a big deal in the grand scheme of things, but it was nonetheless an error in his routine, and an error could land them all in jail, a risk Carlos was unwilling to take.

November was starting to be a lucrative month for Savios's little team. The trio had successfully ransacked a large jewelry store, making off with nearly ten thousand US dollars in a matter of minutes. It was enough money to settle their needs for the month, but Savio was not looking to sustain a way of life but to fund a wealthy hoard of treasure. It was an insatiable quest for him. He always wanted more and was never satisfied.

Each successful job only fueled his passion for wanting more. Savio found success in his work by entering establishments around three in the morning. The way he looked at things, most thefts had already occurred by midnight or one in the morning. At three in the morning, there is a sort of global letting down your guard. This false sense of security made early morning thievery safe and secure for the successful bandits. Up to this point, the group of men had no run-ins with the law, and as far as they were aware, nobody suspected them. Constantly changing the type of loot they would take made it challenging to track them.

"Felipe, how does everything look for taking down the Vino shop tonight?" Felipe had tapped into surveillance cameras at the Vino shop and had a detailed time log of anyone leaving, everyday traffic passing, and local bus routes shuttling by. He was extremely thorough and a perfect expert who made no mistakes. "It's a brilliant plan to nab those expensive bottles of wine, Savio. Don't think I would have thought of that myself." The corrupt comment made Savio smile with satisfaction.

"It's easy to take, slightly tricky to transport, but I can get rid of it quickly and for good money." Savio gloated. "Carlos constructed several carriable crates that hold the bottles securely and prevent any bottles from breaking. The nice thing is that they are easy to carry and don't weigh much. From my calculations, we should be in and out of the Vino shop in less than five minutes." He continued.

"It will be easy for us to get in and out. I was able to zoom in on the alarm keypad when the owner left a few nights ago using their security cameras, which I hacked into. Something so simple makes our entry stealthy and safe," Felipe said, his lips curling up at the corners. Something tells me there is more on your mind than the heist tonight, Savio. You do not usually come in to check up on my work." Savio pushed the office door closed and then took a seat. "You have been working with me for a long time, haven't you? It seems you are starting to know me better than I know myself." Savio said, his tone reflecting something was truly bothering him.

Savio gripped his magic ring and rubbed the one small gem with his index finger, giving the precious stone a polish. "My mind cannot stop thinking about Asher, his ring, and his ability to hide from me. I haven't been pursuing this ring for so long, only to give up when he gives us the slip. He was almost in my hands. I could feel my ring vibrating, nearly as if it could detect the other magical gems nearby. If I had had another minute longer, I could have attacked and undoubtedly secured the ring for myself." Savio grumbled in defeat.

"I didn't think he would have found the tracking device as quickly as he did," Felipe said in frustration. He was quick about it, and it makes me think that somehow or something alerted him that he was being tracked. None the less. I have been digging and think what I have discovered may interest you." Savio, who was now standing, began wringing his hands. "Tell me, good friend, what did you find?" Felipe rapidly wrapped on the keyboard, smashing down on the enter key several times, and wiggled the mouse, clicking and dragging furiously. Grabbing the monitor, Felipe twisted it towards Savio, who was staring intently. "Take a look," Felipe said, beaming at his secretive research.

The words "Christmas Grotto" in bold lettering were highlighted in the middle of the screen. "Excited for Christmas, are you, Felipe?" Savios's usual sarcastic remarks followed. Felipe gave a muffled courtesy laugh and then pointed at a picture on the screen. "Look closer." Savio stepped closer to the computer monitor as Felipe zoomed in on an image of Santa Claus. "It's him, it's Asher. How did you find a picture of him amongst the million other Santa images online?" Savio questioned. "It was a little work, but I did reverse investigating and found him." Felip stood and walked to the dry-erase board on his wall. Taking a blue marker, he wrote Angelos Pizza on it.

"I don't follow you," Savio complained. "Well, after we lost our tracking ability, I reviewed the data from the known locations when we began tracking him. One of the first locations was a pizza parlor down the street from where you almost caught him the night you appeared in his neighborhood. I was able to dig into the security footage of that restaurant and found that Asher is a frequent visitor. Matching the days he was there and the card reader transactions at the time of his leaving, I could see his name, Asher Jupes. A quick search on the internet revealed he was at the Christmas Grotto in Italy last week for a weekend. Apparently, he is liked there and made a big impression."

"So, how does this help me, a picture from something he did last year?"

Savio ranted. "I kept digging into the Christmas Grotto and discovered that the beloved Asher Jupes will return for the opening weekend this Saturday. You can find anything on the internet," a maniacal laughter duet filled the room.

"Great work, Felipe; you are an actual wizard regarding technology." Felipe flashed a quick smile back at Savio, who was now sitting and staring at the computer screen again. So, where precisely in Italy is this silly Christmas Grotto? I want to ensure my surprise attack is well planned and that he cannot escape me this time," Savio said. I've already printed you all the details," Felipe said, handing him several sheets detailing the upcoming event. "You never miss a beat, do you?" Felipe nodded his head, "No, I don't."

Tap, tap, the door swung open, and Carlos popped his head in. "Is that a map of Italy? Are we going there?" Carlos said, pointing at the computer. Did you hear me invite you in? I don't recall either one of us telling you to enter. It's none of your business anyway. What do you want?" Savio roared. "I just came by to inform you the equipment is packed." Savio furrowed his brow, "took you long enough. Did you load the crates as well? I hope your crates work. Sloppy craftsmanship on your part if you were to ask me."

Carlos stepped back from the door. "Yes, I loaded everything. Nothing is missing," he said, closing the door before walking away. "One of these days, I hope I can trust you," Savio yelled at the closed door. Carlos walked down the hall and sat at the front window, staring longly at the families playing in the street.

14

A Portal for Two

A few days had passed since the awkward encounter with Asher's
ex-girlfriend. The quiet walk home from the costume shop
had made things very uncomfortable. Asher could tell that
meeting Emily had really stirred something inside Annabel, but he
wasn't keen on bringing up Emily again. As far as he was concerned, it
was a one-time event, and he would likely never see her again. What
was unusual for Asher was the flood of memories that rushed in the
moment he heard Emily's voice. He could not deny that, at one time,
he had deep feelings for her, and seeing her in front of him resurfaced
many of those suppressed emotions.

"So, have you had a chance to try on your new Mrs Claus suit?" Asher's
voice cut through the heavy silence that enveloped their small London
home. Lost in her thoughts as she whisked the fourth egg into her
mixture of flour, salt, and milk, Annabel was jolted back to the present.
"Pardon?" She replied, her mind still lingering on her own musings. "I
was just wondering if you've had a proper fitting for your new red suit,"
Asher continued his words, keeping the conversation from stagnating.
"Oh, I was just, uh, thinking about the Yorkshire pudding." Annabel's
voice trailed off. Yet, she was not fooling Asher; he knew her better,

and her mind was not absorbed in routine cooking, especially a side dish she had made so many times before. "Are you certain something is not bothering you?" Asher probed a little deeper. "Fine, I am honestly fine. Just my mind wandered a touch." She said, reassuring Asher.

Asher could sense something was bothering Annabel, but she didn't dare bring it up. "Can I help in the kitchen?" he asked. Annabel shook her head. "No, I'm getting along okay, but thank you."

Asher was silent for a few moments before attempting a new topic of conversation. "So, I've been thinking about magic travel with portals, and up to this point, other than that one time when escaping from Savio, I haven't considered trying to bring someone along with me. I don't know if anyone has attempted to do this before beyond emergency escaping or if it could even work." He tapped his fingers on the tiny dining room table. "I was wondering if you would be willing to give it a try with me?"

Annabel stopped mixing the pudding and listened intently. "What do you think? Are you up for an adventure?" he asked.

Annabel set the mixing bowl on the counter and walked over to Asher. "Are you serious? Do you think it could work?" Her voice was full of excitement, the right amount of enthusiasm to remedy the awkward morning silence.

Asher looked up at Annabel with a glint of adventure in his eyes. "I know if I disappear into a portal and someone is holding on to me, trying to keep me from escaping, that person will not pass through the portal but will remain behind. It's definitely a well-built-in safety design."

Annabel nodded in agreement. "So how will I be able to go with you then?" she questioned.

Asher stood and grabbed Annabel by the hand. "Like this," he said confidently. "Perhaps it may work if I hold on to you, not you holding on to me. What do you say we give it a try? Guinevere, I need you again!" Asher called out to his faithful metal friend. Reaching into his front pants pocket, Asher grabbed the glasses and placed them on the table.

"Guinevere, is it possible to take someone with me through a portal when not in an emergency?" Asher inquired of the brass spectacles. Guinevere did not respond but rested on the table like an ordinary pair of glasses.

"Do you think something is wrong with her?" Annabel asked.

Asher stuck his index finger out and gave the glasses a firm but gentle poke.

"Stop that!" Guinevere insisted. "I was taking a nap, and I need my beauty sleep. I can be a bit of a handful, you know."

Asher stepped back from the table half a step. "Sorry to have to wake you from your dreamy slumber, Guinevere. If you don't mind, I have something to ask you."

The metal arms straightened outward to capacity and then upward in a stretching manner. A small grunt came from the glasses, and the lenses stretched to look like a widely opened mouth. Asher wasn't sure, but in his mind, it looked as though she was yawning.

"Very well. Now that I'm awake—and a rude awakening if I say so myself—what do you need, Asher?" Her sarcastic voice murmured.

"Is it possible to be transported through the portal with a companion if not in an emergency escape situation? I know someone can't follow me or hold on to me for evil intent, but what if I hold on to them and invite them to come with me, say a traveling buddy of sorts?"

Guinevere let out a snicker. "Well, color me impressed, Asher. But don't get too big-headed. Yes, it is possible to share the magic portal even in nonemergent situations if the invitation is given willingly, but it still has limits. Kristoff never thought to ask; he just assumed it couldn't be done. The last Santa to transport a traveling companion through the portal was Corbit Hayes during WWI. Now, that was a thrilling duo.

But perhaps that's a story for another time."

A smile stretched across Asher's face, exposing his porcelain white teeth. "Brilliant. Let's give it a go—a test of sorts," he said, grasping Annabel's hand and walking to the front door. "Guinevere, I need to find a portal that can take me to the kitchen," he said, plopping the brass spectacles on his nose. Green and red vapors began to swirl in a kaleidoscope of colors.

"Well, this is a new look," Asher said, snugging the glasses tighter on his face.

"The images will appear different in my lenses when you are traveling with a companion," Guinevere instructed.

"Can you see a portal, Asher?" Annabel asked.

"Not yet, just a mixture of colors swirling around. It's not like the smoke vapors I'm familiar with seeing or like the ones I saw when we escaped Savio together. Wait, I see it—there's a portal just on the other side of the sofa. Is that the portal, Guinevere?"

"Obviously it is," came the snarky reply, accompanied by a burst of vibration that tickled the bridge of Asher's nose.

"Let's head to it." Annabel's heart raced in her chest, her breath quickening with each step. Asher turned his gaze to the four-foot oval circle on the floor. Green and red vapors mixed with orange and yellow bursts, resembling lava, stirred counterclockwise in a liquid-looking puddle on the floor.

"Let's step in," he said to Annabel as if she could see the same magical whirlpool in front of her. But for Annabel, the same dingy floorboards were all she could see.

Just as Asher took his first step, flashes of past companions caught his attention—a wounded WWI soldier, someone in a Civil War uniform with rosy cheeks and dirty brown hair, and a boy about ten years old wearing a simple petticoat with embroidered borders and wavy blond hair, smiling contagiously at Asher.

"What am I looking at, Guinevere?" His voice was tinged with concern.

"These are images of those who have passed as companions in the portal." Images of many individuals appeared one after another, each bearing unique apparel appropriate for their time.

"Get a move on then," Guinevere impatiently exclaimed. "I don't want to be sitting up here on your nose all day."

With those final words, Asher stepped forward into the portal, Annabel clutching tightly to his hand. The instant tug at the navel and free-fall sensation was familiar to Asher but new to Annabel, whose scream bore witness. Asher felt Annabel pull him closer, her arm wrapped around him. The sensation made his cheeks flush and his pulse quicken.

The adventure was over as quickly as the first step was taken, and the pair stood holding each other in the middle of the kitchen.

"It worked!" Asher shouted at Annabel, who was still squeezing her eyes shut. Slowly, Annabel peeked out before pressing her lips against Asher's in celebration. Whether it was the excitement of success or the growing affection in their budding relationship was unknown. But the kiss was mutual and full of emotion.

"Stop it, that is enough of that. The two of you are squishing me!" Guinevere belted out, interrupting the moment.

"Thank you," she said as the two pulled apart. If I'm no longer needed, I will be going now," the brass companion said as she dissolved into thin air. She certainly speaks her mind." Annable chuckled. "Asher nodded in agreement. Yes, there is no filter either. She says what she thinks. She keeps me in line; she does.

"This is marvelous. Taking you on special assignments will be wonderful. Just think: children can see Mrs. Claus with Santa. You'll get to enjoy their reactions to the magic and spirit of the season," Asher said, grinning from ear to ear.

"I will admit, I'm not too keen on that portal thing again. I hate the freefall feeling. I can't promise I'll go on many trips with you, Asher," Annabel said, holding her finger over her mouth and pretending to be sick.

"Ah, you'll be alright," Asher chuckled.

The next several days proved productive as Annabel and Asher made plans for Hyde Park Winter Wonderland. Annabel seemed to have forgotten all about the encounter with Emily, and things felt normal for Asher. During their preparations, Annabel found herself lost in thought about traveling by portal to places she had never been. She imagined visiting Naples, Italy, with its vivid Christmas traditions and nativity scenes scattered throughout the city and its many churches. "I would love to see the live nativity in Piazza San Gaetano," she thought. "We could be involved in the Santa work and maybe do a little sightseeing. After all, we would be there for Santa purposes. What's the harm in a little tourism?" she mused.

"Asher, do you know what they call Santa in Italy?" she asked suddenly.

"What's that? What did you say?" Asher was caught off guard by her question; he had been busy sewing a floppy button back onto his majestic Santa coat. "There, that will do," he said, pushing the threaded needle into a red tomato-shaped pin cushion. "I'm sorry, what did you ask me?"

"What do they call Santa in Italy?" Annabel repeated, her voice slightly more elevated.

"Babbo Natale. Why do you ask?" Asher replied.

"Oh, I dunno, I was just thinking Santa should make an appearance in Italy."

Asher looked up from his newly fastened black overcoat button and made eye contact with Annabel. "So, you think Santa should go to Italy, eh? I'm wondering, do you think Mrs. Claus should go with him, too?"

"What a wonderful idea you have, Asher. How nice of you to invite

108

me along," she said with a slight giggle.

"You know," Asher replied, "they also celebrate La Befana, an older woman who delivers gifts on Epiphany in January. Would you like to dress up as her if we go?" He smirked, inspecting his coat again.

A square pillow sailed across the room, striking Asher in the back. "Not funny, Asher," Annabel said, her voice kind and playful.

Asher picked up the pillow. "Honestly, Annabel, you shouldn't throw pillows like that. No, that was not good at all." Annabel looked shocked and slightly shaken by his reaction to her playful toss. "Oh, I, I'm sorry."

Before she could finish her sentence, Asher had cocked back his arm like a professional baseball player and sent the pillow flying back at her, hitting her square in the stomach. "That is how you throw a pillow!" His playful instructions were an invitation to engage in a well-needed pillow fight.

Laughter, giggles, and flying pillows filled the room until both were red-faced and breathing heavily. "Okay, okay, I give up," Asher shouted, his breathing slightly labored.

"The victory is mine. Kneel at my feet, Asher. You have lost the battle."

Asher, playing along, knelt before his victor. "What do you demand from me, oh great pillow warrior?"

Annabel stroked her chin in mock contemplation. "A trip to Italy, that is what I demand."

Asher nodded. "Yes, great Pillow Goddess, a trip to Italy is what you will receive. Do you demand anything else?"

Annabel walked a slow circle around Asher, who was still kneeling, then paused. "Stand, arise before me," she playfully demanded.

Asher stood, his eyes locking with hers. "What more do you demand?" he asked once again.

Annabel closed her eyes. "My victory kiss, of course."

Though Annabel had emerged victorious in their pillow fight, Asher couldn't shake the feeling that he had won something far greater. As they shared a needed embrace and exchanged a warm, tender kiss of victory, it was a moment they both cherished, the sweetness lingering just long enough to be treasured.

"Well, thank you, Mrs. Claus. I sure love losing battles to you. I'm thinking of a rematch later in the week. What do you think?" Asher asked with a playful glint in his eyes.

Annabel nodded, her smile mischievous. "I think I'm up to the challenge, Asher. But be ready to pay up if I win again."

"Yes, Mrs. Claus. I think I can handle it."

"Mrs. Claus… how strange that her name is not known. Only Mrs. Claus," Annabel mused, lounging back on the couch.

Asher settled down on the couch beside Annabel. "Well," he began, "she has always had a name." In the past, her name was kept secret from the public as a way of protection. There has always been evil that battles the good. In old times, keeping her name secret was a way of keeping her from being detected or known when she was out on the streets or in places of concern," Asher explained, inspecting his Santa suit again.

"I don't mind being called Mrs. Claus, but I often found it strange that she is only referred to as Mrs. Claus. Now I know the reason, and I can't help but admire the men who loved these women so deeply that they wanted them to be safe and protected. Things have changed a lot since those old times and practices. I think it's time she has a name." Annabel's voice was thoughtful, reflecting her newfound understanding.

Asher looked up from his suit, a warm smile spreading across his face. "You're right, Annabel. She does deserve a name. And I can't think of anyone better than you to bring that change."

"Do you want to be known as Annabel Claus?" Asher asked with a grin.

"No, not named after me. After all, I'm just dressing up like her. I'm not even the real Mrs. Claus, and we're not married," Annabel replied, her tone light but thoughtful.

Asher dropped his gaze to the floor, running his fingers through his hair—a telltale sign of his discomfort. Annabel had noticed this quirk over the years they had worked together. It wasn't that Asher wasn't interested in her; he just wasn't sure if he was ready for a serious commitment. Asher was used to being alone since his adoptive parents had been killed in a car accident while he was away on his first assignment as a young news reporter. Though time had healed many wounds, he feared growing close to someone, worried they, too, would be taken from him.

Recognizing his feelings, Annabel quickly shifted the conversation back to the name, steering clear of the topic of marriage. "I think she needs the name of Santa's first-ever wife. Do you know their names?" Annabel asked, watching Asher as he placed his oversized red Santa coat on a thick wooden hanger.

"I don't recall coming across their names or talking with Kristoff about them. It's likely recorded in the lost book of our forefathers," Asher replied, thoughtful.

Suddenly, something red streaked past Asher's head, followed by a gust of wind that knocked over a spool of thread and sent the pin cushion tumbling to the floor. Asher whipped his head around just in time to see a velvet red fabric bag land on the coffee table in a crumpled mess. The soft bag gathered itself together and stood up vertically, its corners acting like feet, and then it shook violently like a dog shaking off after a bath.

"Mr. Baggins. You surprised me," Asher admitted to his cloth friend. "Is there another mission?"

The silent bag twisted its top back and forth in a gesture resembling a head shake. "So, what brings you here today, good sir?" Mr. Baggins bent over, and a rolled-up paper no more significant than the length of a toothpick rolled out. The kind bag straightened up and inclined its top in a pointing gesture toward the rolled parchment. "You brought me a letter, have you?" Mr. Baggins dipped his head in affirmation, then floated a few inches up in the air before turning and flying horizontally, evaporating into thin air just inches from the wall.

Annabel reached down and inspected the tightly rolled parchment. Its paper was thicker than cardstock, with a slightly soft, almost leathery feel. At first glance, it appeared to be ancient thin leather, tied closed with a hemp string. "Well, go on then, read it," Asher insisted.

Annabel hesitated. "How do I know it's not for you to read?" she asked.

"Well, aren't we in this together?" Asher replied.

Nodding, Annabel agreed and began to gently remove the dry, rough string. The leather parchment began to unwind slightly on its own, and then Annabel had to roll it out flat on the table. "Well, what do you see?" Asher asked, raising his eyebrows. "What does it say?"

Annabel leaned forward, her eyes narrowing to a squint. "They are names. Gideon, son of Ezra, and Candace, daughter of Abiel." Annabel beamed. "Are you thinking what I'm thinking? These must be the names of the first Santa and Mrs. Claus."

Asher walked over to the dining table and plopped himself into a chair. "Yes, I believe you are correct. These are ancient names for sure," he said thoughtfully.

Annabel clasped her hands together. "That's it! That's how I will introduce myself at the Christmas Grotto tonight. I will be Candace Claus. Maybe in time, this name will remain for generations to come. I can't think of a better way to honor the first in line of many amazing women."

Feeling resolute, Annabel hurried to her room to change into her new Santa suit. "This is going to be a great night at the Santa Grotto. I'm more excited than ever!" she shouted behind the closed door.

Asher approached the dining room table, where his Santa coat hung on a chair. He removed the coat from the hanger and stared at the closed bedroom door. "You definitely should be Santa's wife," he whispered, dressing himself for the big night at the Grotto.

15

Santa's Grotto

T he couple, dressed in their festive Santa attire, stepped out of their flat and strolled down Piccadilly Street toward Hyde Park. With only a couple of miles to cover and the brisk mid-November air invigorating them, they decided the walk would be a welcome form of exercise. It didn't take long for passersby to notice the vibrant red duo.

"Hi, Santa!" a red-faced boy shouted from across the street. The couple turned, their eyes lighting up with an infectious joy. Without missing a beat, Asher raised his white-gloved hand and offered the warmest wave. "Oh, Annabel, I just adore the little ones," he exclaimed, his voice filled with a childlike excitement. "Their joy fills me with such anticipation for Christmas. It's like I'm a child again, eagerly awaiting the magic of the season. And now, I get to be the one bringing that magic to others."

Something about the moment felt truly magical for Annabel. Perhaps it was the novelty of wearing the new suit or the exhilarating experience of traveling through a portal. Whatever the reason, she couldn't shake the feeling of joy and wonder bubbling up inside her. As they continued down the street, they were met with smiles and greetings from passersby.

"Imagine if they only knew you were the real Santa walking down the street in broad daylight," Annabel remarked, nodding toward a family with three small children who were pointing excitedly in their direction.

Asher turned and waved at the family, returning their smiles. "Oh, they believe I'm real," he replied with a chuckle, his voice filled with a playful twinkle. "It's the parents who have stopped believing. Funny how life works, isn't it? I never believed in Santa, and now here I am." He patted his round belly playfully, adding to the jovial atmosphere.

Annabel reached over and gently stroked his soft white beard. "Did I ever tell you I find a man with a beard very attractive?" she said with a mischievous shimmer in her eye. Not entirely comfortable with the flirtatious compliment, Asher cleared his throat and then erupted into a loud "Ho, Ho, Ho," causing a nearby cat to scramble from its perch atop a trash can.

The familiar Santa shout alerted two sisters down the street, who began racing towards Annabel and Asher. "It's them, it's really them. I know it is. I can see it and feel it," the older girl with the dark fishtail braid shouted. The younger one, about five years old, did her best to keep up but stumbled on an uneven section of sidewalk, crashing to the ground with a whimper.

"Ella, get up; we're going to miss them." The little girl struggled to her feet, her knee-torn stockings revealing a scraped knee. "Ella, Mum is going to have a fit when she sees your new stockings torn like that." Tears filled Ella's eyes, streaming down her red cheeks.

Annabel hurried over, took Ella's hand, and helped her stand. "Are you alright, little one?" Ella only stared up at Annabel, tear-soaked and silent.

"She'll be alright, ma'am... uh, Mrs. Claus. She falls a lot at home. She's just that kind of girl, I guess," Ella's sister reassured.

115

Annabel nodded. "Yes, some folks are just a bit wobblier than others. You must be the big sister. What's your name?"

"Lily. I'm Lily, and I'm eight years old. I've been a good girl all year, Mrs. Claus."

"Call me Candace. Mrs. Claus is so formal."

"Pleasure to meet you, Candace. Wow, Candace is my best friend's name at school, but we call her Candy. Do people call you Candy, too? Did they name the candy cane after you?" Her giddy comments came rapid-fire.

"Well, she is as sweet as a candy cane, that is for sure." Asher smiled.

"Santa!" the two wide-eyed sisters shouted in unison.

"Hello there, Ella and Lily," Asher greeted warmly.

Lily's eyes widened even further, her tear-soaked eyelashes fluttering as she looked up at the towering figure before her. "How do you know our names?"

Asher tapped the side of his head with a knowing smile. "Magic, of course. Your names popped into my head the moment I saw you."

"See, I was right! It is the real Santa!" Lily exclaimed.

"Very observant of you, Lily. And I want you to know that you've been a very good girl this year. Being a big sister is a special blessing, and you've done an excellent job looking out for Ella. I look forward to visiting your home this Christmas. But until then, I have something for you." Asher reached into the deep pocket of his majestic red coat and pulled out two white, pencil-length candy canes. "Here you are. Two special flavor canes for two special girls."

Lily grabbed her treat, examining it closely like a scientist scrutinizing a specimen. "Hey, these candy canes don't have red stripes, Santa."

"You're very observant, Lily, and you're right. These candies are special."

Lily frowned in thought. "So not having a red stripe makes them special?"

Asher chuckled, his eyes twinkling. "That's part of it, but there's more. Let me show you. Lily, what's your favorite candy flavor?"

The little brunette closed her eyes, tapping her lips as she pondered. "Strawberry!" she declared.

"Oh, that's a fantastic choice, one of my favorites too. And you, Ella? What's your favorite flavor?"

Ella didn't hesitate. "Watermelon!" she shouted, her voice full of excitement.

"Brilliant. Now, think of your favorite flavor when you pop the candy in your mouth." The two sisters peeled back the wrapping on the hard candy and, as instructed, thought of their favorite flavors. "Mine tastes just like strawberries!" Lilly exclaimed, a huge smile lighting up her five-year-old face. Ella, dancing in a small circle, chimed in, "Strawberry! Strawberry!"

Asher chuckled, "Now, are you ready for even more magic?" The girls looked up in wide-eyed wonder. "More magic?" Ella asked.

Asher nodded, "Yes, more magic. Take your flavor cane out of your mouth and think of a new flavor, something that you really like." The girls did as instructed, then popped the flavor cane back into their mouths. Asher and Annabel watched eagerly for their reactions.

"Wow, it tastes just like a s'more! I can taste marshmallows, chocolate, and even graham crackers!" Lily announced excitedly.

"What about you, Ella? What flavor do you taste?" Ella's eyes widened, then closed softly as she savored the burst of flavor in her mouth. Suddenly, she blurted out, "Macaroni and cheese!"

Annabel, Asher, and Lily all burst into laughter as Ella kept her mouth closed tightly around the white cane. "Well, they are called flavor canes. I imagine if she loved a good turkey dinner, it would taste like that, too," Asher said, doing his best turkey impression. They spent the next few moments enjoying the magical encounter.

Annabel glanced at her watch. "Well, we need to be on our way, girls."

Her words were met with a disappointed but understanding "aww" from the sisters.

"Candace is right; we are expected in the Santa Grotto shortly. You girls best get back to your parents. I'm sure they will be looking for you before long," Asher added.

"Thank you, Candace. Thank you, Santa." Lily's gratitude was heartfelt, and Annabel smiled warmly at the girls.

"Lily, look," Ella said, pointing to her knee. Where there had been a tear in her stocking, now it was restored as if by magic. The girls exchanged amazed glances.

"You are a good girl, Ella. Perhaps slow down a little in the future, eh?" Asher suggested gently.

"Merry Christmas, Santa," Ella said, grabbing Asher around the waist in a hug of gratitude. Asher looked down at her and patted her back. "Merry Christmas, Ella."

"Come on, Ella, let's go tell Mum!" The two sisters turned and headed back down the street, skipping and giggling all the way.

"That part never gets old," Asher said, his voice radiating the charm of the moment.

Annabel and Asher resumed their walk down the long sidewalk, making their way to the Santa Grotto. Continuous shouts from the streets and stares from passersby accompanied them the entire way.

"We made it," Annabel said, pointing at the entrance. An enormous sign welcoming visitors to the park stretched across the walkway, adorned with images of Santa and children with toys. Towering leafless trees lined the street, all decorated with thousands of vibrant lights that twinkled even in the early afternoon light.

The street was filled with strollers, children, and adults making their way through the magical winter wonderland, bundled up in scarves, gloves, hats, and waterproof jackets. The air was calm and heavy, with culinary delights wafting in from all directions, mingling into a delightful fragrance that made tummies rumble with hunger.

"Oh, I just love coming here each year. This year feels busier than last," Annabel remarked, pointing at the carousel loaded with children. She was correct; more people than ever filled the streets and lined up at the circus tent, Bavarian Village, and even waited in line to board Asher's favorite, the Christmas tree ride.

"Looks like we'll have to wait a few minutes to get on the Christmas tree ride," Asher said, his disappointment evident. Annabel peered over at the large mechanical Christmas tree with golf cart-sized ornaments bobbing up and down with patrons.

"Why do you like that simple ride so much?" Annabel asked.

Asher shrugged. "Well, it has a great view of the park, and it's not as fast as some of the other rides."

Annabel pointed at the magnificent Munich Looping rollercoaster filling the low skyline. "Not fast like that one, is it?"

Asher held his stomach and made a nauseated face. "Yeah, I don't do well on those. Let the younger crowd enjoy those high-velocity twists, flips, and dips."

The red-dressed couple weaved their way through the crowds to Santa Land, where a sizeable sleigh display being pulled by fake reindeer marked the entrance. "Well, let's head in and let them know we are ready," Asher said, holding the wooden door open to the festively decorated A-framed cabin.

16

The Last Visitor

S tepping into the Santa Grotto, a familiar warmth and coziness enveloped the air, more akin to a log cabin than a cavernous hideaway. The scene exhibited a sense of nostalgia with its brick chimney facade adorned by a wooden mantle carefully decorated with garlands and pine cones. A grand wooden chair occupied a prominent spot next to the chimney, complemented by a wicker basket resting on an antique oval rug of varied hues. Adjacent to the Santa chair, a rustic bench draped in fur awaited children eager to visit Santa. A smaller, festively adorned Christmas tree and assorted wrapped gifts completed the Christmas setting. Above the mantle, the clock displayed 2:59 pm, signaling it was time for Asher to assume his role.

"A bag of gifts for the children has been placed next to your chair, Mr. Jupes. It's lovely to have you back again this year," said a mature woman in traditional red attire adorned with white fur cuffs and a fluffy collar. You look like you are all set for your three-hour shift this afternoon," she continued.

Asher's heart swelled with joy as he approached the Santa chair, Mr. Baggins snug in his pocket. He gently placed the little toy in the wicker basket, which was filled to the brim with small toys for the children. "So wonderful to see you too, Agnes. I can't believe it's been a year since we last stepped into this Santa Grotto," he said, his voice brimming with warmth and nostalgia, a testament to the joy that the Christmas season brings.

Agnes, a pillar of the Winter Wonderland since its opening in 2005, radiated a sense of dedication and warmth. The Winter Wonderland was a sight to behold with its snow-covered trees and twinkling lights. Her years of hard work and commitment to the Christmas festivals were etched in her silver hair, the deep wrinkles at the corners of her eyes, and the creases around her mouth. Despite the physical signs of aging, her eyes sparkled with the same youthful enthusiasm that had enchanted visitors for nearly two decades.

"Can I get you anything before we start sending in the children? A bottle of water, perhaps?"

Asher nodded. "That would be wonderful. Agnes, you have always been so accommodating to us. You make coming here a pleasure. It feels like home to us." The warmth of Agnes's presence enveloped them like a cozy blanket on a cold winter's night.

Agnes smiled warmly at Asher and Annabel before stepping out of the Grotto. "I'll just be a moment." Her smile, a reflection of the warmth and joy she brought to the Winter Wonderland, radiated in the air, filling the space with a sense of comfort and joy.

Asher and Annabel exchanged a glance, their hearts filled with the familiar warmth and joy that Agnes's presence always brought. The festive decorations around them twinkled under the lights, casting a magical glow that enchanted everything. The Christmas tree, adorned with shimmering lights and delicate ornaments, danced joyfully. The wrapped gifts, their colorful paper reflecting the twinkling lights, added to the festive atmosphere, creating a scene straight out of a Christmas fairy tale.

Annabel walked over to a picture-framed mirror on the wall, her heart fluttering excitedly. She swept her long bangs away from her eyes, tucking them behind her right ear. Then, she pulled a small red tube from her handbag and glossed her lips, a final touch to her transformation into Mrs. Claus. "You look radiant tonight, Annabel. Fitting and marvelous as anyone could imagine Mrs. Claus to look like. You keep up those good looks, and more people will come to see you than me." Annabel caught Asher's eyes in the mirror and gave him a wink, then dropped the lipgloss back into her handbag. The room seemed to sparkle with the anticipation of the enchanting festivities.

"Would you like a chair as well, Annabel?" Asher asked. "No, thank you. I prefer to stand. Besides, I like walking each child up to see you. Seeing the kids beam excitedly is my highlight of the evening. Asher returned a smile, acknowledging the shared sentiment.

"Here you are, my dears," Agnes said, holding out two water bottles. "I also grabbed something special for you, Asher. I had it shipped all the way from the United States, and it arrived just two days ago." Agnes set the water bottles on the fireplace mantle, then pulled a glass bottle with a yellow label featuring red underlined blue and white lettering from a shoulder bag. Gently agitating the chilled bottle, she twisted the cap, sending a stream of chocolate foam dribbling down the side.

"A Yoo-hoo? You got me a Yoo-hoo? Agnes, you sure know how to make people feel special." Asher twisted the bottle cap completely off, guzzled its contents, and then wiped his beard with his sleeve. "Oh, this is just what I needed. A million thanks, Agnes."

"There is quite a line formed already. Are you ready, Santa?" Agnes asked, a knowing smile on her face.

Asher fluffed his beard, straightened his belt, and plopped down in his Santa chair. "Ho, Ho, Ho!" His thundering voice echoed out of the grotto, sending children into a cheer. "Let's get started," Asher called out to Annabel, who was eagerly waiting for the signal to begin.

A lanky nine-year-old ginger-haired boy with numerous freckles dotting his nose was first in line. "Good evening, Mrs. Claus. My name is…" But before he could continue, Annabel hushed him gently.

"Shh, don't tell us your name; that is part of tonight's magic. Oh, and please, call me Candace, Candace Claus." The thin boy looked up at Annabel and smiled. "Nice to meet you, Candace Claus."

Annabel beamed. "Nice to meet you, too. But there is no need to whisper; my name is no longer a secret. Come, let's go say hello to Santa, shall we?"

Annabel and the freckle-faced lad approached Asher, who was eagerly anticipating his first visit of the evening. "Good evening, Oliver," Asher greeted warmly. He patted the fur-covered wooden bench beside him. "Sit here, Oliver. I want to chat with you for a few moments."

Oliver nodded and perched himself on the edge of the bench, his eyes wide with curiosity. "Santa, how did you know my name?" he asked.

Asher raised his eyebrows with a knowing smile. "Santa knows these sorts of things, Oliver. If you recall, there's a Christmas song about me that sheds a little light on what I know. Can you help me with those words? Let me start you out, and you can finish." Asher cleared his throat and began to sing, "He sees you when you're sleeping…"

Oliver jumped to his feet, his face lighting up with recognition. "I know this song! 'He knows when you're awake, he knows if you've been bad or good…'" His song stopped as abruptly as it had begun, and he looked at Asher with concern. "Santa, I've been good, haven't I?"

Asher adjusted his Santa cap, snugging it down comfortably. "Yes, Oliver, you have been very good indeed. Why, just last night, when you were visiting your grandmother, you did the dinner dishes for her without being asked."

Oliver's mouth gaped open slightly in amazement. "How did you know that?"

A satisfied grin stretched across Asher's face. "Magic! Pure and simple magic." Asher reached into the wicker basket beside him and pulled out a toy that had been specially prepared for his young visitor. "I have something for you for coming to visit me tonight. But before you go, would you like to tell me what you want for Christmas this year?"

Oliver leaned over and whispered his Christmas wish into Asher's ear as he received his gift. Before reaching the exit, Oliver turned back and shouted, "Merry Christmas, Santa!"

Asher watched the boy leave with a smile, his heart warmed by the exchange. The magic of Christmas, he thought, was alive and well in moments like these. "Am I next?" a little girl with dark hair in a pink raincoat asked, her eyes wide with anticipation. One after another, each child waited eagerly to see Santa, their excitement palpable throughout the evening.

Bong, bong, bong. Asher counted the chimes of Big Ben in his head. Bong, bong, bong. "Six o'clock already," he murmured. "That went by so quickly."

"Well, that's it then. Thank you for coming in again," Agnes declared, a note of satisfaction in her voice. "I think this was a bigger crowd than last year, don't you?" She added with a knowing smile. "I'm starting to see a trend, Asher. You absolutely draw bigger crowds than the other Santa helpers we have."

"Asher, it looks like someone holding a baby is standing right outside to see you," Annabel said, pointing at a dark silhouette just out of reach of the twinkling lights hanging in the trees. "Do you think you can see one more, Asher?" Agnes asked politely.

"Oh, it's been a good day of seeing little ones. Let's see one more before we head out for the evening," Asher replied, settling back into his wooden chair. Annabel waved her hand, gesturing for the individual to come over. "Come on over; Santa said he can stay for a few more minutes before he heads back to the North Pole."

The shadowy, slender figure dipped its head in acknowledgment and slowly approached the grotto, stopping briefly to adjust the bundled baby blanket before continuing onward.

Something feels wrong, out of place, not right at all, Asher thought, his senses heightened. Cautiously, he settled himself back into his chair. "Step this way; Santa is excited to see you," Annabel said, ushering the way to Asher. A few paces away, Asher realized it was not a bundled baby being carried but a dark military-style backpack.

Asher felt his breath quicken, keeping up with his racing heart. "Annabel, Agnes, run!"

The cloaked intruder, realizing he no longer held the element of surprise, lifted his gaze toward Asher and dropped his pack to the ground. Asher sprang to his feet, locking eyes with the unveiled assailant. "Savio, how did you—?" But before he could finish his question, Savio launched himself at Asher, and they tumbled to the floor together in a heap, crushing the wicker basket and smothering Mr. Baggins.

"Help! Someone help us!" Annabel shouted to a now-vacant waiting area outside the grotto. "Everyone has left the area, Annabel!" Agnes alerted her. "We've got to do something to help him," Annabel pleaded.

Asher felt a searing pain at the back of his head, his vision darkening as his ears filled with a deafening silence. Laying face down, he had pinned down both Guinevere and Mr. Baggins, who flailed and twisted, attempting to be freed. Savio grabbed Asher's ring finger, grasping it with all his strength. Asher's skin blistered beneath the ring, vibrating violently.

"Aah!" Asher screamed, the pain in his finger unbearable and unrelenting. He could feel the ring holding on, refusing to leave but slowly losing the battle. Suddenly, he heard a loud thump, and the pressure of Savio's knee digging into his lower back stopped. Savio crashed to the floor, landing on his right side, eyes closed. Annabel stood above both men, holding a four-foot wooden candy decoration she had used as a makeshift bat.

"Asher, are you alright?" Annabel's voice reflected the surge of adrenaline in her body.

"I'm fine. Let's tie up Savio. Quickly, grab the rope garland from the Christmas tree. We can use that to secure him," Asher instructed.

Annabel turned and headed toward the small Christmas tree a few feet away. Savio cracked open his eyes slightly, focusing on what appeared to be a child's lost stud earring on the floor a few inches from his face. "Quick, Annabel, he's waking up," Asher urged, getting to his knees. Mr. Baggins, now freed, flew upward and perched himself on the mantle. Asher reached down to his pants pocket and tapped it, feeling the metal glasses but detecting no movement.

Savio unexpectedly scooped up the discarded earring from the floor in a flash, stood to his feet, and ran to the Grotto opening, where he grabbed his pack before leaping out the entrance. In a vibrant green flash and a crack of thunder that rattled the Santa Grotto's wooden frame, he disappeared.

Annabel returned, garland in hand, her face a mix of confusion and concern. "Where did he go?"

Asher shook his head, still trying to process what had just happened. "I don't know, but he's gone. We need to regroup and figure out what to do next. This isn't over."

Annabel nodded, her determination matching Asher's. "We'll get through this, Asher. Together."

Asher smiled, feeling a renewed sense of resolve. "Yes, together."

"Are you two okay? What was with that guy?" Agnes asked, emerging from behind a stack of Christmas-wrapped boxes. "This world is getting scarier by the day," she continued.

"It does seem like there has been an uptick in violence, Agnes. But I still believe there is more good than bad happening all around us. Just look at the families that visited tonight and fill up this park every evening. That gives me such great hope for the future," Asher replied.

Agnes nodded in agreement. "I will call security and see if they can find him. I need to report this. Do you need any medical attention? He really knocked you over."

"No," Asher said, rubbing his finger and ignoring the pain in his back and shoulder. "I should be okay. Annabel and I will head out for the evening if it's alright with you."

"Oh, absolutely; you guys should get going. I hope this won't deter you from returning in the future," Agnes said. "We definitely want you to come back every year."

"Not a chance this will deter us! We won't let something like this stop us from sharing the spirit of Christmas," Annabel's words lifted Asher's spirits.

Asher reached into his pocket and carefully pulled out Guinevere. The brass frame was bent awkwardly, and the right lens was spider-cracked in all directions. "Guinevere, oh dear. She does not look good at all," he said with concern.

"How rude!" Guinevere's snarky remark broke the momentary silence. "Telling a gal she doesn't look good. I thought you knew better than that. If you would lose some weight, perhaps your crushing heft wouldn't have mangled me like this!" Her sassy comments were a relief to Asher, who had feared the worst.

Asher felt her thin frames quiver in his hands, straightening the bent arms into a perfect curvature. Guinevere began shaking herself, forcing the cracked glass to reverse into a spotless clear lens. "There, better than new," she complimented herself, then darted out of Asher's hand and into his side coat pocket.

"Well, it appears Mr. Baggins and Guinevere can go anywhere they please unless restrained by Santa," Asher said. "Who knew?" Mr. Baggins floated upward from the mantle and then vanished into thin air.

"I think that may have stressed Mr. Baggins out a bit, being squished like that and unable to help," Annabel observed.

"Right you are, Annabel—I should probably check on him when we get home. Best to let him rest a bit for now," Asher agreed.

"How's your finger feeling? It sounded like a howler of an injury." Annabel asked, her voice full of concern. Asher rubbed his finger and then rolled the ring around it, inspecting for pain.

"Wait, what? Oh no, another gem has come loose. Annabel, help me look for it on the floor."

Annabel's stomach lurched. "I think I saw Savio swipe something from the floor before he dashed out. Oh, this is not good. Do you think he took it?"

Asher's head dropped to his chest. "This is very bad indeed."

17

We Are Never Truly Alone

A re you feeling okay?" Annabel asked, concern evident in her voice. "You seem a bit under the weather."

For the first time since becoming Santa, Asher felt less energetic and slightly fatigued. He stood up slowly from his chair, arching his back in a good stretch. "Keen observation, Annabel. Curiously enough, yes, I do feel a bit rundown today."

Annabel retrieved a tall, clear glass from the cupboard and filled it with chilled orange juice. "Here you go, drink up. This always perks me up when I'm feeling sluggish—a sugar pick-me-up with vitamins."

Asher thanked Annabel for her remedy, grabbed the frosty glass, and guzzled down its contents. "They must have used the sweetest oranges to make this juice. It's like liquid candy," he said, licking his sticky lips. Asher placed the empty glass down on the table and then wiped his mouth with his hand before returning back to his seat. Flashing a puzzled look in Annabel's direction. "I can't help but wonder if my new onset of fatigue is related to another gem missing. Perhaps my own immortality weakens as the ring loses power.."

Annabel lifted the empty glass from the table and made her way over to the kitchen sink. "I wonder about that too, Asher. I don't think it's a coincidence that you began to feel this way after the gem was lost."

Asher dropped his gaze to the table, slowly stroking his beard. "You look lost in thought, Asher," Annabel observed.

Asher remained silent, continuing to stroke his beard for several moments before responding. "If the loss of the gem is affecting me this way, I wonder if it will inhibit my magical abilities." His voice reflected his alarm. "What concerns me even more is Savio's unknown abilities. He might have gained more power."

Annabel nodded in agreement. "Do you think he'll keep trying to take the ring from you?"

Asher rubbed his finger over the vacant spot where his ring once sat. "Savio is obsessed with power and won't stop pursuing us until he's accomplished his goal. We need to be on high alert."

Annabel pulled a chair away from the table and sat next to Asher. "Is there a way to stop him or get the gems back?"

Asher tapped his finger on the table rhythmically. "Those very questions kept me awake late into the night, Annabel. I don't have the answers yet. If only I had access to the Great Forefathers of Christmas book. It contains the magical secrets, including those of my enchanted ring. All the secrets and wizardly abilities are detailed in that book, and I believe Savio has it."

Annabel's eyes widened with concern. "Then we must find a way to retrieve that book and the gems. We can't let Savio continue to amass power."

Asher nodded, a resolute look on his face. "Yes, we must. But first, we need a plan. We need allies, information, and a way to counter Savio's growing influence. We have to act quickly before he becomes unstoppable."

Annabel placed a reassuring hand on Asher's arm. "We'll figure this out together. You're not alone in this fight."

Asher managed a small, grateful smile. "Thank you, Annabel. Your support means more to me than you know."

The two sat in companionable silence for a moment, each lost in their thoughts, contemplating the challenges that lay ahead and the strategies they would need to devise to thwart Savio and reclaim the lost magic.

Asher's voice broke the silence, "I think I want to go for a quick walk to clear my head," he said, standing up and heading towards the door.

"I'm going to stay here and get a few things done before we head out to the Children's Hospital today," Annabel replied, pushing her chair back towards the table. "Don't forget, we need to arrive by 2 p.m., and visits to the rooms start at 3:00."

Asher gave a thumbs-up and closed the door softly behind him.

The cool mid-morning air was invigorating, brightening his spirits and refreshing his senses. The moist sidewalks offered a sense of renewal as he walked, the street coming to life with early patrons and tourists eager to explore Piccadilly Street. With each step, Asher's mind churned over the previous night's events—the missing gem, his increasing fatigue, and the growing threat posed by Savio.

Could the ring be dismantled one gem at a time? Was it possible that Savio could forge a new ring for sinister purposes? The questions loomed large in his mind, each one more troubling than the last.

Asher passed a bakery, the scent of fresh bread and pastries momentarily distracting him from his worries. He paused for a moment, inhaled deeply, and let the aroma comfort him.

"Enjoying the smell?" a sultry voice enquired.

Asher whipped his head around and found himself staring directly into a familiar pair of attractive chestnut eyes. "Emily! Wow, how crazy to see you again. I thought you would be at work right now. What brings you here so far from Ann's Relics and Gowns?"

Emily's full, smooth lips widened into a smile that complemented the blonde waterfall curls caressing her heart-shaped face. "I love this bakery. They have the best beignets stuffed with spiced pumpkin cream this time of year."

"Sorry if I seemed a little out of sorts when I ran into you at work. I was a little in shock and didn't know quite how to react or what to say," Asher admitted.

"It was a little awkward for me as well," Emily's bronze face now glowed a soft red.

"So tell me," Asher continued, "what have you been up to? How is life going?"

"Things are going well. As you know, I have my own shop now, and I feel very fortunate that business has been good, especially after the pandemic. I'm still single, but I have a guy friend, and he treats me well."

"A guy friend, eh?" Asher joked playfully.

"It's not what you think, Joseph. I have only known him for a short while, but he treats me well, and he is becoming a close friend. I don't foresee it becoming a romantic relationship, but it is nice to have a guy friend to talk with."

Asher felt a pang of nostalgia at being called Joseph again. Emily reached up and tugged gently on Asher's beard. "What is this? It is so white and super soft. It's kind of Santa-like."

Asher chuckled. "Makes me look old."

Emily's hand slid down Asher's arm to his hand and then gave his fingers a tiny squeeze. "I think it is very cute on you."

Asher cleared his throat. "Oh, I uh… thanks. Well, I better get along. I have some things to tend to."

"Well, it was so good to see you again. Now, Joseph, don't be such a stranger; come by and see me sometime," Emily said, entering the bakery. A few steps inside, she turned and caught Asher's eye, giving him a wink.

The feelings of his former relationship flooded back, and as he walked further down the sidewalk, his mind began to drift over memories of the two of them.

Observing the people around him—a young couple, hand in hand, oblivious to the world, an elderly man feeding pigeons—he felt a pang of envy. Their lives seemed untouched by the dark currents that plagued him. *I need to stay focused and think strategically*, Joseph told himself. *If Savio had access to the Great Forefathers of Christmas book, he would have crucial knowledge that could shift the balance of power.* His thoughts continued to race. One thing was for certain for Asher: he would have to stay ahead of Savio and anticipate his moves.

Turning a corner, Asher found himself in a small park where children played on swings and slides, their laughter a stark contrast to the turmoil within him. He took a moment to sit on a bench, watching the joyful scene. It reminded him why the ring and its magic were so important. As the children's laughter echoed around him, he remembered his appointment at the children's hospital. *"I better get heading back,"* he thought.

Asher retraced his steps back to his place on Piccadilly, knowing Annabel would be ready to head out to the children's hospital. He hadn't realized how far he had walked, lost in thoughts of the missing gem. Passing the bakery again, he couldn't shake the memory of Emily's eyes and her sultry voice. The encounter was like drinking a sweet poison; he longed for more, even though the pain she had caused in the past was unforgettable. He had given his whole heart to her, but the gesture was not reciprocated, leaving him alone as she moved on to a new relationship.

Twisting the doorknob, Asher pushed open his front door to find Annabel decked out in her new Mrs. Clause suit. "Ah, you made it back, and just in time, too," Annabel said, laying out Asher's Santa suit on the couch. "Go and get ready. We have many children excited to see you." Asher walked over to his vibrant red suit, sweeping it up into his arms. "I'll be just a moment. Thanks, Annabel. You're the best.

After a quick cab ride and a few amused glances from onlookers, the Christmas duo arrived at the Children's Hospital right on schedule. The multistory redbrick building showcased the craftsmanship of the 1800s, with long rectangular windows and a smoothly curved brick wall that gracefully followed the street corner. In contrast, the hospital's entrance was modern, featuring a magnificent glass roof that led to automatic sliding doors. Inside, vibrant colors and cartoon murals adorned the walls, creating a welcoming and non-threatening environment for the children.

"Welcome back, Mr. and Mrs. Claus," an enthusiastic voice greeted them. It belonged to a middle-aged woman with salt-and-pepper hair tied up in a bun. "My name is Becky, and I will be assisting you today and helping you navigate the event."

"Thank you. It's wonderful to be here. We are looking forward to visiting with the children," Annabel replied.

"Like the last time Santa visited, we have our meeting room set up with decorations and treats. We have created a schedule to allow the children to visit safely. As you can undoubtedly understand, not all children are well enough to leave their rooms. We have arranged a special delivery to their rooms, which will include a small gift, a signed letter, and a photo of the two of you."

"That is very gracious of you," Asher said softly. "Oh, how I wish I could make things better for these little ones. So much needless suffering."

"This is why we are here, Mr. Jupes. To provide the best help we can," Becky reassured him. "Come, let's get you inside," she continued.

Passing by the reception desk, several children stared and pointed. One dark-haired girl, who had been teasing her younger brother in the waiting room, froze in her steps, transfixed by the pudgy, red-cloaked visitor with a snow-white beard. Numerous giddy kids watched the magical couple walk down the hospital corridor until they were out of sight.

"Here we are, just in there. Ernie has set up his camera for the photos, and there are plenty of candy canes in a cloth sack next to your chair. I'll be out in the halls coordinating your visitors. The first will be arriving shortly," Becky informed Asher and Annabel, then turned and slipped back through the door and out of sight.

"Hello there," said Ernie. "I'll be snapping all the memories today. Don't mind the camera flash. Your eyes will adjust later tonight," he added with a friendly smile. Ernie was a slender man in his early thirties with slicked-back hair and a straggly goatee.

"Very well. Mrs. Claus, known to some as Candace Claus, and I will get ourselves ready," Asher said.

The afternoon visits with the children passed in the blink of an eye. Kids with masks over their noses and mouths filed through the doors one by one, each with beaming eyes, eager to share their Christmas wishes. The event was heartfelt, and everyone felt a sense of happiness and gratitude for the spirit of hope and peace that filled this small section of the hospital. Everyone felt at peace except for one. Asher couldn't shake the feeling that he needed to visit the children, who were unable to leave their rooms.

"Thank you for coming in and giving the children some well-needed hope," Becky said.

"We were happy to be here. Can I ask something from you?" Asher inquired. A twinkle sparked in Becky's eyes.

"Certainly, what can I help you with?"

Asher glanced around, ensuring no one else was in earshot. "I was wondering if I could pass by a few rooms where the kids can't leave. I won't go in, but it would mean a lot to me if I could wave to them from the hallway."

Becky drew in a long breath. "Some of the kids in those rooms may be under sedation for medical reasons. I can probably let you pass by a few rooms, and hopefully, you will be able to wave to a couple of kids. We need to be stealthy about it. The providers in the hospital get cross when non-family visitors roam the halls."

Annabel and Asher nodded in agreement. "Follow me; we'll make this a quick visit," Becky said, pointing to the floor above. Moving with the precision of a well-practiced team, the three walked down the hall and up an old staircase reserved for employees. "Here we are. Be as quiet as you can. I'll go speak with the staff and distract them. After you pass by the rooms, return to this door and head to the lobby. I can give you about five minutes. Be swift." With those last words, Becky turned and headed down the hall toward the nurses' station.

The corridor was mostly quiet, with only intermittent electronic beeps breaking the silence. The door to the first room was open, revealing several family members in chairs, interacting with a seven-year-old girl with a stocking on her head and an IV line attached to her arm. The girl was talkative but had dark circles under her eyes, evidence of many restless nights.

As Annabel and Asher passed by the doorway, the young girl's mother said something to her and pointed in their direction. The instant Asher made eye contact with the small, infirmed girl, her reddened eyes seemed to brighten, and a toothy grin emerged. Asher closed his eyes for a brief second, then, upon opening them, gestured for her to look under her pillow. The little girl reached behind her head and wiggled her tiny hand under her fluffy headrest. Grasping something rectangular and firm, she removed a slender red box with a gold bow fastened tightly around it. The now-beaming-eyed girl looked back at Asher, who returned a wink before walking toward the next room.

Annabel leaned close to Asher's ear and whispered, "What was in that little box?"

Reaching up, Asher wiped a small tear from the corner of his eye; his reply was incoherent and jumbled.

Annabel placed her hand on his shoulder, rubbing it tenderly. "Try again, Asher. I didn't quite get that."

Asher cleared his throat quietly. "Sorry, I got a little choked up. Her wish was for her mom. That sweet little girl, in her sick bed, wasn't worried about herself but was only concerned about her mother seeing her daughter ill. She wanted to give her mother a beautiful bracelet, something special to always remember her by. In that little box are matching gold bracelets with mother-daughter charms holding hands and engraved words: 'Families are forever.'"

With humbled hearts, Annabel and Asher continued down the hall, visiting room after room in a similar fashion. The hearts of both recipients and givers swelled with compassion and Christlike love. However, it was the last room visited today that made the most profound impression on the loving Christmas couple.

The patient's room was quiet and still. A nine-year-old boy slept in a darkened room attached to several monitors. The family had been absent, likely stepping away momentarily after many long hours. Asher felt a steady vibration and tumbling in his coat pocket. Instinctively, he reached in and retrieved Guinevere. The sassy brass spectacles were more subdued and reverent today. Speaking in a hushed tone, the glasses bid Asher to look into the room through the lenses.

Without hesitation, Asher followed her invitation, revealing a room full of family members who had passed on from this world. Numerous ancestors stood by the bedside, looking at the child with loving care. A short-statured, gray-haired woman who had been a grandparent to him in this life now stood valiantly as a guardian angel, resting her hand on top of the child's hand. A mixed group of men and women of various ages stood in a circle, appearing to pray.

Sharing the scene unfolding in front of him, Asher whispered to Annabel, "We are never truly alone." Gently placing Guinevere back in his pocket, Asher and Annabel made their way to the stairwell and back out to the lobby.

18

A Sinister Ring

Savio sat at his desk, a jeweler's loupe pressed firmly against his right eye. "Just look at this gem! Holding it in the light, it looks blue, but as I tilt it to the right, it now looks green. If I twist it to the left, it changes to yellow. I can't figure this thing out."

Felipe, who had been quietly working at his laptop, glanced up briefly before returning to his screen.

"I can't thank you enough, Felipe, for finding them. Without your clever detective work, I wouldn't be holding this gem right now."

"So, how did you find him anyway?" Savio asked, curiosity stirred. Felipe looked up again, a hint of pride in his eyes."It's all right here on the internet. It took some time because there was so much to sort through. I started by going back to the time you first encountered him and noticed his ring. By hacking into numerous live-feed cameras, door cameras, business cameras, and even security cameras, I was able to get a decent facial and body image."

Felipe stood, placed his laptop down, and shuffled toward Savio, who was starting to zone out.Felipe's exuberance bubbled up inside him, fueled by the adrenaline rush of hacking into supposedly secure sites.

"The next thing I did was run his image through facial recognition. It didn't take long to learn everything about him—his house, his favorite places to eat, and the friends he spends most of his time with. It was by finding these pictures that I discovered he had been at the Santa Grotto in the past, and after a little more searching, I learned that he was coming back this year. The rest is history," he said proudly.

"Well done indeed, Felipe," Savio complimented his right-hand man, causing Felipe to beam with pride. "My proudest moment, however, was discovering his true alias. Using facial recognition for Asher, Jupes pulled up a younger-looking man just a few years ago working for the Gazette—a well-known reporter, in fact, the one and only Joseph Amesbury. His new legal name, Asher Moby Jupes, was just a clever anagram rearranging the letters in his former name, Joseph Amesbury. Digging deeper into Mr. Amesbury's past, I now know everything about him. From his deceased adoptive parents to an old girlfriend, all of which has already proven to be useful information."

Savio flashed a sinister grin at Felipe, who was now doing a one-man parade march around the office. "Most impressive work, Sherlock," Savio said, patting Felipe on the shoulder. "Where is that no-good Carlos?" Savio snarled.

"Probably hiding so he doesn't have to work," Felipe complained.

"Must I do everything around here?" Savio muttered as he carefully placed the gem in a small plastic bag and dropped it into his front shirt pocket for safekeeping.

Stepping out of his office, Savio wandered down the hall to a back room filled with bookcases, cabinets, and worktables cluttered with various tools. The air was thick and warm from an electric furnace on a back table, which also held a well-cured crucible, a gas torch, and some powdered flux. Broken antique gold and silver earrings and necklaces littered the tabletop, waiting to be transformed. "Carlos? Carlos, where are you?" Savio's voice was deep and demanding.

A hunched-over Carlos emerged from a shadowy corner, grasping a sketch pad and a shortened pencil with a worn tip. "I'm right here, Savio, just finishing the drawing of the new ring you wanted me to design." Carlos had matured into a skilled jeweler over the years under Savio's forceful hand. Moving and selling looted precious metals and jewelry was done by melting down the plundered materials and molding new jewelry or small metal bars for easy dark alley transactions.

Savio reached his hand forward, demanding to see the sketch. "Let's see how you incorporated the jewels into my design." Savio's eyes widened, and a thin smile of satisfaction stretched across his face. The center of the ring was a skull missing the lower jaw, and the band of the ring had been artistically designed as a snake-scaled body that would wrap around the finger, its intricate cobra head stretching across the front of the skull just above the orbits, which were designed to hold the two magical gems he had obtained from the Master Santa ring.

Satisfied, he returned the penciled draft back to Carlos. "When can you start?" Carlos pointed at his workbench, "I was only waiting on your approval of the design. My equipment is ready to begin."

"This better be your best work. I expect nothing less than your very best. Savio thundered as he exited the room. Since obtaining a second enchanted gem, the intrigue of the new gem and any magic properties related to it had consumed him. Savio's obsession had escalated, and his lust to obtain all the gems had become insatiable.

Halfway to returning to his personal office, Savio stopped in the hall, pulled the small clear plastic bag out of his pocket, and inspected its contents. Satisfied that they were secure, he replaced them and hastily made it back to his desk for further testing. Pulling the soft plastic bag once again from his pocket, he laid it upon the finger, donning his magic ring. Immediately, a steady, low vibration rattled the crude golden ring with a low electrical charge. Pulling the small clear envelope away from his finger, the ring would rest, and all vibration ceased. Curiously, Savio felt stronger, more electrifying, and more powerful when the two gems reunited.

This must be the source of his mortality. I remember reading something about this in that old book, Savio thought. Savio approached the bookshelf in his office and pulled several books off the top shelf. Reaching to the back of the shelf, he slid the back panel to the side, exposing a hidden compartment. Hefting the large book from its resting place. Savio placed it on his desk and wiped the dust from the cover, exposing the title. The Great Forefathers of Christmas. It looks like I will be spending more dedicated time with you now," he said, thumbing through the pages.

The book was as large as an old encyclopedia, its leather cover binding together thick pages of discolored parchment. The text appeared to be handwritten in old English, with looping letters crafted by a quill. Savio skimmed the vast pages quickly but came to an abrupt halt when he saw the name Joseph Amesbury. Scanning further, he noted it had changed to Asher Jupes. What truly stopped him cold was seeing his own name.

"Savio?" he muttered in disbelief. "How is this even possible?" He flipped through the book, his heart pounding, until he reached the last entry. The remaining pages were blank, but the final inscription had a pulsating inkblot, like a cursor on a document ready to type. "Is this book recording events as they happen?" he wondered aloud. "This book is enchanted," he declared, slamming the ancient tome shut.

"Perhaps my reading can wait a day or two," Savio said to no one in particular, returning the book to its secure hiding place.

A few moments late, Felipe broke the pensive moment when he tapped lightly on the doorframe. "Sorry to disturb you. I wanted to let you know that You Know Who emailed you again and is open to meeting up with you again this evening."

"Did she say where?" Savio fired back.

"The same place as before. I think she finds the coffee shop a safe place to meet," Felipe responded.

"A safe place? Does she consider me dangerous?" Savio pressed.

Felipe half-suppressed a laugh. "I think you are dangerous. But that's beside the point. Honestly, she doesn't suspect that you are up to anything. I believe she just sees the coffee shop as a neutral environment, not a romantic setting that might lead a man on."

"Leading me on... That should be the least of her concerns," Savio snickered, wringing his hands. "This woman is already under my power and completely unaware. I just need to keep my visits frequent, or the enchantment will begin to wear off. I must be extremely careful—she will prove to be the key to my success."

"Did you find Carlos?" Felipe asked, entering the office and settling onto a rickety metal folding chair beside Savio's desk.

"Yes," Savio replied with a nod. "He was finishing up the design for my new ring. His crude drawing and sloppy hand are all I have to work with. But if a miracle is granted, it might turn out the way I hope it does." Savio's words dripped with disdain, masking the twisted truth of his nature. Not a single fiber in his being could muster a genuine compliment towards Carlos. Savio's core was a festering pit of selfishness and indifference, befriending people solely for his own gain. His true loyalty resided within the smallest of circles—a circle limited to just two faces: his own and the one in the mirror.

"I'll keep my eye on him while you are away," Felipe said, his curiosity piqued. I'm eager to see how this ring turns out. Once we have both gems bonded in gold, the magic will be enhanced, and there is no telling what abilities you may gain." Felipe stepped out of the office. " I'll be right back."

Savio slid out the new gem from his pocket, holding the small baggie close to the desk lamp. The transparent rock shimmered under the light, casting a mesmerizing array of colors across the room. "I have already started feeling the effects of the gem just by carrying it with me. Once the two enchanted stones are connected as one, I will gain unimaginable power. I believe as I am gaining power, Asher is losing his magic, and that will give me the extra strength I need to wrest this ring from him once and for all."

Savio dropped the gem bag back into his shirt pocket, patting it delicately. "I think I'm going to change and head to the coffee shop a bit early," he said. Felipe slid forward in his chair, "So, what is your plan with her today?" Savio leaned back in his leather office chair and propped his feet up on the desk. "Now that she feels safe with me, I'm going to start digging into her past and get vital information. I will let her lead the conversation but cautiously navigate it.

Savio began picking at a loose black thread on his shirt's sleeve cuff, his gaze distant and contemplative. "It all began very innocently. I noticed it years ago when I first encountered Carlos. On each visit, he seemed increasingly willing to do whatever I asked, adopting a more servile attitude. I started paying closer attention to what I might be doing to influence this change. After careful observation, I realized it was my handshake. Not the handshake itself but the ring touching his hand. Somehow, his flesh touching the ring created a loyalty to the ring. I wear the ring, and he became loyal to its bearer, completely unaware of it. The less contact he had with the ring, the more he reverted to his old ways. So, I ensured that I greeted him with a handshake each time, maintaining my control over him. Now, I no longer need the ring to touch him; simply being in his presence is enough to exert influence. How do you think I've been able to control him for so long? He is entirely under my command."

"Do you think that is one of the gem's magical properties?" Felipe asked, curiosity etched on his face.

"It is my suspicion that something sinister altered the gem when it was in Hitler's possession," Savio said, stroking his chin thoughtfully.

"Whatever the cause, it matters not to me. What I'm learning is that the gem has more magical powers than I ever imagined. Having two gems in my possession is only the beginning.

19

Picture-perfect

W ell, you are looking more like yourself today, Asher," Annabel said, grinning at him as he stretched his arms upward from a restful nap on the couch.

"I'm starting to feel more like myself these last few days. Losing that gem really impacted me physically, but I think the remaining gems have stepped up," Asher replied, his voice reflecting renewed strength.

"That's wonderful news to hear," Annabel cheerfully responded, walking toward the calendar hanging on the wall near the kitchen. "Thirty-one, thirty-two, wow, thirty-three Polar Express visits are scheduled for December. This is a bit more than last year. Are you up to it, Asher?"

Asher got up and moseyed over to the kitchen to inspect the calendar. Polar Express appearances in many locations throughout the United States and several countries had all been written in blue ink and underlined in red.

"I think I can handle it. We will definitely be traveling by portals. Looks like Guinevere will get a good workout over the next several weeks. Without this ability to travel, it would not have been possible."

Asher walked to the refrigerator, slid a can of Yoo-hoo to the side, and grabbed the fresh orange juice that Annabel had prepared for him earlier in the day. His daily vitamin C intake routine seemed to have helped with his energy levels and his ring regenerating.

"Look here, Asher. Annabel blurted, pointing at the calendar. You have a confirmation request in person today down the street. This is the only appointment we had that requires you to fill out forms in person. It must be something new with this scheduling company," she deduced. "I'll head over there right after this O.J.," Asher replied, taking a sip and savoring the fresh, tangy flavor.

"Should we do lunch out today?" Annabel hinted. "There's a wonderful new cafe not too far from where you're headed to fill out those Polar Express forms. I need to run an errand, but afterward, how about we meet up?"

"Yes, yes indeed. We both could benefit from a little change in dietary repetition. I imagine you're getting tired of my limited menu options." A soft laugh escaped him.

"Don't cut yourself short, Asher; you seem to know your way around the kitchen pretty well," Annabel replied.

With the lunch date established, Asher made himself ready and departed. "It's only a twenty-minute walk, and besides, I could use the exercise," he mused, poking his grumbling stomach as if it were listening. Apart from his glass of orange juice earlier, his stomach was running a bit on the empty side since he had slept through the early breakfast hour that day.

The sidewalks were bustling as usual in London, and the storefronts seemed to have been transformed overnight. Christmas lights adorned the windows, wreaths greeted customers at the door, and numerous Christmas sales and discount prices were posted in all directions. The Christmas season was here, and there was no mistaking it. Though Asher's wardrobe did not resemble Santa in any way, there was a sense of magnetism about him that drew long looks from awestruck children along the way.

Today's afternoon walk had a slightly bitter bite, and the wind tussled the long white whiskers on Asher's face. *I haven't been to this part of London in years.* He realized, looking up and down the street at the many new towering buildings. "Excuse me, ma'am. Do you know the Bancroft's office supply store? I'm a bit turned around but I think it wasn't too far from here," Asher questioned an elderly lady with a bright pink umbrella. "The woman was slightly taken back and let out a half-scared, half-embarrassed chortle. "Pardon me, caught me off guard you did, consumed in my thoughts." the startled woman apologized.

"The apology is mine," Asher reassured her. "I haven't been this way in a while, but I used to visit an office supply store nearby. Mr. Bancroft, the owner, was a kind man. I thought I might drop in on him."

The woman paused, scanning the area as if searching for something. "Are you talking about that old four-story brick building with the white window frames and the pale green door on the ground floor?"

"Yes, that's the one," Asher confirmed.

"Oh, that store closed some time ago. It's a military relic store now. It's not really my cup of tea, so I've never gone in. It's two streets over that way," she said, pointing her frail, aged finger to the north. "I'd best be on my way. Good luck, dear."

With a mix of gratitude and sorrow for the store's change of hands, Asher thanked the kind woman and set his course toward the old redbrick building. Visiting the store hadn't been in his plans when he left home moments earlier, but something inside urged him to go there. These feelings happened frequently enough for Asher to recognize that it wasn't just his imagination but a very real, unmistakable sensation akin to a whisper from his subconscious. Listening to that proverbial voice in his head had always steered him in the right direction.

It didn't take long for Asher to make his way down the street, where he found himself standing outside what used to be Bancroft's office supply. The building, for the most part, looked just as it had the last time Asher was there years ago. Bancroft's had been his favorite store, and over time, he had grown fond of Mr. Bancroft, coming to appreciate the friendly discount on his much-needed office supplies during his days as a reporter. Though the building still bore a resemblance to those earlier days, its windows were no longer plastered with posters advertising paper and pens. Instead, they showcased a collection of military relics, a silent testament to the store's new identity.

The old wooden door's hinges emitted a brief, high-pitched squeal as Asher stepped inside. "I don't need an entry bell or electric chime to let me know I have a visitor," declared an older, thin man sitting in a wooden chair behind the counter. "If I spare grease on the metal, I keep money in my pocket. I figure it's a win-win situation," the man continued with a touch of humor.

"How long have you been here?" Asher asked.

"Oh, I moved in about six months after the previous owner passed away. It was quite sudden for him. One day, he was working his store, and the next, he was gone. I believe it had something to do with his heart."

Asher dropped his gaze to the floor. "I'm sorry to hear that. I was friends with him, but I'd been away in the US for a while and lost my regular contact with him. He was a good man."

"Well, I don't have any office supplies to offer you, but feel free to look around. Who knows, you might find something useful or interesting that you can't live without," the seasoned salesman encouraged with a wry smile.

The old supply store had indeed undergone a transformation. The space was quiet and still, with dim lighting casting long shadows. Several light bulbs were missing, likely an attempt to save on electricity. The shelves and display cases were meticulously organized, showcasing an array of military artifacts. It was clear that the majority of the items were from World War II, with a few uniforms and relics dating back to the First World War. Asher found the museum-like display captivating, each artifact telling its own story of the dark times of the past.

In a dusty corner of the store, Asher noticed a box filled with framed photographs from the Second World War. Though faded with time, the images still held the weight of history. "Mind if I take a look at these pictures?" Asher called out to the clerk.

"Sorry, I haven't gotten around to putting those out for display yet. But you're welcome to look through them. Remember, everything's for sale," the clerk said, his voice laced with a hint of salesmanship.

Asher carefully removed each framed picture, blowing the dust off the glass with gentle puffs of breath. Beneath the obscuring layer of dust, each photograph revealed a piece of preserved history. One by one, the images unveiled military men in crisp uniforms, standing with pride and determination.

One photograph in particular caught Asher's attention—a poignant scene of soldiers bidding farewell to their loved ones at a train station. The image was frozen in time, capturing what might have been the last moments those couples ever spent together. The reality of war's reach, its extended fingers grasping at the very heart of humanity, was sobering. It was a stark reminder of the personal tragedies hidden behind the larger narrative of history.

The next picture caught Asher by surprise: a black-and-white photograph of a Nazi squadron of five men leaning against a Panzer tank. Though the image was grainy and of low quality, the faces of the men were remarkably clear. Three of them were strangers to Asher, but the other two faces sent chills down his spine—Kristoff and Eckerd, standing side by side, immortalized in the photograph.

This is impossible. Asher's thoughts raced, trying to reject the reality before him. How could this be? He scrutinized the image further, his eyes narrowing as he flipped the frame over. The corner of the photograph was slightly curled, revealing an eerie inscription in faded pencil markings that made Asher's breath catch. *An J.A. Von K.C.*

At first glance, it seemed like an innocent inscription, easy to overlook. But Asher's magical ability to understand languages and hidden meanings revealed its true significance. *To J.A. From K.C.*—the message was unmistakable. *To Joseph Amesbury from Kristoff Kristkindle*

Lifting the bent, curled backing of the frame, Asher peeked inside and glimpsed a small, neatly folded parchment tucked away. Was this a secret note intended for me to read? He wondered. Since the backing was firmly secured except for the lifted corner, removing it would require some careful dismantling of the frame with household tools.

"I'll take this old-time picture I just found," Asher said, handing the frame to the bored elderly store owner. The man took the frame, dusted the glass with a well-worn rag he kept behind the counter, and made a remark, "A group of Nazi thugs, eh?" He placed the picture into a plastic bag and stuffed wadded paper around it to protect the purchase.

"Sometimes, you can't judge a book by its cover, and sometimes, you can't judge a man by his uniform," Asher replied, his tone laced with meaning.

The elderly man responded with a dismissive "Whatever!" and added, "Come back again if you're in the area," his words, ushering Asher out the door and back onto the street.

There was only one thing that could keep Asher from rushing home to open the picture frame: his lunch with Annabel. "Opening you up will have to wait a little longer," he murmured, eyeing the frame in his bag. Determined to meet her on time, Asher quickened his pace, eager to complete the Polar Express paperwork without further delay.

The detour to the military relics store had already added nearly forty-five minutes to his journey, putting him at risk of being late again. The memory of his last tardy incident at Angelo's Pizza still haunted him.

151

This time, however, he hoped the intriguing find might help soften the blow if he were late. Regardless, he was resolute in not making Annabel wait. Completing the Polar Express forms swiftly became his top priority.

After a hurried jog that felt like an eternity, Asher's luck began to turn. The Polar Express paperwork, completed more swiftly than he had anticipated, allowed him precious time to meet Annabel. He thanked the receptionist and turned to head back toward the lobby.

Just steps from the door, a soft, tender voice called out, "Joseph, I thought that was you."

Asher snapped his head around, his gaze meeting the radiant chestnut eyes he had known so well. "Emily? What are you doing here?"

"Well, it's not every day you see a white-bearded man moving like a young man. It caught my attention," Emily said, her voice warm with a hint of amusement. "After seeing you a couple of times now, I realized it was you again, and I just had to say hi. That first time we bumped into each other at the gown shop, it was a bit... crowded, if you know what I mean."

Asher felt a twinge of discomfort but was intrigued by her renewed interest. He lingered, though he felt a growing sense of unease.

"It's strange to run into you so many times in such a short span," Asher admitted.

"Maybe it's not so strange after all. Maybe it's meant to be," Emily replied, stepping closer and placing her hand on his forearm.

Asher was momentarily frozen. He wanted to avoid appearing rude but was unsure how to handle her increasing proximity. Slowly, he took a half step back, but Emily followed, closing the gap between them. "Looking into your eyes takes me back to when we were dating," Emily said softly, tracing his cheekbone with her finger.

At that very moment, as Asher tried to retreat, a voice from behind him cut through the tension. "So that's how it is, then, huh?"

Asher turned just in time to see a visibly upset Annabel storming out the door.

"Annabel, wait!" Asher called out, but she was already too far gone. He spun around, locking eyes with Emily, who wore a smirk that deepened his frustration.

"She'll be fine, Asher. Why all the fuss? What's done is done," Emily said, her tone nonchalant.

Asher shook his head in disbelief, his heart pounding with a mix of regret and anger. Without another word, he turned and headed for home, each step feeling heavier than the last.

20

Together as One

The walk home felt like the longest of Asher's life. His mind swirled with guilt and confusion, knowing how the scene must have looked through Annabel's eyes. *How will I ever explain this?* His thoughts churned, his stomach twisting in knots as he replayed the moment she stormed off. *What was with Emily today? I've never seen her act like that before.*

Asher approached the front door, took a deep breath, and pushed it open with a heavy heart. Inside, Annabel was on the couch, her suitcase half-packed, tears streaming down her face. The sight of her weeping struck him like a blow.

"Annabel, we need to talk," Asher pleaded, his voice tinged with desperation.

"There is nothing to talk about, Asher. I saw everything I needed to see," Annabel snapped, her words sharp as she slammed the suitcase shut.

Asher quietly closed the door behind him and walked over to her, his heart aching at the sight of her pain. "You have every right to be upset, given what you walked in on," he began, his voice steady but gentle.

"I'm not talking about this, Asher," Annabel shot back, her voice thick with anger and hurt as she turned and headed into the bedroom, yanking clothes off hangers.

Asher felt a wave of relief as Annabel listened to him, her earlier anger slowly giving way to understanding. "I don't blame you for wanting to leave," Asher said softly, following her. "But before you go, before you walk out on a misunderstanding, I beg you to give me just two minutes more of your time. Please, just hear me out."

Annabel tossed the handful of clothes she'd yanked off the hangers onto the bed and returned to Asher, who was sitting on the edge of the couch. She sat across from him, her lips pursed, waiting. "Thank you," Asher said, grateful for her willingness to listen. "I assure you, what you saw is not what actually happened. You've known me for years, and you know I'm a man of my word. What I'm about to share will change your mind and mend your heart."

Annabel remained silent, though she unfolded her arms, a small sign that she was open to his explanation. As Asher carefully recounted the events, he noticed the tension gradually leaving her body; her shoulders relaxed, and she traced the carved wooden armrest with her finger, deep in thought. He paused, giving her space to process everything.

"I'm sorry," Annabel finally broke the silence, her voice heavy with remorse. "I misunderstood and misjudged you." Asher dipped his head in acknowledgment. "I, too, need to apologize. I should have stepped away the moment she got too close. Maybe then, this whole misunderstanding wouldn't have happened."

Annabel nodded, wiping a tear with a tissue. "I couldn't imagine my life without you. I was just so hurt. My feelings for you are deeper than I've ever let on, and the pain was so intense I just had to get away." She paused, pulling another tissue from the box. "We have something special, Asher, but I don't know where we're headed or what we are. I've stayed by your side through everything, but I need to know if we have a future together, a real one."

"I have a remedy for that," Asher said, standing and moving closer to her.

"A remedy? What are you playing at?" Annabel asked, puzzled.

"I'm not playing at anything," Asher said, his voice steady but betraying a tremor of anticipation. He hadn't planned for this moment to happen today, and certainly not under these circumstances, but something deep inside told him it was now or never. As his thoughts tumbled into place, certainty settled in—a certainty that both excited and unnerved him. Butterflies swarmed in his stomach, and his hand began to tremble, not from doubt but from the weight of what he was about to do. The moment felt charged, electric, like the air before a storm, and despite the whirlwind of emotions, Asher knew he was exactly where he was meant to be.

"Mr. Baggins, the time is now. I need your help." He called out,

Almost instantly, his velvet companion appeared, floating gracefully to the floor beside Annabel. Asher reached into the bag, pulled out an item, and then dropped to one knee.

Annabel's eyes widened as she saw the most elegant golden ring in his hand. Butterflies of nervous excitement fluttered wildly in her stomach, her breath catching in anticipation."This ring was once worn by Lorelei and given to her by Kristoff, the Santa before me. It gave her immortality and bonded them during their time on earth. It's been in Mr. Baggins' possession, waiting for this moment."

With care, Asher slid the slightly loose-fitting ring onto Annabel's left hand. "Annabel, I love you deeply, more than words can express. Will you be my companion and my helpmate? Will you stay with me forever? Annabel, will you marry me?"

Annabel's excitement overflowed like a dam breaking, her heart racing as she helped Asher to his feet, his hands trembling in hers. "Is this really happening?" she whispered, her voice quivering with joy. Her eyes sparkled like stars, and she let out a soft, disbelieving laugh. "I've dreamed about this moment for so long." Tears of happiness welled up as she gazed at him, barely able to contain herself. "I love you, Asher, more than anything. Of course, I'll marry you!"

Her words tumbled out in a rush, and without thinking, she threw her arms around him, pulling him into a passionate kiss. As their lips met, the gold band on her finger seemed to come alive, resizing itself to fit her perfectly. A wave of warmth and energy surged through her, leaving her feeling lighter, almost as if she were floating. She wasn't just becoming Asher's fiancée—something deep and magical had awakened within her, filling her with a sense of wonder and a love that felt boundless.

"I feel different now," Annabel said, examining herself with curious eyes.

Asher nodded, a soft smile forming on his lips. "I do, too. I'm now an engaged man. This does feel different. But different in a good way."

"Yes, different in a good way," Annabel agreed, "but more. I feel more energy, more alive than ever—something magical."

"Well, I've been known to have that effect on women," Asher joked.

Annabel grinned, but her focus remained inward as she continued to examine herself, stroking her arms and legs, her fingers gently pressing into her forearms. "But seriously," Asher continued, "you must be experiencing magic—or maybe even immortality. I expect even more enchanted changes will come the moment we are bonded in matrimony."

"If this is how you feel every day, this is amazing. I cannot remember ever feeling this way—not ever," Annabel admitted, her voice filled with awe.

"I have something more to show you," Asher said, walking to the front door and retrieving the bag he had carried from the military relics store. Setting the bag on the coffee table, he dashed to the kitchen and returned with a screwdriver in hand.

"What's in the bag?" Annabel asked, curiosity piqued.

Asher carefully pulled out the framed picture of Kristoff and Eckerd, recounting the story of how he had discovered it. "See right here—both mine and his initials," Asher said, pointing to the faded letters. "But it's what's behind the backing of the picture that's drawing my attention. There's a folded piece of paper tucked inside. I think Kristoff might have left it there for me to find. I was drawn to the store and this picture by some unseen force."

"So, which one is Kristoff?" Annabel asked, her eyes narrowing as she tried to discern the faces in the old photograph.

Asher wiped the remaining dust off the glass with a tissue. "That one right there. And the guy next to him is Eckerd," he said, pointing at the young man with curiously large ears.

Annabel took the frame from Asher and brought it closer to her eyes. "Oh, he was quite handsome, wasn't he?" she said, rubbing the dirty glass covering Kristoff's face.

"He was a great man, and Eckerd was as loyal a friend and supporter of the Santa Order as one could hope for. Both of those men and their sweet wives gave such care and service to the needy. There have been, and always will be, men and women who serve selflessly in this world. It doesn't always take magic to make miracles happen; it just takes a willing heart and a desire to make a difference," Asher declared, his voice filled with admiration.

"Let me see that frame again, Annabel. Let's see if we can get a better look at the hidden note inside." Asher twirled the screwdriver in his hand as he spoke. The screws holding the backing to the picture frame were tarnished and deeply embedded. The wood was aged yet held the screws securely. With some effort, Asher managed to remove enough screws to slide the backing away from the frame. Inside, a three-inch yellowing paper had been carefully folded, its edges squared and creased with precision. No words were visible on the outside; the note's secrets remained hidden within the folds of the parchment.

Asher carefully removed the aged paper, unfolding it with deliberate care to avoid any tears. As he slowly revealed the message, he realized it was handwritten but upside down. Gently rotating the paper, he read the words Kristoff had left behind: "Joseph, protect the ring at all costs. Trust nobody."

The weight of the message sank into Asher as he set the paper back on the disassembled picture frame, leaning back on the couch, his mind a whirlpool of thoughts. Annabel, sensing the gravity of the note, picked it up, her eyes scanning the faded words. "Was this really written after the war? How is that even possible? You weren't even born yet."

Asher stroked his chin whiskers, deep in thought. "Things are revealed to Santa as needed. This must have been a revelation to him at some point early in his Santahood. Enough of a revelation that he knew my name and the situation I would find myself in many years in the future from the time he wrote the letter."

"It would have been nice if it said a name or someone to look out for," Annabel criticized the warning note.

"I don't think he needed to," Asher replied. "Think about it—on my way to sign those papers, I felt strongly prompted to go to the relics store. Not after I signed the papers, not before our lunch date. It was right on my way to sign the papers. And who did I happen to run into after I signed them?" He paused for effect, answering his own question. "Yes, you guessed it: Emily."

Annabel's brow furrowed with concern. "Do you think it was set up? That someone knew you would have to show up to sign those papers?"

"It's difficult to say," Asher admitted, pacing the floor, his mind racing. "But she was very aggressive toward me, and it was so out of character. How could she even know about the ring in the first place?"

"Maybe Savio has something to do with it," Annabel suggested. "It seems unlikely, given that he's from Argentina and she's from the UK. Still, it's the only logical explanation. It's the only common thread in the mystery. There must be a connection."

Asher nodded, considering her words. "It's possible. Savio might have a way of reaching out or influencing people beyond what we know. The timing is too perfect to be a coincidence. One thing is for certain: Savio will not stop until he has the ring, and his powers will increase, especially now that he has another gem. I think I need to confront Emily and see if I can get down to the bottom of this once and for all. It's not easy trying to defend the ring and still fulfill Santa's duties."

"It looks like Savio's closing in on us again," Annabel said, her voice tinged with concern. "If he's found Emily and knows about your past, it's only a matter of time before he tracks us down."

Asher nodded, his own worry surfacing. "You're right. We need to leave, and fast. But where do we go?"

Annabel's eyes scanned the room, searching for a solution. Her gaze landed on the note lying on the picture frame. "What's that?" she asked, pointing at it. It was as if, by magic, new words had appeared in different handwriting. "It's in German, and I can't read it," she said, a hint of frustration in her voice.

"Let me see," Asher said, quickly moving to the table. He examined the note, his eyes widening in surprise. "Different ink... this is incredible."

"What does it say?" Annabel pressed.

Asher read the message aloud. "It's from Eckerd. He wrote, *My home has been handed down from one generation to the next. I now leave it to the Santa Order for whatever you need and to help Keep the work going. Eckerd.* And there's an address."

"Where is it?" Annabel asked, her curiosity piqued.

"Lübars, a small village on the outskirts of Berlin," Asher replied. "It sounds like our next destination. Let's use the portal to get there. Guinevere, we need your help."

From inside, Mr. Baggins, still resting on the floor, came a familiar, slightly muffled voice. Asher swiftly retrieved the brass spectacles, a wave of relief flooding over him. "Are you going to put me on or leave me here to gather dust?" Guinevere's sassy tone elicited a smile from Asher. "Let's get this over with. I'm sure you're eager to find the portal to Eckerd's house in Lübars," she continued, her voice tinged with excitement.

Asher donned the glasses and began to scan the room for a portal, but initially, nothing appeared. "I don't see a portal, Guinevere. Can you offer a bit of guidance?" he asked, feeling the glasses subtly vibrate on his nose. "Did it ever occur to you to open your front door?" Guinevere chirped. "Actually, no," Asher admitted with a chuckle. "Not surprising," came the playful retort.

Opening the front door revealed a mesmerizing sight: green and red vapors swirled and danced on the ground a few paces away, shimmering with an otherworldly glow. "Grab your suitcase, Annabel. You're already packed. We can settle in once we get there. I'll return here to fetch a few more items. Come on, let's be off. Lübars awaits us."

Annabel, grasping her suitcase, locked the front door and then stepped forward, her fingers entwined with Asher's as they approached the portal. "I'm not as nervous this time, now that I've done this with you a few times. I just hate that stomach-drop sensation," she confessed. "Ah, you'll get used to it," Asher reminded her, leading her into the portal. The familiar sensation of free-fall tugged at Asher's stomach, but the warmth of her hand was absent, leaving him with a strange, unsettling feeling.

When he opened his eyes, Eckerd's house came into view, its quaint charm well-preserved. Wooden beams, darkened with age, crisscrossed the ceiling, supporting a roof of traditional thatch. The walls were adorned with ancient portraits and aged oil paintings, each telling a story of a bygone era. "Where is Annabel? Why didn't she come through the portal?" Asher's voice echoed in the empty house, his concern palpable.

"Losing another gem from your ring has significantly weakened your magical abilities," Guinevere's voice resonated through the glasses, her tone grave. "The full extent of this weakening will only become apparent when you attempt specific magical tasks." Her brass voice held a note of glumness. "Show me the portal back home, Guinevere. I need to get back to Annabel." Asher's urgent request was met with a swirl of red and green vapors within the lenses. Stepping into the portal, he left Eckerd's house behind, the air crackling with lingering magical energy.

21

A Not-So-Lucky Cab Ride

Annabel stood outside the house, her suitcase still clutched in her hand, a look of confusion etched across her face. She scanned the surroundings, bewildered by how she had been left behind while Asher had seemingly vanished. "I don't understand. What just happened?" she asked, her voice tinged with frustration.

"The ring's magical abilities have been compromised," Asher's voice came from inside the house, startling her. She turned to see him emerging from the reopened doorway, folding Guinevere with a practiced motion and tucking the brass spectacles back into his pocket. "I had no idea the ring's enchantments had weakened so significantly," Asher admitted, his brow furrowed with concern. "I thought it was only my health and strength that had been affected."

Here, let me grab your suitcase," Asher said, guiding Annabel back inside with a reassuring smile. "This definitely complicates our plans," he added, a hint of frustration in his voice.

Annabel walked over to the dining room table and took a seat, her shoulders sagging slightly. "Well, it looks like we'll have to do things the old-fashioned way," she said, trying to sound upbeat despite the unexpected setback. "I'll book a flight for myself, and you can meet me there. I'll handle the arrangements."

Asher nodded in agreement, heading to the closet to retrieve a small duffle bag. He began packing essential items for their new destination, his movements precise and purposeful.

"From what I can gather, the flight from London to Berlin is about an hour and forty minutes," Annabel said, her fingers dancing over her phone screen as she confirmed her flight details. "After that, we'll need to drive from Berlin to Lübars, which should take around thirty minutes. See how much you can get done with technology, Asher? Her words poked at his determination not to own a smartphone.

Asher finished packing and glanced at Annabel, his expression a blend of determination and concern. "We'll manage," he said, a touch of optimism in his voice. "It's just a detour, and we'll be back on track soon. Oh, and by the way, who needs a smartphone when I have magic?" His words carried a playful edge, though his eyes betrayed a hint of frustration.

Annabel met his gaze with a grin, her eyes twinkling with amusement. "You know," she teased, "if the magic in that ring keeps weakening, you might want to start reconsidering a cell phone plan." Her tone was light and humorous, a welcome contrast to the earlier frustration of the situation.

"So, did you get enough time to see Eckerd's house?" Annabel asked, shifting the conversation.

"I got a quick glimpse," Asher replied, emerging from the kitchen with his duffle bag. "It was like stepping into a time capsule. Everything was exactly as if Eckerd had just left it. I'm looking forward to going back with you and exploring it more. Even in that brief moment, the house had an almost magical aura. I can't help but wonder if its connection to the Santa Order has something to do with it."

Asher's eyes narrowed thoughtfully as he absently tapped his chin, lost in speculation. "When are you heading back to Eckerd's place?" Annabel asked, her voice brimming with curiosity. "By the way, we should really consider renaming it something cool. Something like Santa Headquarters, General Headquarters, or even better, Command Post," she suggested, her eyes lighting up with enthusiasm.

"Command Post sounds very official," Asher replied, a smile tugging at his lips. "I like it. It gives us that movie-like feel." He chuckled, imagining the grandeur of their new title. " To answer your earlier question, I figure once you board your plane, I will port travel and meet you there. When is your flight?"

"I head out first thing in the morning. I can take a taxi if you want to travel by the magical port from here," Annabel suggested, her tone light yet practical. "I'll be fine heading to the airport, and this will give you time to tidy up the new place before I arrive," she added with a playful hint in her voice.

"Settled then," Asher replied, nodding in agreement. "I'll lock up the moment you leave for the airport. Everything will be ready by the time you get there."

As the evening hours rolled in, Asher and Annabel slipped out of the house for a last-minute engagement celebration dinner. A mutual decision was to try the new All Day Cafe that Annabel had been desiring to go to earlier that day. The atmosphere of the cafe was peaceful, and for the newly engaged couple, it was an escape from the unusual past few weeks.

"What a day this has been," Asher said, his voice heavy with fatigue. "Just think about everything that's happened in the last 12 hours alone." His eyes seemed to drift beyond the window as if he were seeing something far off in the distance.

Annabel reached across the table, gently interlacing her fingers with his. "I think it was the most beautiful day ever," she said softly. "I'm not focusing on the odd or unusual things that happened. I'm choosing to see the beauty and the amazing moments that today brought."

Asher looked up, meeting her gaze. "You're right," he admitted, a warmth spreading through him. "You're perfect for me. You've always had a gift for seeing life as a cup half full, while I've often seen it as half empty." He leaned back in his chair, contemplating her words, feeling a deep appreciation for her perspective.

"I've been lost in thought today. Ever since Savio obtained the second gem, my mind has been racing, trying to figure out how to stop him," Asher said, scooping up a bite of his smoked haddock kedgeree with a poached egg.

"And have you come up with any ideas?" Annabel asked, leaning over to wipe the corner of his mouth with a cloth napkin. "You had a little something right there," she added with a giggle.

"Thanks," Asher replied, wiping his beard, slightly embarrassed. "What I've realized is that we need to go on the offensive. If we keep waiting for Savio to make the next move, he'll always have the upper hand." He took another bite of his dinner, his mind clearly working through the plan.

"I get the idea of hunting him down, but what are we going to do once we find him?" Annabel asked, taking a small bite of gnocchi.

"I believe the key is removing his ring. My ring can't be taken from me unless I willfully give it up, but I think that only holds true when all the gems are intact. Savio managed to almost remove it once before, which made me question the ring's power to stay on my finger. Now that two gems are missing, I believe he might have more success if he tries again. But I also think the same applies to his ring. His ring never had all the gems, and with only two, it might still be difficult to remove, but with a struggle, we can likely take it. If we remove the ring, we strip him of his power. The question is, how do we find Savio?" Asher's brow furrowed slightly, and his lips pressed together as he gazed into the distance.

"I think the most pressing thing right now is leaving London and getting to Lübars, where we can be safe and figure out our next move," Annabel suggested with a smile. "Maybe the answers will come to us once we're in the right environment—you know, at the Command Post." She paused, her expression turning serious. "I feel like we've pushed our luck here in London. And besides, Savio is on to us."

Asher nodded in agreement. "Yes, we need to stay a step ahead of him if we're going to be on the offensive. That was a fine meal, Annabel; thanks for the suggestion. I really enjoyed the smoked haddock kedgeree," he added, smoothly changing the subject.

"Shall we head out? We've got a big morning ahead of us." He took Annabel's hand, and together, they headed home, the weight of their situation balanced by the comfort of each other's presence.

The following day greeted Annabel and Asher with a clear, sunny sky, though the air was damp and cool, carrying a sense of new beginnings. A feeling of hope accompanied them as they prepared to leave. "Well, this is it," Asher said, locking the door behind them. "I don't imagine we'll be back here until we've dealt with Savio and his quest. Hopefully, we can accomplish this soon. At least we're only dealing with one person, which should make things easier." Asher hadn't really considered that there might be more than just Savio involved in the ploy to obtain the ring, but the thought now lingered in the back of his mind.

They stepped out of the house, the weight of the situation pressing down on them as Asher kissed Annabel on the cheek. "I'll see you soon," he promised, slipping on Guinevere's glasses once again. The portal, which had shifted slightly down the hall, continued to swirl with green and red vapors. With one last glance at Annabel, Asher stepped through the portal and disappeared from sight, leaving the familiar behind.

Annabel wasted no time making her way down the street, her eyes scanning for a cab. Spotting one parked conveniently at the curb, she hurried over and climbed in.

"Lovely day, ma'am, isn't it?" the driver greeted her with a cheerful tone.

"Indeed it is," Annabel replied, settling into the seat. "What luck to find a cab parked just outside my place. That never happens," she admitted with a hint of surprise, adjusting her bag on her lap.

"The name's Carlos. Where are you headed?" The man's Latin accent was thick, but his English was clear enough.

"London Heathrow, please," Annabel replied. "Can you get there quickly? I'm in a bit of a hurry."

"Claro que sí, ma'am. I'll step on it," he assured her with a confident smile.

"Thank you," Annabel said, her tone gracious. After a moment, she added, "Your accent—it's not from around here. Where are you from?"

"Argentina, ma'am. The land of excellent music, food, and dancing," Carlos replied, his voice filled with pride.

"Argentina? That's quite far from London. What brings you here?" Annabel asked, curiosity piqued.

"My boss sent me here to do a little surveillance work. Seeing if things can be profitable for him," Carlos answered, casting a brief look in the rearview mirror at Annabel.

"Well, that's very ambitious of him," Annabel remarked. "How long have you worked for him?"

Carlos's eyes left the mirror and focused back on the road. "All my life, I've been with him. But things won't always be this way," he added, his voice tinged with a hint of somberness.

"So, the airport—where are you headed?" Carlos asked, attempting to shift the conversation.

Annabel glanced out the window, choosing her words carefully. "Oh, just getting away for a time. A little change of pace, if you know what I mean. Will you be heading back to Argentina soon?"

Carlos met her gaze in the mirror, his dark brown eyes thoughtful. "I imagine I'll be heading back the moment I have something to report," he said, his voice trailing off with a sigh.

As they pulled up to the bustling entrance of London Heathrow, Carlos spoke again, "Here we are. Have a safe flight, ma'am."

"Thank you, and best of luck to you," Annabel said, stepping out of the cab. "Maybe I'll run into you again on a future taxi ride."

"Perhaps we will meet again," Carlos nodded, his tone carrying a quiet finality as she walked away.

Annabel stepped out of the cab and hurried down the walkway toward the airport entrance. Meanwhile, Carlos remained in the idling cab, his eyes tracking her as she weaved through the crowded sidewalk until she was out of sight. He pulled out his phone, dialing with an urgency that matched his tension.

"Carlos, what do you have to report?" The voice on the other end was sharp, demanding.

"She's alone and on the move, leaving from Heathrow. She didn't disclose her destination when I asked," Carlos replied, his tone steady.

There was a brief pause before the voice responded, "She's likely meeting up with Asher. I'll have Felipe hack into the airline ticket sales. They can't stay hidden from me. Ditch the cab and get back here—I'm sure by now the authorities are on the lookout for a stolen cab."

Carlos shoved the phone back into his pocket, the weight of his situation pressing down on him. He started the cab, driving away with a grim expression, frustration simmering beneath the surface as the reality of his continued servitude weighed heavily on his mind.

22

A Passage and Pearls

The thirty-minute cab ride from Berlin to Lübars was a visual feast. Green fields stretched endlessly, their vastness meeting a gray skyline heavy with rain-filled clouds. As the cab rolled through the landscape, the village of Lübars unfolded like a scene from a storybook, seemingly untouched by time. Traditional half-timbered houses, their steeply pitched roofs, and brightly painted shutters nestled among lush greenery dotted the countryside, each one a testament to the enduring charm of rural life.

Annabel gazed out the window, her eyes drinking in the beauty around her. Horses grazed peacefully in the meadows, their gentle movements adding to the serene atmosphere. The cab turned onto a winding cobblestone street, the pathway lined with rows of apple trees, their branches casting dappled shadows on the moist, lush grass. The village, with its timeless allure, welcomed her with open arms, offering a moment of calm and a deep connection to the natural world.

The cab rolled to a stop in front of a house with a steeply pitched roof covered in red clay tiles, weathered by time, giving it a rustic yet enduring appearance. Brightly painted red shutters framed the windows, hinting at the personality of the previous owner and complementing the tiled roof above. Flower boxes that once brimmed with geraniums now sat empty on the window sills, void of the vibrant vegetation they once held.

The entrance was modest, but the sturdy wooden door, adorned with intricate carvings, offered a warm welcome. As Annabel stepped out of the cab, she noticed a low stone wall toward the back of the property, likely enclosing a private garden. The house, with its timeless charm, seemed to invite her into a space where the past and present coexisted, connected by the enduring beauty of nature.

"There you are," Asher greeted Annabel as he opened the large front door. "Oh, Asher, it's exquisite. I think I am home. Annabel said, craning her head in all directions, trying to soak it all in. "The only thing that could make this house a home and more beautiful is you in it. Let me help you get your things," He said, giving her a peck on the cheek.

Asher had arrived hours earlier, preparing the house for Annabel's arrival. Though the home had been well-preserved, a light layer of dust had settled over the furnishings and counters. After wiping everything clean and organizing the space, the house now radiated charm. An old wooden table with two well-worn bench seats sat under a large window, where the sun's rays cast a warm light over the fresh flowers Asher had placed in a vase at the table's center. The cream plaster walls were adorned with several antique portraits and oil paintings, just as Asher had described to her after briefly visiting by portal the day before.

"Come here, Annabel. Look at this portrait," Asher said, pointing at a picture on the wall. Annabel stepped closer and noted that the photograph was modern, with vibrant colors and crisp quality, though its frame was old, likely passed down through generations. "That's Eckerd, Dennis, Kristoff, and their wives. It's clear they used this place in the past, just as we plan to now. See, this was taken right in front of the house," Asher explained, his finger tapping the house in the background.

Annabel's eyes widened with delight. "Look how happy they were. They look like family," she remarked, her voice full of sincere respect. Asher shared her sentiment, his grin stretching into a full smile.

"Let me show you around," Asher offered. "I've arranged a room for you down the hall, and I'll be staying upstairs. I think you'll find the room comfortable and private. It looks like some additions have been made to the house over the years. I'll use the bathroom over here," he said, pointing to a closed door in the hall. "You actually have your own connected to your room."

"You sure made good work in a short time!" Annabel said, a hint of admiration in her voice. "Why don't I unpack my things? Then we can start exploring the house's hidden secrets."

"Sounds like a good plan," Asher agreed, turning to walk away. "We'll also need to head into town later this evening to get groceries. I checked the refrigerator, and everything's in working order. It seems like Eckerd left the house in a sort of hibernation state. And one thing I've quickly discovered is that the house is powered by something unearthly," he added, glancing back with a knowing smile. "We have electricity and plumbing, yet we're not connected to any external sources. You might say the house is enchanted."

"I can't wait to see what else we can discover here!" Annabel shouted after him, her excitement palpable as she watched him disappear down the hallway.

Asher shared her enthusiasm. The house, though not enormous, had a distinct architecture that hinted at secrets waiting to be uncovered. The narrow corridors and oddly placed rooms suggested there could be hidden compartments or perhaps even a concealed passage or tunnel. The thought of uncovering such mysteries added a thrill to the air, making the old house feel even more alive with possibilities.

Annabel popped open her suitcase and began sorting her clothes. She carefully hung a coat and two dresses inside the armoire, which stood as a sturdy sentinel of the room's history. A small nightstand, a wooden vanity with a cushioned stool, and an aged rocking chair completed the furnishings, each piece holding a quiet elegance. One by one, she unpacked her belongings, folded them neatly into drawers, and placed small personal items on the vanity. As she settled in, she felt a deep sense of belonging—this place, with its timeless charm, felt like home. A place where she could imagine spending her life with Asher.

Annabel reached into her suitcase and retrieved the last item: a velvet bag slightly larger than a standard pencil case. It wasn't fancy, but it had traveled well, securing its contents with a dependable zipper closure. She pressed the soft bag to her chest, drawing in a deep breath before carefully unzipping it to inspect what was inside. The sunlight refracted off the princess-cut diamond earrings, causing sparkles to dance across the room. Her heart swelled as she reminisced about the evening Asher gave them to her as a birthday gift years ago. Several necklaces, bracelets, and brooches filled her prized cloth bag.

Stepping over to the vanity, Annabel selected the top middle drawer to store her jewelry safely. As she slid open the drawer, she suddenly shouted in surprise.

"Everything okay?" Asher called from the front room.

"I just found our first treasure!" Annabel's voice was excited and slightly higher-pitched.

"I hope it wasn't a rodent," Asher teased. "Come take a look, Asher. I think you'll be as surprised as I was."

Asher quickly made his way to the back bedroom, where he found Annabel holding an elegant pearl necklace in front of her. The pearls were perfectly round, with a lustrous sheen that caught the sunlight and displayed subtle hues of pink, cream, and silver. They were strung together in a delicate line, their smooth surfaces cool to the touch.

"Wow! Where did you find those?" Asher asked, intrigued.

"They were in there," Annabel said, pointing to the open drawer.

Asher tilted his head, examining the drawer from a different angle. "Is that a note in there?"

Sliding his hand into the drawer, he retrieved a small envelope with a note folded inside. Annabel walked over to the hanging oval mirror on the wall and modeled the necklace, twisting her shoulders back and forth, watching the pearls' colors and sheen dance in the light.

"Hey, these were Linda's pearls," Asher said, holding the note in his hand.

"Who was Linda?" Annabel asked, captivated by the necklace.

"She was Eckerd's wife. I remember Kristoff talking about her when I first interviewed him. I know Eckerd loved her dearly. These pearls were left to you as a gift from them."

"And how do you know they were left for me?" she asked, still admiring herself in the mirror.

"It says your name on this note," Asher replied, amazed.

Annabel stopped her swaying and took the letter from Asher's hands. Scanning the note, she confirmed what he said.

These pearls were given to me by the man I love so much. I cannot take them with me when I depart this world, so I prefer that they be worn by a woman who is as deeply in love with a man as I am. Kristoff has seen you in a vision, and I want to leave this necklace to you, Annabel, as I know it will reflect the love that Joseph and you share.

God bless you in your service to others,

Linda

Annabel carefully tucked the letter back inside its envelope.

"You truly look radiant in those pearls, Annabel. I can only imagine how they will complement a wedding gown," Asher said, his voice filled with admiration. "Why thank you, kind sir," Annabel replied, her voice reflecting a hint of giddiness.

Annabel slipped off the necklace and zipped it securely into her soft velvet bag. She placed it on top of the vanity and gently closed the drawer. "Well, I'm all unpacked. Shall we start exploring the house?" she asked, her excitement bubbling over. Asher nodded and gestured toward the open door. "You lead the way."

The curious couple spent the next hour or so exploring every nook and cranny of the house. They opened cabinets, looked behind portraits, and tapped on walls for any sign of a hidden passageway, but to no avail. Apart from some old garden gloves and a spool of thread that had gotten lost under the couch, there were no other secrets to be found.

"I think the only secret we'll find is that necklace, Annabel," Asher said, his voice tinged with disappointment.

Suddenly, there was a crash. An old porcelain decorative plate slipped from Annabel's hands, shattering into pieces on the floor.

"Dang, I don't know how that happened. It just slipped right through my fingers," Annabel said, embarrassed by her clumsiness.

"No matter, it's just an old plate. I'll fetch the broom," Asher reassured her.

Within moments, the broken pieces were swept up, and Asher returned the broom to the mudroom closet. As he placed it back, he noticed the rear panel of the closet shift slightly. Curious, he pressed his hand against the back wooden panel and felt it give as if mounted on hinges.

"A false back wall?" Asher mumbled to himself, giving the panel a more forceful push. The hidden door opened slightly before slamming shut again, its closure aided by a strong coiled spring on the backside. Though it had closed quickly, it was enough time for Asher to see that this, indeed, was a passageway to a hidden room behind the closet.

"Annabel, you won't believe what I've just found," Asher called out, his heart racing with excitement. Annabel rushed to his side and peeked into the broom closet.

"Push the back wall," Asher instructed.

Annabel pressed the panel, and just like before, the secret door swung

175

open, only to snap closed again. Her excited eyes met Asher's. "Do you happen to see a torch in one of the cabinets, by chance?" she asked.

"Actually, I did, and I put fresh batteries in just moments before your arrival," Asher replied a hint of pride in his voice.

He quickly retrieved the flashlight and clicked it on, illuminating the inside of the broom closet. The beam revealed a few old cobwebs, wadded-up dust cloths, and a dustpan hanging on a rusty nail.

"Why don't you go first?" Annabel suggested, ushering Asher forward.

With the torch in hand, Asher led the way, and they passed through the false wall. The door snapped shut behind them with a resounding click, sealing them into the darkness of the hidden passage.

23

A Table for One

sher and Annabel stepped through the narrow passageway cautiously, their footsteps softly echoing against the aged, dry wooden walls. Annabel's heart raced with a mix of anticipation and unease, propelling her forward into the unknown. The passage widened as they passed through the door, revealing an empty storage room. In the center of the room hung a broken light bulb from the ceiling, its glass shards scattered on the floor.

"An empty room. Nothing here at all," Annabel grumbled, her earlier excitement now tinged with frustration.

Refusing not to give up, they began searching for any sign of another hidden passageway or false wall. "Use the torch and tap the walls; maybe one of them will sound hollow," Annabel suggested, her voice full of hope.

Following her lead, Asher moved the beam of light across the plaster walls, tapping and pushing against them, but the room gave no secrets away. "The walls sound solid. I think this might just be an abandoned secret room," Asher admitted, his head slightly lower. The only thing in here is that broken light, " he said, pointing up at the fractured lightbulb dangling above him.

A thought popped into Asher's mind the moment he looked up at the ceiling. Reaching up, he gave the metal chain attached to the light socket a firm tug. Instantly, the far wall began to shake, slowly lifting and revealing a stone staircase that descended into the unknown dark basement below.

Annabel's eyes widened, excitement rushing through her. "It looks like the room wasn't empty after all," she whispered with awe and anticipation.

Asher nodded, his earlier defeat replaced with a steely determination. "Let's see where this leads," he said, leading the way down the stone staircase. The torchlight highlighted the ancient walls as they pressed deeper into the mysterious passage.

Asher's torch beam sliced through the darkness, casting eerie shadows on the stone walls as it swept across the room. His eyes narrowed on an old bookcase lining the back wall, its shelves packed with books of varying sizes, their spines well worn. The sight of the bookcase sparked his curiosity, but Annabel's hand found the light switch on the wall before Asher could move closer to it.

With a flick, a small pop echoed through the room, followed by the flickering light of the old lightbulb overhead. The dim light revealed the rest of the room, illuminating an antique desk in the center, complete with a cushioned office chair that had seen years of use. A worn lounge chair sat off to the side, inviting in its faded upholstery, while an end table beside it held a Tiffany-style lamp, its stained glass casting a warm glow.

But what caught their attention most was a large wooden trunk near the room's far corner. Reinforced with metal bands and secured with a heavy lock enchanted with swirling green vapors and yellow sparks, the trunk seemed to hide secrets inside. The air in the room was thick with anticipation as they exchanged glances, knowing that whatever lay inside must be a well-guarded secret.

Annabel scanned the spines of the books—*Santa Through the Ages, A Night of Impossible Magic,* and *Divine Miracles*—each title enhancing her curiosity. Meanwhile, Asher rifled feverishly through the desk, searching drawer after drawer for the key to the locked chest. Frustration crept in as each search turned up empty, and he finally slumped into a chair, puzzled.

"Maybe it's hidden in one of the books," he suggested, getting up and pulling one from the shelf.

"I was thinking the same thing," Annabel agreed, joining him. Together, they started the task of inspecting each book, hoping to stumble upon the elusive key.

Asher's hand paused on a large volume, its title catching his eye. "Hey, Annabel, look at this," he said, pointing to *Corbit Hayes History Vol. 1 of 3.* Flipping through the pages, he found a chronicle of the Santa Order's founder. "This records his entire ministry. I'd love to read about his adventures," he said, excitement coloring his voice.

A vibration in his pocket caught him off guard as he reached for another book. He pulled out Guinevere's spectacles, noticing a change— her smooth, rounded right arm had morphed into a skeleton key, swirling with green vapors and emitting yellow sparks that echoed the glow from the trunk's lock.

"Looks like I just found the key," Asher said, grinning. Annabel's eyes widened in surprise and delight as she saw the key-shaped arm of Guinevere's spectacles. The discovery of the key in such an unexpected place added a new layer of mystery and excitement to their adventure."

"Be careful with me; I'm more spectacles than a brass key," Guinevere grumbled, a hint of impatience in her tone.

Asher knelt beside the trunk, carefully guiding Guinevere's key-shaped arm into the lock. With a quiet *click,* the lock yielded, swinging open to reveal its guarded secrets.

"Oh my, how beautiful!" Annabel gasped, her hand flying to her mouth as she took in the sight before her. Asher carefully lifted the ancient Santa robe from the trunk, its majestic red fibers catching the dim light.

"This looks centuries old," Asher murmured, turning the coat in his hands to examine it. The rich, dark red fabric was deeper in color than the Santa robe he was familiar with, and its long coat tails cascaded down to mid-thigh. Intricate shapes and unusual symbols were meticulously stitched into the fabric, giving evidence of a divine origin. From a side pocket, a more vibrant red stocking, reminiscent of modern Santa robes, peeked out. Asher pulled it free and immediately noticed the matching symbols and stitching on both the coat and the stocking. These were not just any Santa robes, but the original robes of the Santa Order believed to possess magical powers."

"Put it on, Asher; let's see how it looks on you," Annabel urged, pointing to the hat in his hand.

Asher nodded, placing the hat on his head and giving it a slight tug to secure it. "How do I look? Ancient, right?"

Annabel's expression shifted from admiration to confusion. "Try invisible. Where did you go?" she asked, her hands reaching out to where he had been standing. Asher looked down in surprise, realizing that he, too, couldn't see his own body. Experimenting with the strange effect, he waved his hand in front of him, marveling at the sight—or rather, the lack of it.

"I think I may incorporate this hat into my wardrobe," Asher mused, placing it gently on the desk. "It's a tribute to its original owner and useful to have."

Piece by piece, he examined the items from the trunk—boots, belts, and various other wardrobe pieces—all with their own stories and magical elements piled up on the lounge chair, each item whispering its history.

Asher lifted one particularly worn jacket, its fabric marred with bullet holes. "This one might have been Corbit Hayes's jacket," he speculated, tracing his finger over the ragged tears. "Only dark magic could have caused such damage."

A hint of concern crossed his face as Annabel stepped closer. She ran her fingers along the old fabric, examining the same holes. "I agree, Asher. It looks like dark magic had something to do with these holes. Ordinary bullets would not have been able to do that. From what I can gather, evil forces have been targeting the Santa Order, and they won't rest as long as the Order remains."

Asher's stomach rumbled loudly, and instinctively, he poked his belly with a sheepish grin. "Hungry, Asher?" Annabel asked, her tone teasing.

"Well, it is approaching dinner time," Asher replied, chuckling.

"How about we finish up here, head into town, and find a good place to eat? I'm sure we can discover a great spot," Annabel suggested as she began putting the magical items back into the trunk and locking it securely.

Asher started reshelving the books, one by one. When he reached volume three of Corbit Hayes's history, he thumbed through it quickly, lingering on an intriguing entry. His eyes widened as he read about an ability tied to Guinevere. "This is fascinating. It says that if I wear Guinevere and place my hands on a tree trunk, I can see back in time, witnessing everything around the tree throughout its life."

Annabel leaned closer, curiosity piqued. "How do you think it works?"

Asher traced the words with his finger, scanning further. "It seems to have something to do with the tree's rings, which could transport me to specific moments in its past. I definitely need to read more of these books." He closed the book with a thoughtful pat and returned it to its place on the shelf, his excitement and anticipation mingling with his hunger.

"Let me go and change my shoes real quick, something more appropriate for walking into town," Annabel said, shutting the broom closet door behind them. "Yeah, I want to wash up a bit before heading out, all those old clothes and antique books," Asher replied with a smile.

Stepping outside was invigorating. The clean air greeted them as they emerged into the afternoon light, with puffy clouds floating above, their shadows intermittently softening the sun's golden rays. "It's not too far of a walk, and I love our freedom here. I can hardly imagine anyone finding us," Annabel remarked, her gaze darting around as if expecting someone to appear. Her thoughts returning to Savio reminded her of the taxi ride from their home to the airport before arriving in Lübars, where she had spoken with the driver from Argentina on a temporary assignment.

"Not to bring up a grim moment, but where did you say Savio was from?" she asked, her tone edged with curiosity.

"South America. Why do you ask?" Asher replied, his curiosity piqued.

"Yes, yes, I remember it was in South America, but where in South America?" Annabel pressed.

"Argentina, to be exact," Asher answered. The response flooded over Annabel with a tsunami of concern, a frown briefly flickering across her face. "What troubles you, Annabel?" Asher asked. Noting her concern

"Do you think Savio is working with others?" She asked with speculative concern.

"I do often wonder this. Why do you bring it up?" Asher's face reflected curiosity.

Annabel spent the remainder of the walk into town recounting the man in the taxi and his curious remarks. "He parked his car and watched me walk into the airport until I was out of sight," Annabel concluded with a hint of alarm.

Annabel halted, her eyes meeting Asher's, concern mirrored in both expressions. "This confirms what we feared, Annabel. Savio likely has people loyal to him spying on us and planning something sinister. He knew where we lived in London and who you were. He could have tracked your travel and discovered where we are now if he's skilled enough. We need to stay vigilant."

"I think the cab driver's name was Carlos, but I'm unsure. He didn't seem as loyal as you might expect. He talked about wanting to go in a different direction than his boss, who I'm now certain is Savio. But let's not let this ruin our evening. I'm sorry for bringing it up on the way to dinner, but I didn't want to forget to tell you," Annabel explained, her voice softening.

"There's no need to apologize," Asher said, taking her hand with a reassuring squeeze. "Come on, let's enjoy the evening."

They continued walking until they reached a bustling restaurant filled with the scent of Croatian cuisine. "What do you think? Should we give it a try?" Asher suggested.

Annabel smiled. "It sounds perfect."

As they approached, they noticed a crowd waiting to be seated. "Looks like there might be a bit of a wait," Asher remarked, glancing around for alternatives. His gaze was drawn across the street to a quieter tavern, where a few patrons sat outside, enjoying the cool evening air.

One woman, sitting alone at a small table, caught his eye. Asher's heart skipped a beat. "Is that Emily?" he murmured, a sense of dread creeping over him.

24

The Intruder

S tand behind those people over there so she can't see us," Asher whispered, nodding toward a family in line. "Do you think she saw us?" Annabel asked, her voice tinged with concern.

"I'm not sure it's even her. Let's try to get a better look," Asher replied, bobbing his head to peer through gaps in the crowd.

"You stay here and keep our place in line, just in case it isn't her. I'll be right back," Annabel said, darting behind several people and slipping out of sight.

Asher continued to watch from a distance, but the shadowed corner and shifting crowd made it difficult to confirm the woman's identity. The woman remained seated, scanning up and down the street as if looking for someone. From his vantage point, Asher saw Annabel stealthily inching closer. His heart quickened with concern. Suddenly, he spotted her taking a seat at a nearby restaurant patio, using a menu to shield her face. The woman didn't notice Annabel and continued her watchful scanning. Lowering her menu slightly, Annabel peered over the top, her eyes locked on the blonde woman sitting alone.

Asher focused intently on Annabel's every move. She angled her menu to remain hidden from the woman sitting several tables away but exposed her face to Asher. Shifting his position behind a woman and her son, Asher caught Annabel's eye. She mouthed the words, *It is her*, then stood and walked back towards him.

Asher's attention snapped back to the half-hidden Emily, who suddenly stopped scanning the area and stared directly in his direction. His stomach knotted, and he froze, trying to avoid detection. But before he could react further, Emily stood up slowly, pushed in her chair, and began crossing the street, her eyes locked on Asher's location. Annabel, clearly noticing Emily's approach, froze for a moment before taking several steps backward and ducking inside a nearby boutique.

She must have spotted me—or thinks she has. Asher's mind raced. He crouched down, sitting against the restaurant's front wall. After a quick glance to make sure no one was watching, he reached into his sports coat pocket and pulled out a rolled-up red cloth. "Good thing I brought you," he whispered, placing the old red cap he found in the locked trunk snugly on his head, its pointed tip falling over his right ear. In an instant, he vanished from sight.

Asher remained still, observing Emily's every move. She approached the same line Asher had been standing in moments before and slowly walked by each person, looking them up and down. Frustrated, she pushed her way to the front of the line and into the restaurant. Asher stood and walked towards the Boutique where Annabel had ducked into. Standing on the opposite side of the street, he noted Emliy exiting the restaurant, turning, and heading down the street, clearly upset that her stakeout did not yield the results she had hoped.

Annabel had laid low in the boutique, waiting for the right moment to slip out unnoticed. She bought a scarf, wrapped it around her head as a disguise, and headed outside. "Nice scarf you've got there," Asher's voice whispered from behind her, though he was still invisible. Startled,

Annabel let out a quick, quiet scream. "Asher, that's not even funny! Where are you?"

"Right behind you, wearing my new hat. I think it suits me," he chuckled.

Annabel glanced around nervously. "It looks like she stormed off in that direction. Do you think she'll come back?"

Asher shook his head. "Not likely. She's already searched the line and inside. It's probably safer than ever now to eat."

Annoyed by the tip of the red stocking cap draped over his right ear, Asher subconsciously flipped the cap to the other side, its tip falling over his left ear. Like someone had flipped a switch, Asher reappeared instantaneously.

"Well, look who's back," Annabel said, playfully poking Asher in the belly.

"So that's how it works," he said, flipping the hat to the other side and disappearing again.

"Stop that, Asher. Someone's going to see you! Reappear out of sight and meet me back in line. I'm ready to eat," Annabel said, her voice firm and determined.

The evening turned into night, and Annabel and Asher finally enjoyed a meal, though their eyes were constantly scanning the surroundings for any sign of Emily. "I wish I had thought to follow her while I was invisible," Asher mused. "If I had, I might've been able to see who she's with. It's clear now more than ever that she's under some kind of influence. Her mannerisms were so scripted, almost robotic. The way she inspected the line and barged through the entrance has to be Savio's doing. He's using her to get to us. Makes me wonder if the taxi driver's under the same spell."

Annabel, finishing her meal, nodded thoughtfully. "If he has control over them, who knows how many more he could have under his power?"

Wiping her mouth with a napkin, she placed it on her emptied plate.

"Shall we head back? It's getting late," Asher suggested.

"After you, kind sir," Annabel replied, following his lead.

The walk back felt quicker than their earlier trip to town, perhaps because they had already crossed that path before, but more likely because their minds were caught up in the evening's events. A few steps from the front door, Asher abruptly halted and pointed to the door, which was slightly ajar. "Someone's been here while we were gone."

Annabel furrowed her brow, squinting to see the door better in the dim moonlight. "I'm positive I locked it securely before we left. I even tugged on it."

Asher whispered, "Let's go around to the back," motioning for her to follow.

As he twisted the back doorknob, Asher leaned close to Annabel's ear. "If a struggle breaks out, you run. Got it?"

Annabel nodded but then hesitated. "Shouldn't we go to the police?"

"And how are they going to help against the dark magic of Savio?" Asher reminded her.

"Good point. Do be careful, Asher."

"Stay here, and I'll investigate," Asher said, pressing the backdoor open.

"I'm not staying here while you go in by yourself. We're a team, right?" Annabel's voice began to rise.

"Keep it down; we don't want to lose the element of surprise," Asher urged, squeezing her hand. "We definitely are a team. Keep close to me."

They tiptoed in with cautious steps, their eyes adjusting to the dark house as they made their way toward the front room, where a lamp had been turned on by the intruder.

"Someone's sitting on the sofa," Annabel whispered. "He's alone and not doing anything but sitting."

They stayed still, observing the man in silence, when suddenly he reached up and clicked off the lamp, plunging the room into darkness.

Instinctively, Asher lunged, tackling the sitting figure and sending the sofa crashing over with them. The lamp shattered on the floor, and the intruder grunted under Asher's weight. "I'm not here to hurt you; get off me, por favor; you are so heavy." The voice came in a thick Latin accent.

"Annabel, the lights!" Asher shouted, keeping his grip on the man. "Get to your feet slowly," he ordered.

The intruder turned over, and Annabel gasped as she saw his face. "Carlos!"

Asher tightened his grip. "This is Carlos?"

"Sí, soy Carlos," the man admitted.

"Did Savio send you?" Asher demanded.

Carlos nodded. "Yes, but it's not what you think. I'm done with him. I came to warn you."

"Then why did you turn off the light and break into our house?" Annabel asked, her voice sharp.

Carlos sighed, rubbing his sore back. "I started feeling guilty for breaking in and realized how it would look when you came home. I decided to turn off the lights and leave, hoping to find you tomorrow under better circumstances."

"Have a seat," Asher said, flipping the couch back over and adjusting the cushions. "How do we know we can trust you? How do we know you're telling the truth?" His questions were sharp and direct.

Carlos settled on the couch, edging himself to the front of the cushion. "Two reasons. First, I didn't fight back," he replied, still rubbing his back. "And second, this." He reached into his pocket and pulled out a small cloth bag with a drawstring no larger than a matchbox. "Hold out your hand," he instructed, holding the bag out to Asher.

Asher hesitated but then extended his hand, palm up. As Carlos held the bag over Asher's hand and tilted it, the ring on Asher's finger began to vibrate. With a gentle tap, Carlos released a small translucent gem that rolled onto Asher's palm, immediately gravitating toward his ring. As soon as the gem touched the band, it melted seamlessly into the gold, reclaiming its original place.

A surge of energy coursed through Asher, and a gust of enchanted air tousled his hair and beard. "My stolen gem. How did you get it?" Asher asked, confusion etched on his face.

"Let's just say Savio has no idea I'm here—and even less that the second gem in his ring is a counterfeit, taken from some of the jewelry he looted in the past." Carlos's grin widened, satisfaction evident in his expression.

"Annabel, come in here, it's safe," Asher called out, his voice steady. Annabel stepped cautiously into the room, her eyes meeting Carlos's for the first time since the taxi ride. "Hello again, ma'am," Carlos greeted her with a warm smile. "Hello there," she replied softly, her tone inviting yet laced with curiosity. "I heard you say that Savio doesn't know you're here. Are you sure? And how did you find us?" Annabel's questions mirrored Asher's own thoughts.

Carlos leaned back on the couch, resting his arm on the armrest as he began to explain. "When I forged his new ring with both magical gems, Savio was in the room the entire time, watching closely. He trusts no one. I had already devised a plan to switch the gems, thanks to the sleight of hand I perfected over the years as a forced thief. I knew I couldn't remove both gems—he would notice something wrong with the new ring immediately and suspect me. So I decided to take just one gem, leaving some magic in his ring. I timed my escape perfectly, slipping away while he was distracted by his new prize. It's been a few days now, and I feel like the magic Savio had over me is finally gone. I'd forgotten what freedom felt like," Carlos confessed, his voice tinged with emotion.

Annabel sat beside him, gently rubbing his shoulder. "How did you know where to find us?"

"I followed the right person," Carlos replied, pulling a picture from his wallet. "I learned that this woman, Emily, is under Savio's evil enchantment, and she had a past connection with Asher. I gave her a ride in London when Savio was meeting with her. She was polite, and it was easy for Savio to enchant her. He pretended to be her friend, using that pretense to get closer and keep her under his control."

"Savio knows Emily, the girl in your picture?" Asher's voice was tense. Carlos nodded, "Yes, he discovered she was your past girlfriend, and that's when he hatched a plan to use her to get to you. He's been obsessed with possessing the ring's power for as long as I've known him."

Asher stroked his beard thoughtfully. "How did Savio find out about my past and my identity?"

"That was Felipe's doing," Carlos explained. "He's an evil tech genius—there's nothing he can't hack into."

"How many are working with Savio in total?" Annabel asked.

Carlos held up two fingers.

"Only two people?" Asher's eyes widened in surprise.

"There were three, but now that I've deserted him, it's just Felipe and your old girlfriend that he's controlling."

"We saw her yesterday," Annabel interjected. "We think she might have seen Asher or believed she saw him. We barely escaped undetected. She looked like she was waiting for someone at a café in town. Was she planning on meeting you?" Annabel questioned.

Carlos shook his head. "No, she has no idea I'm here or that I followed her. If she was looking for someone, it could only be one person... Savio!" Carlos's voice trembled with fear.

25

A Step in the Right Direction

Finding Carlos sitting on the couch was unsettling for both Annabel and Asher. Still, it solidified their resolve to stop Savio once and for all and reunite the missing gems from Asher's magical ring. With Carlos now on their side, they invited him to stay with them for a while, hoping it would provide him with stability and give them an extra pair of eyes on the lookout for Savio and Emily.

The following day, Carlos was pleasantly surprised to wake up to the comforting smell of fresh bacon sizzling in the frying pan and the soothing sound of early morning chatter from the kitchen. "Did you sleep okay, Carlos?" Annabel asked, removing several bacon pieces from the pan and placing them on a paper towel-draped plate.

"Pillows are an amazing thing. I never knew they were so soft to sleep on," Carlos replied, a hint of wonder in his voice. Asher looked up from his plate, wiping a dribble of yolk from the corner of his mouth.

"What kind of pillow are you used to using, Carlos?" Asher asked.

"Well, if you count a sack filled with old T-shirts as a pillow, that's what I'm used to," Carlos admitted.

Annabel paused, touched by his response. "How do you like your eggs,

Carlos?" she asked, ready to cook them to his liking.

"Scrambled, if it's not too much trouble," he replied, sitting next to Asher at the table. "So, is this your place?" Carlos asked politely.

"It's actually home to the Santa Order," Asher answered, biting off the end of his bacon strip.

"Santa Order? What's that?" Carlos inquired, curiosity piqued.

Asher finished off his orange juice and set the glass down. "The Order is made up of family, friends, and those entrusted with the secrets of Santa. It's about sharing the work of helping give hope and miracles to those in need."

"Come with me real quick. I want you to see something." Asher stood up, and Carlos followed him into the front room, where Asher pointed to a portrait of Kristoff, Eckerd, Dennis, and their wives. "This was the previous Santa Order. A great group of people," he said with deep admiration.

"So, how does one become part of the Santa Order?" Carlos asked sincerely, with a hopeful tone.

Asher turned and led him back to the kitchen. "Come on, your breakfast is probably ready." The silence that followed made it clear that joining the Santa Order couldn't be quickly done. Carlos understood that it required more than just interest; it demanded trust and proving oneself worthy. Quietly, he hoped that returning the gem to Asher might have been the first step toward joining a noble cause.

"These eggs are wonderful, ma'am. Thank you," Carlos said gratefully.

Annabel turned and addressed him with a warm smile. "If you're going to spend more time here, you'd best start calling me Annabel."

Carlos nodded. "Yes, ma'am—uh, Annabel, ma'am."

Annabel placed another heap of eggs on his plate, her smile growing. "Just Annabel. Nothing more."

"Carlos, you mentioned another person working for Savio, someone with tech skills. I'm a little concerned about him. It explains how Savio always seems to be a few steps ahead of us, making it hard to stay hidden for long," Asher said, worry creasing his brow.

Carlos set his fork down and cleared his throat. "You won't need to worry about Felipe anymore," he said with a hint of satisfaction.

"Why do you say that?" Annabel asked, joining the conversation.

"Before I left, I anonymously tipped off the local authorities, revealing everything about Felipe and Savio. Savio had to leave before they arrived, probably to meet Emily, but Felipe... I imagine he's sitting behind bars by now, far away from his precious computers."

Carlos pulled out his phone quickly, typing into the search bar. He then held up the screen for Annabel and Asher to see. "They captured him," he said, showing them a news article from Argentina. "Savio's still on the loose, though."

"This evens the playing field a bit, so to say," Asher said with a light grin and a sense of relief. Annabel's eyes sparkled with hope, and Carlos's shoulders visibly relaxed. The news of Felipe's arrest had lifted a heavy burden off their shoulders.

"So why is he using Emily?" Annabel asked.

Carlos leaned forward, his tone serious. "Originally, she was just a pawn to get to you," he said, pointing at Asher. "Savio planned to use her to lure you in and then, at the right moment, attack and force the ring from your finger."

Asher instinctively rubbed his ring, feeling the returned gem securely in place. "A few months ago, I would've told you that removing the ring without my consent was impossible," Asher admitted, showing his growing trust in Carlos. "But I've learned that when the gems are removed, the ring loses its ability to stay in place. Thanks to you, Carlos, it's nearly impossible for him to take it now." Relief washed over both Asher and Annabel.

Carlos furrowed his brow, deep in thought. "I wonder what his angle is with using Emily at this point."

"Savio is desperate, obviously," Asher replied. "It sounds like his plan was to lure me in through Emily, then catch me off guard and attack. But with Felipe arrested and his own name plastered across news articles as a wanted man, he must know his plan is falling apart. Now he's scrambling, and Emily's caught up in the whole mess, probably without even realizing it."

"So, what can we do to help Emily?" Carlos asked. After a brief pause, Asher came up with an idea. "Perhaps I can play into Savio's hand. Purposely be found by Emily. See if I can get any information from her or see what she might be up to."

"It sounds a little risky," admitted Annabel, "but I think it's the best plan we can work with."

The following day, their plan was in full swing. Asher ventured into town alone, under the guise of running errands, while Carlos remained at the house, just in case Savio had discovered their location. Annabel, wearing older clothes left behind in the closet, disguised herself and planned to observe Asher from a safe distance, careful to remain unseen.

Asher believed that the early hours of the day would be the best time to find Emily. Figuring she might frequent the town bakery or coffee shop, he set off in that direction, fully expecting to encounter her.

The early sun rays pierced through the gray clouds, casting golden beams on the cobblestone streets and red-tiled rooftops. Asher's gaze landed on an A-framed, pale yellow building with two large chimneys poking out the top. Cement steps led to the front door, shaded by a small overhang. The hand-painted red lettering on the front window drew him in, promising a cozy spot to observe the morning crowd.

"Welcome to the Lübars Café. You're new here, no? Are you passing through or staying for a while?" a young brunette asked from behind the glass display counter filled with pastries. Asher approached, scanning the delectable treats before making eye contact with her emerald-green eyes.

"Very observant," Asher replied. "Yes, I'm new in town and staying for a while. Such a charming little place." He glanced around, admiring the well-decorated coffee shop.

"Seems like we've had an uptick in new faces lately," the young woman remarked.

"Really?" Asher asked. "Other new faces?"

"Ja, neu." The polite saleswoman gestured toward a small round table by the window. "Just yesterday, a man sat there, talking with an attractive blonde woman. I thought you might know them."

Asher furrowed his brow. "Why would I know them?"

"She sounded like you—spoke with a thick British accent. I just assumed you all came together to see Lübars."

Asher's eyes narrowed. "Have you seen them before?"

"The woman? Yes, I've seen her a few times. The man, though, that was the first time I'd seen him. They make a cute couple. He seemed to pay her close attention and held her close."

Asher stroked his beard thoughtfully. "Does she come in here every day? Maybe I can meet her and see if she's from London like me."

The clerk wiped the glass display with a damp cloth, brushing off powdered sugar. "Ja, she's been here around this time every day for the past three or four days. You should definitely introduce yourself. By the way, has anyone ever told you that you look like Santa?"

Asher's mouth stretched into a delighted smile. "Yes, I've heard that before," he chuckled. "I'll take a seat at that table and wait to see if she shows up." He pointed to the window-side table. "Could I get a water and one of those franzbrötchen? They look amazing."

The sweet pastry in the glass display case beckoned to Asher. Its layers were carefully folded, filled with cinnamon and sugar, and topped with a buttery glaze that had caramelized into a sticky, irresistible surface. He couldn't pass it up. "Ja, ja, I'll bring it right over with several napkins," the young waitress said with a smile. As she turned to go, Asher called after her, "How rude of me—tell me your name."

She stepped from behind the counter, carrying a large glass of water, several napkins, and the Franzbrötchen on a glossy white porcelain plate. "Liesel. They call me Liesel," she replied with a smile.

"Well, Liesel, it's been a pleasure to meet you. My name is Asher, but if you happen to call me Santa by accident, I'll probably respond," he said with a playful chuckle. Liesel pivoted on her heels, letting out a giggle that matched her charming demeanor as she headed back to the counter.

For the next forty-five minutes, Asher sat at his table, watching the steady stream of early morning patrons rushing in for pastries and coffee. Yet, despite his anticipation, there was no sign of Emily. He knew Annabel, stationed across the street as a lookout, was likely growing impatient.

Another half-hour passed before Asher caught Liesel's gaze from across the room. She shrugged her shoulders in a silent apology, mirroring his frustration. Just as he considered abandoning the plan, the front door creaked open. Liesel's eyes darted to the entering patron, then back to Asher. She raised her eyebrows twice in a playful, universal signal—*look who just walked in.*

"Asher?" Emily reacted, turning her head sharply toward him. "What are you doing here?"

"It's wild running into you in Lübars," Asher said, feigning surprise.

Emily hesitated, then changed direction and dropped into the chair across from him. Her expression was blank, her eyes staring into Asher's without saying a word.

"Is everything okay?" Asher asked, concern evident in his voice.

"Did he follow me in?" she whispered, terrified.

Asher quickly scanned the café and the walkway leading to the entrance. "I don't see anyone. Who's following you?"

"It's nothing. Nobody," Emily replied, shaking her head, but her face betrayed her fear. Asher knew she was referring to Savio. "It's nothing, Asher. Leave it alone."

Emily's demeanor puzzled him. It was as if two people were fighting for control inside her. She reached out and grasped his hand, tracing hearts on his palm.

"I've missed you, Asher. I can't live without you. Can't we start all over again?"

Asher pulled his hand back quickly. "Emily, you're not yourself. What's going on?"

But Emily snatched his hand back, repeating her actions. "I've missed you, Asher. I can't live without you. Can't we start all over again?" Her words carried a hypnotic rhythm.

"It's Savio, isn't it?" Asher asked, pulling his hand away again.

Saying Savio's name seemed to snap her out of the trance. "Did he follow me in?" Emily asked, her voice trembling.

"Emily, can you hear me? No one's following you."

But Emily's demeanor shifted again. She stared blankly at him, reaching out once more. "I've missed you, Asher. I can't live without you. Can't we start all over again?" she repeated, once more under Savio's control.

Asher realized the keywords were triggering her trance. "Savio," he said firmly.

Emily's eyes darted to the door. "Did he follow me in?"

Asher stood and grabbed her hand. "Yes, he followed you in. Come with me—I can help."

He led her toward Liesel, who stood at the counter, placing small pastries into a paper bag. "Liesel, do you have a back door?" Asher asked urgency in his voice.

Sensing something was wrong, Liesel nodded and pointed to the back kitchen. "That way, just through there. So, you knew her after all, eh?" she said with a hint of satisfaction.

"Yes, you were right. It's a long story. Thanks for your help, Liesel," Asher replied, guiding Emily carefully into the kitchen.

As they stepped out the back door and onto the street, Asher waved to Annabel, who had been watching from a distance. "Follow us back to the house," he called out to her before continuing on with Emily.

26

More to the Order

C arlos, hurry! We need your help!" Annabel's voice was urgent as she assisted Emily and Asher into the house. Carlos dashed to the front door and swiftly guided Emily to the couch.

"No, keep going—to the back of the house. Annabel, go open the passageway to the basement," Asher directed urgently.

Without hesitation, Annabel hurried to the vacant storage room, tugging on the chained light above to reveal the hidden passageway to the basement. Moments later, Carlos and Asher entered, each holding one of Emily's hands, carefully guiding her.

"Annabel, take her hand and assist Carlos in getting her down the stairs. I'll go ahead and unlock the trunk. There's something in there that might help," Asher instructed, his voice brimming with determination.

Asher urgently rifled through the trunk's contents as Annabel and Carlos helped Emily navigate the steps. "Hurry, Asher! Something's happening to her—her body's getting rigid! It's like she's trying to stop us from reaching you," Annabel exclaimed, panic rising in her voice.

Asher tossed aside a pair of black boots, then a bullet-riddled Santa coat, his hands moving frantically through the items. "It's not me she's avoiding—it has to do with what is in the trunk. She can sense its power," Asher explained, his tone hurried. "Here it is!" he announced, reaching deep into the trunk.

Suddenly, Emily halted, her head dropping as a deep, Latin-accented voice erupted from within her. "I will not let you take her from me!"

"Hold her tightly! I don't know how she'll react to this," Asher warned, concern evident in his voice.

"Take this, Emily! I'll hold her arm. Carlos, hold on tight," Asher ordered, his voice filled with unity and strength.

"What is it?" Annabel asked, her voice tense.

"Open your hand!" Asher shouted, struggling to restrain Emily as she fought to break free. Annabel quickly opened her palm, and Asher rolled a beautiful wedding ring into her hand. The vibrant yellow gold band featured a translucent gem center stone, delicately held in place by intricately carved roses on either side.

"Hold still, Emily," Annabel and Carlos repeated, trying to calm her. With their firm grip on her wrists, her wild swinging was contained, though the thrashing persisted.

"Hurry, slip the ring on her finger!" Asher urged, his voice filled with urgency.

Annabel was quick to respond. After a bit of a struggle, she successfully pushed the ring over the knuckles of her finger, securing it on her hand.

"Nothing's happening!" Carlos shouted in frustration. "What do we do?" Annabel's voice quivered with anxiety.

Out of nowhere, Mr. Baggins launched himself from inside the trunk, crashing into Asher and collapsing onto the floor in a crumpled heap. Then, as if by magic, a piece of parchment paper floated out of a soft velvet bag, fluttering down like a feather. Annabel snatched it from the air, her eyes locking onto the message.

"What does it say?" Asher shouted.

Annabel held up the paper for him to see. One word was scrawled across it in large letters: SAVIO. The revelation of this word left them all in a state of anticipation and curiosity.

Asher furrowed his brow, then, as if a lightbulb had gone off in his mind, he shouted, "Savio!"

Instantly, Emily's body went limp, crumpling to the hard floor.

"What happened? Where am I?" Emily's voice was intermingled with confusion.

"It's Joseph. We're here to help you," he reassured her as he and Carlos helped her to her feet.

"Joseph?" Carlos stopped, taken aback. "Did you say, Joseph?"

"It's a long story. Let's get her back upstairs to the couch. She needs to recover," Asher said. Annabel, are you okay?" Asher's thoughts immediately turned to Annabel.

"I'm fine—just a little on edge after all that," she replied, brushing some ash-like dust off her arms. "What is all over me, anyway?"

"That ashy dust is all over us. I'll explain when we get back upstairs. Could you close the trunk while we get Emily to the couch?" Asher asked, grabbing one of the aged books on the shelf. Carlos and I will help Emily back up the stairs."

Steadily back toward the couch, Emily's ability to carry herself returned as she slowly stepped forward with Carlos and Asher on either side. "Come in here and sit on the couch," Carlos's invitation was kind and inviting. Resting comfortably on the couch cushions, Carlos raced to the kitchen and retrieved a cool glass of water. "Here, drink this, it might help." Asher watched with interest as Carlos attended to Emily compassionately. "Thank you, the water is very refreshing. I'm sorry, but who are you?" Emily asked, sipping the cool water. "My name is Carlos. I am here with Asher. Let me know how I can help you feel more beautiful, uh…that is, more comfortable. Sorry, my English is not so good. "Emily's cheeks flushed; thank you, Carlos," she said softly, flipping her hair over her shoulder.

"I see the men tending to your needs, Emily. Are you feeling better?" Annabel asked, noting Carlos's proximity to Emily. Emily nodded. "Yes, this kind man is very attentive," She said, patting Calos's forearm.

"That is excellent news," Annabel responded. You were quite distressed a few minutes ago."

Emily looked Annabel up and down. "Aren't you Asher's friend who was shopping for a dress?"

" Yes, that was me looking for a dress that day. And, I'm actually his Fiance." She said, holding up her ring finger, her voice thick with pride. A wide smile crossed Emily's face, exposing her porcelain white teeth. "That is so wonderful. You are a lucky lady, and I'm sure you will make a fine couple." Emily smiled in Asher's direction and then looked back at Annabel. "What part of London am I in exactly? Is this your place?" She asked Annabel, scanning the room."

"We aren't exactly in London, Emily," Asher interjected, grabbing a couple of chairs from the dining room. He gestured for Annabel to sit beside him. "Looks like we owe you an explanation."

After a long conversation about why Joseph was now called Asher, followed by a light lunch, the group began to bond, easing the earlier tension. "So, you're Santa?" Emily said, fanning herself with her hand. "This is all so wild—just this morning, I didn't believe in any of this folklore. But now, I can't deny what I've been seeing. It's a lot to take in."

Annabel gently patted Emily's knee. "It takes time to process, but yes, Santa is—and has always been—real."

Annabel then pointed at the new ring wrapped around Emily's finger. "So, explain the ring, Asher. And what was all that ashy dust all over us?"

Asher stood and walked over to a picture on the wall, pointing to an image of the previous Santa. "Look at the ring on Linda's hand. It's the same one now on Emily's finger. I recognized it when I was digging through the trunk downstairs. I didn't think much of it at first, but when Emily fell into that trance, the image of the ring popped into my mind, along with its exact location. I'd like to take credit for the idea, but it was as if someone was guiding me. I just followed the impressions as they came."

Annabel gasped slightly. "So, this is the same ring Linda wore?"

Carlos, sensing the shift in tone, asked, "You act like that's a bad thing. Is it?"

Asher turned from the photo and sat back down beside Annabel. "No, it's not bad. It's a magical ring. I think Annabel realized that it was the ring keeping Emily alive. It's an immortality ring—the same as the one I wear, the same as Annabel's, and the same type that members of the Santa order once wore. The shocking part is that Emily must have been on the brink of death, caught under some dark magic."

"But in another way, it's a good thing I'm wearing it, or I will likely not be here right now, correct?" Emily's voice was low and heavy with the new reality.

Asher locked eyes with Emily. "It's no coincidence you're wearing that ring, Emily. Something bigger than us is at play here, guiding the Santa Order. One thing is certain: you've been chosen. You're now part of the Order."

Emily leaned back on the couch, the weight of the revelation settling in. "I'm not entirely sure what this all means, but I'm just happy to be alive and grateful you saved me."

Carlos brushed a thin layer of dark soot from his arm. "So, what's this black dust all over us?"

Asher walked over to the lamp table and picked up the worn book he'd brought from the basement. Dusting off the cover, he showed the title to the group *Magic of the Ages Defined*. "I found a really interesting section about magic that can be performed by simply touching a tree. I felt an urge to bring this book up, and maybe it'll help us understand the dust."

He thumbed through the pages and stopped at a passage, tapping it with his finger. "Here's something. It says when dark magic is destroyed, it leaves behind a black, powdery substance—amorphous carbon, more commonly known as soot."

"Well, we were definitely covered in soot, so I'd say the dark magic's been dealt with," Annabel remarked, satisfaction in her voice.

Emily brushed off her sleeves, sending puffs of soot into the air. "One thing's for sure: I feel like my old self again. I haven't felt this free or in control for ages."

Annabel stepped forward, pulling her into a warm embrace. "You're one of us now, Emily. Welcome to the Santa Order."

Carlos glanced up at Emily, a deep longing in his eyes. His heart yearned to be part of the Order, but something more stirred inside him. From the moment he'd met Emily, he couldn't stop thinking about her. It wasn't a fleeting crush based on her beauty, though she attracted attention wherever she went. No, this was something deeper—a flame burning within him, and Emily was the spark. The only question on his mind was whether she felt the same.

27

Where Do We Go From Here?

Several days had passed since Emily's rescue from the evil enchantment, and the stress of an imaginary organized crime ring trying to seize Asher's ring had faded from his thoughts. Knowing Savio was now alone in his quest was encouraging, but his evil intent and unknown magical abilities still weighed heavily on Asher's mind.

The mood in the house had lightened considerably, and a sense of happiness filled the air. Emily had regained her strength and quickly bonded with Annabel, which was both comforting and, at times, unsettling for Asher. Every so often, he would catch the two giggling together, only to look up and find them smiling at him—clearly sharing stories about him from their past.

Annabel stepped out several hours earlier in the morning with a shopping list for tonight's dinner. The newly formed Santa Order felt it would be nice to have a wonderful meal together on the back porch while enjoying the sunset. Asher had not had tonight's menu in some time, and Annabel insisted on doing something nice for him after all he had been through. The evening cuisine would be Asher's favorite, bangers and mash. Deciding to add some color to the dish, Annabel placed green peas on her list of necessary items.

Asher sat on the living room couch, thumbing through *Magic of the Ages Defined*, but his attention kept wandering. Emily and Carlos were busy in the kitchen, getting everything ready for the outdoor dinner.

"Carlos, can you find a step stool? I see a nice set of dishes up there that have been placed for safekeeping." Emily pointed toward the set of porcelain dinnerware, the intricate blue blooms and geometric patterns gracefully aged with time.

"Certainly, I think I remember seeing a stepladder on the back porch. I'll go and fetch it for you," Carlos replied with a warm smile, hurrying out the door.

Asher peeked over his book just in time to catch Emily watching Carlos leave, her gaze lingering a little longer than expected. Her spirits were clearly high today—her hair styled perfectly, makeup immaculate. She was dressed to impress.

Moments later, Carlos returned with the ladder. "Here you go," he said, positioning it near the shelves. Emily gave him a grateful smile as she stepped up, carefully reaching for the plates.

Whether by accident or intent, Emily's foot slipped on the top step, sending her tumbling into Carlos's waiting arms. "Oh, thank you, kind sir," she giggled, her voice light with gratitude. "It was my pleasure, Emily," Carlos replied, his cheeks warming as he held her securely in his strong arms.

Asher softly closed his book and watched them, noting the comfortable dynamic between the two. There was something more in the way they interacted—a quiet connection that hadn't been there before. It was good to see Emily in such a positive mood, laughing lightly with Carlos. But even as he observed them, the lingering threat of Savio gnawed at the back of his mind, a reminder that the peace they were enjoying might not last.

The morning hours slipped by so quickly that Asher had lost track of the time since Annabel had stepped away. Shaking his watch, he looked again, noting how long she had been gone.

"Out of curiosity," Asher's voice carried a heavy tone of concern, "have either of you heard from Annabel this morning?"

Carlos gently set Emily down, her feet touching the wooden floor. "Come to think of it, no. She has been gone an awfully long time." He glanced at Asher. "I'm worried, something doesn't feel right."

Emily's anxious voice followed, "Neither have I."

Carlos and Emily joined Asher in the living room, sitting beside him. Carlos hesitated before speaking. "You don't think…"

Asher's gaze remained fixed, staring out the window. "Yes, Carlos, I'm concerned about exactly what you're afraid to say." Breaking his stare, Asher looked directly at Carlos.

"We've been avoiding cell phones and living off the grid out here," Emily added with frustration. "It has its blessings, but no way to track her whereabouts. What do we do, Asher? How do we find her?"

Asher drew in a deep breath, his voice steady. "Let's try to stay calm and think this through. There's no reason to assume Savio is involved with her being late." His words were measured, though his concern was clear. "I'm just as worried, but we need to be rational. Maybe we should head to town and look for her. It's possible she's just enjoying some time out window shopping. I've known her to do that now and then." He tried to maintain an air of calm, concealing his growing unease.

Suddenly, Emily screamed, clutching her ring finger. Carlos whipped his head toward her, heart racing. "What's wrong?" he asked, his voice tight with concern. Emily let out another scream, her hands desperately tugging at the enchanted ring, trying to twist it off.

Asher leaped to his feet, his own hand trembling as he clutched his ringed finger, grunting in discomfort.

"What's going on?" Carlos shouted, alarmed.

Emily curled into a fetal position on the couch, her fist pressed hard into her gut, moaning in pain. Carlos dropped to his knees, stroking her arm, hoping to soothe her agony.

Asher slumped to the floor, leaning against the wall for support. "It's as bad as it can be," he muttered, his voice low and filled with dread.

Carlos, his face twisted with confusion, looked at Asher. "What's bad? What just happened?"

"Savio has Annabel," Asher answered, his voice trailing off.

Carlos stared in disbelief. "Are you sure? How can you know that?"

Asher's eyes were clouded with pain and certainty. "The pain Emily and I just experienced—I've felt it before. When someone with evil intent tries to remove the ring, it reacts. Someone must have tried to take Emily's ring forcefully, and our rings reacted in unison. There's a power that connects the rings. When one ring is in distress, they all feel it."

Carlos squinted at the ring Emily was massaging. "Wait—are you saying the ring is alive?"

Asher nodded solemnly. "Yes, in a magical sense. The rings are enchanted with living magic. That magic is woven into the metal, the gems—everything. It's what grants immortality to those who wear them."

"Emily, are you okay?" Asher's voice was calm and caring. Still rubbing her aching hand, Emily managed a weak reply. "I'll be okay... I just need a minute." She took a deep breath. "The pain was so overwhelming. All I could think about was getting the ring off. But something in my mind kept telling me not to, and the more I tried, the louder the warning became."

Asher knelt beside her, his concern evident. "You're safe now, Emily. But we need to act quickly. Savio won't stop."

Emily tilted her head, puzzled. "But how are we going to find Annabel? She could be anywhere."

Asher reached into his pocket and pulled out the brass spectacles. "Hopefully, with these," he said, raising Guinevere proudly. "We'll need every bit of magic we have to track her down—and fast."

Carlos shrugged, looking eager. "What can I do to help?"

"You'll be more useful than you realize," Asher said, his voice filled with quiet confidence. "You've spent years around Savio; you know him better than any of us. You might be the key to finding her."

Carlos's eyes brightened, surprised but hopeful at Asher's words.

"Let's head into town," Asher added, tucking Guinevere back into his pocket. The trio united in their determination, stepped out the front door and made their way toward town, their pace quickening as the weight of their mission hung over them.

It didn't take long for the group to arrive in town. The village was bustling with weekend shoppers, and a small farmers' market had sprung up overnight. Stalls brimmed with fresh produce, hand-crafted goods, and homemade treats, bringing a sense of life to the quiet village streets.

"Where do we go from here?" Emily asked, scanning the crowd.

Carlos glanced around, his brow furrowed. "There are so many people here today. She could be anywhere."

Asher remained silent, his expression unreadable. Slowly, he wandered to a nearby park bench beneath a large, twisted tree. Its branches stretched high above, casting intricate shadows on the ground. Settling onto the bench, Asher closed his eyes, slipping into a meditative state.

Emily and Carlos stood back, exchanging glances but saying nothing as they waited. The vibrant energy of the market continued around them, but their attention remained fixed on Asher. After several minutes, Asher opened his eyes, his expression clearer, as if something had come into focus. Without a word, Asher approached the tree, kneeling as he pulled Guinevere from his pocket and carefully set the brass spectacles on his nose. "I read this in the book I found back at the house," he murmured, breaking the silence. Reaching up, he pressed his palm against the rough bark of the tree, his touch firm and deliberate. He began in a low, rhythmic whisper, almost like a prayer, "Show me this morning, show me this morning. I want to see Lorelei; show me this morning."

He repeated the chant, his hand still resting against the tree, until he abruptly stopped. Rising to his feet, he slid his hand upward along the tree trunk, keeping contact with the bark. He peered through Guinevere's lenses, scanning his surroundings slowly, methodically.

Carlos, watching intently, spoke up. "Do you see her, Asher? Can you see her now?"

Through the enchanted glasses, the sunlight took on an airy glow, revealing an earlier version of the town, bathed in the soft, warm morning light several hours before. Asher's gaze swept over the empty streets, the quiet shops, and the open fields stretching out beyond.

Then, he froze, his eyes locking onto something. "Look, look!?" Guinevere exclaimed energetically, her brass frame vibrating on the bridge of his nose. Asher raised his hand and pointed down the street, his heart pounding. "I see her," he whispered, his voice catching in his throat. "I see Annabel."

Carlos and Emily watched Asher's head slowly turn, tracing his beloved's path that morning as she approached the town.

"There, it happened there," Asher said, pointing to a small boutique store down the street with a large sign in the window with bright orange writing.

"Well, get a move on; go get her back!" the high-spirited Guinevere urged. Asher slid the glasses off his nose, pushing them deep into his pocket. "You heard her," Asher said, waving his hand for Emily and Carlos to follow him. Let's go get Annabel back!"

28

More Than Magic

The village was lively, with excited street patrons gathering around the tables under pop-up tents at the local farmers' market. In the distance, a young girl with auburn hair sat on a picnic blanket, her focus on several oranges laid out in a line in front of her. Holding up a plump baseball-sized peeled orange to her mouth, she sunk her teeth deep into the soft, fleshy slice, the sweet juice seeping through the corners of her mouth and dribbling down her forearms in a sticky stream. Laughter, chatter, and the scent of fresh produce filled the cool afternoon air, all completely unaware that the sinister Savio was holding Annabel captive behind closed doors only steps away.

With his eyes focused on the boutique store seen in Guinevere's enchanted lenses, Asher pressed on like a bloodhound on a mission to find Annabel. As the trio neared the boutique's front door, the faded orange-lettered sign caught Asher's eye. It was weathered, cracked, and revealed the truth—this store had been closed for quite some time. Though the building appeared empty, an unusually palpable dark energy seemed to encapsulate the aged edifice; its eerie aura sent shivers down the trio's back, a haunting reminder that something more sinister awaited them inside.

"Carlos, go around the rear of the store and make sure Savio doesn't slip out the back door," Asher whispered, pointing to the shadowy alleyway. "Emily, stay here and out of sight. I need to get his ring out of his possession and neutralize the threat he poses. Once I have Savio's ring, I'll signal you to call the authorities."

"As long as he has that ring, he's dangerous," Asher continued. "But once it's gone, he won't be able to intimidate law enforcement. He'll finally be nothing more than a powerless criminal, subject to the law."

"I will head around back and await your signal, Asher," Carlos said, pointing to the back alleyway. Emily nodded in agreement to her assignment, her face tense but determined as she kept her distance from the store's wall, hiding herself behind an outside rack of souvenir t-shirts at the neighboring store.

Asher neared the front door quietly, carefully pulling out his trusty spectacles and placing them gently on his nose. "It's going to take all the magic we have if we are to succeed," he murmured to Guinevere, slipping her brass arm over his ear.

"I am with you, Asher," Guinevere's voice was firm, her usual sass giving way to a rare, steady resolve.

Closing his eyes, Asher bowed his head, his snow-white whiskers cascading down to his chest. He drew in a slow, deep breath through his nostrils and, in hushed reverence, summoned his enchanted bag. "Mr. Baggins, your help is requested and needed. The time is at hand. Please join us on our mission."

A sharp crack in the air was followed by a flash of green light that illuminated the space just above Asher's head. As before, the magical bag appeared, floating down as wisps of luminescent green hues trailed from its edges like smoke. Grasping the bag with care, Asher tucked the ensorcelled cloth under his belt. Glad you are with me, Mr. Baggins.", he said with a gentle tap of affection.

With everything in place, Asher took another deep breath and reached for the cold brass doorknob in front of him. The moment his fingers made contact, a dark vapor swirled around him, and his ring began to vibrate violently, searing his skin beneath it. A sharp pain shot through his hand, but before he could react, both the front and back doors of the building flung open with force, revealing a thick, ominous vapor that now filled the entire space.

"Annabel, are you in there?" Asher called out, his voice cracking under the weight of fear and concern. For a moment, there was only silence, and then a faint, muffled whimper came from the back of the room.

Asher's heart pounded, the realization of Savio's dark magic bearing down on him, but the sound of Annabel's voice spurred his courage. He gripped the enchanted bag tighter as he pressed forward into the darkness. The thick black vapor was impenetrable to the eyes; even donning Guinevere did very little to help him see. Asher groped the air, taking careful steps towards the moaning Annable in the distance. "Annabel!" Asher shouted. This time, no reply came. The air was still, cold, and hauntingly quiet. Asher halted in his steps, straining his ears for any sound. A tearful sniffle to the right of where he was standing broke the silence. Asher pivoted his feet and pressed onward, squinting and waving his hands in the dark in a desperate search.

Unexpectedly, Guinevere shrieked in agony, her brass frame thrashing violently on the bridge of Asher's nose, and in an instant, her lenses splintered into cracks that spread in every direction. Asher winced, instinctively squeezing his eyes shut as a sharp pain shot through him, jolting him with an intense electrical shock. He reached up to pull her off for safety, but as his fingers touched her, Guinevere's once lively metal arms fell limply from his ears, sliding off his face.

The fragile remnants of her cracked lenses and bent frames tumbled to the ground with a dull clatter, landing in a crumpled heap at his feet. Asher stood frozen for a moment, staring towards the floor at the shattered pieces of his trusted companion, a surge of helplessness and anger rising within him.

Mr. Baggins wriggled free from Asher's belt and raced to the floor, his fabric form hovering over the crumpled remnants of Guinevere, unsure of how to assist. Leaning in closer, he stretched his material and gently stroked the remains of his faithful companion. His movement was tender, but before he could fully react, a thundering crack split the air, startling Asher and filling his ears with a painful, high-pitched ringing.

In an instant, the thick black vapor that had enveloped the room dissolved, vanishing as quickly as it had appeared. Asher's eyes darted to the ground where Mr. Baggins had been—only to see an unraveled mess of threads piled next to the twisted metal of Guinevere. His heart sank into his chest, the weight of sudden loss heavy. "No! This can't be happening!" Asher shouted. Memories of their magical adventures, caring for those in need, and providing for the poor all flashed through his mind. His loss was palpable and unconsoling, and in less than a minute, both of his most trusted magical allies had been destroyed, leaving him alone, vulnerable, and facing an enemy that would now have to be fought without the help he had grown to depend on.

His moment of anguish was interrupted by a black-cloaked figure standing in front of him. An antique wooden chair next to him served as a restraining seat for Annabel. Her hands were tied behind her back, and her legs were secured tightly to the spindly legs of the chair. Her head hung downward in defeat, salty streams flowing down her face and over the tear-soaked tape binding her mouth.

"Can't you see you have no power over me? Your magical bag and your flimsy antique glasses are laughable." Savio ringed his hands, a sinister chuckle in his throat. "So this is the big-bellied magical man that children admire. You are nothing more than an old man with simple parlor tricks and a magic ring preserving your life."

Asher did not respond; he only stood listening, staring defeatedly at his captured fiance.

Savio stepped behind Annabel and tightened the lashed ropes on her wrists; her face grimaced as she groaned. "Still, that gold band on your finger has many mysteries about it. Savio's gaze fell upon Asher's ring. "Undoubtedly, it possesses magic you don't even comprehend. Its full potential with all the magical gems together would be better off with me, someone who can use its full powers for a better purpose.

Asher discreetly slid his hand inside his pants pocket and kept his ring out of the sight of Savio's lusting eyes. "So you think you are more powerful than me, and my magic is a parlor show?" Asher used his question as a stall tactic to buy time and craft a plan. "If my magic is so inferior, why have you been hunting me down, trying to get it from me?" Asher's voice was commanding and unnerving to Savio.

Savio's eyes gleamed as he tapped the false gem on his ring, completely oblivious to the swap Carlos had made. "You know as well as I do that Hitler obsessed over power and believed in magic. His Nazi Party's devotion to occult forces and magical relics was supposed to grant the Nazis unlimited power. He may have lost the war, but in a way, he proved his belief in magic was real. He found relics—items that defied understanding. The ring I wear now was forged with a gem taken from your very ring," he said, pointing at Asher. "And now I possess two gems."

Savio's confidence oozed as he continued, "A portion of your ring's power is with me. Hitler's discovery proved that magic exists and holds abilities beyond anything we've ever comprehended. Finding this ring among my grandfather's Nazi plunder has given me that same understanding. Magic is real, Asher, and I wield it."

Asher looked down for a moment, gathering his thoughts before locking eyes with Savio once more. "If my ring is more powerful than yours," he began calmly, "what makes you believe you can overpower

215

me?"

Savio, clearly eager to justify his obsession, launched into an explanation, but Asher wasn't fully listening. Out of the corner of his left eye, he spotted Carlos and Emily carefully peeking around the frame of the open back door. Catching their attention, Asher subtly raised his eyebrows and gave a slight jerk of his head toward Savio, signaling the pair to slip inside while their enemy remained distracted.

"I don't just believe I can overpower you, Asher. I know I will," Savio declared, his voice filled with dark confidence as he remained oblivious to Emily and Carlos stealthily slipping into the room. Raising his hand, he gestured toward the ring on his finger. "Yes, this is a powerful ring, but the gem it holds pales in comparison to the ancient magic contained in this one."

Savio lifted his opposite hand, displaying a golden ring shaped like two intertwined serpents, their eyes gleaming with an eerie light. He tapped it with a sinister grin, the weight of his words hanging heavily in the air. "This is true power, Asher. A power that not even your enchanted trinkets can stand against."

Asher's eyes narrowed, unsure of the significance of the ring, but his expression remained composed. He noted Savio's arrogance, the gleam of triumph already in his eyes. If he could keep him talking a little longer, Carlos and Emily might have the opening they needed.

Savio's monologue took him a few steps away from the helpless Annabel and closer to Asher. You probably don't even realize the significance of this ring; it is ancient Egyptian, a Heka, the god of magic. Hitler and his party learned of its ability and magic when it was discovered amongst the treasures of the pharaohs. Nazi scientists and archeologists discovered that the heka's magical abilities were neither evil nor good, only magical.

Asher noted Emily crouching low and approaching the back of Annabel's chair. Carlos remained behind, hiding in the shadows, a few paces away from Savio.

Asher walked further from Annabel and closer to the wall to his left, hoping to draw Savio along with him. "What proof do you have that the ring or supposed Heka even worked? It's all just hearsay." Asher's voice was tinged with sarcasm.

"How do you think the Nazis were able to produce such superior weapons at such a rapid pace? Savio's tone was harsh and agitated. "The use of the one-gem ring and the Heka ring helped them see the technology of the future, and they attempted to replicate what they had witnessed in those enchanted visions." Savios stepped and closed the gap between him and Asher. "Their biggest blunder," he continued, "was not knowing how to wield such power; otherwise, the outcome of the war would have been much different. Fortunately for me, the ring made it my way via my Nazi grandfather." a sinister grin stretched across Savio's face, "And my power continues to grow daily as I learn its abilities.:

Time was slipping away, and Asher knew they had to act swiftly. "Carlos, now!" he shouted.

Carlos sprang from the shadows like a lion pouncing on its prey. "What the—?" Savio muttered in surprise, whipping his head just in time to see Carlos lunging toward him. Without hesitation, Savio raised both hands, crossing his left wrist over his right in an "X" formation. Carlos collided with an invisible barrier mid-air, crumpling to the ground unconscious.

Savio's eyes narrowed as he twisted his head to the right, his gaze landing on Emily, who was frantically untying Annabel. "So, there you are, Emily," he thundered, his voice dark and menacing.

Emily froze, her eyes locking with Savio's intense glare. Her hands trembled as she stood upright, abandoning her desperate effort to free Annabel. Fear surged through her, but she knew she couldn't falter—not now.

It was at that moment, with Savio's back turned, that Asher tackled him to the floor, sending both men crashing down in a cloud of dust. Savio reacted swiftly, driving his elbow sharply into Asher's gut, forcing a painful grunt from him. Winded but undeterred, Asher's resolve to defeat Savio burned stronger. With a surge of adrenaline, Asher delivered a solid blow to the back of Savio's head, sending the black-cloaked figure sprawling motionless on the floor, his hands curled limply in front of him.

Without wasting a second, Asher lurched forward, seizing Savio's hand. He gripped the Heka ring tightly and yanked it off with a sharp pull, sending the twisted gold serpent ring skidding across the floor and out of sight.

But Savio wasn't finished yet. Pulling his knees under him, he pushed himself upright and lunged at Asher, sending him tumbling backward. It was then that Savion noted the Heka just steps away. Dashing over, Savio grasped the Heka and held it tightly in his hand. "So, you're a fighter, are you?" Savio sneered, pulling something from a leather sheath at his side.

Asher raised both hands defensively, trying to reason with him. "Savio, it doesn't have to be like this!"

But Savio's eyes gleamed with cold fury. "It's too late for that!" he shouted, leaping forward, thrashing wildly in a desperate attempt to remove Asher's ring. The moment Savio's hand touched Asher's ringed finger, searing pain erupted under the master ring, the metal vibrating violently. Savio gritted his teeth, grabbed Asher by the wrist, and slammed his hand hard against the floor.

A sharp crack echoed through the room as the impact knocked two of the gems loose from the master ring. The stones clattered onto the floor, their magical energy flickering in dim pulses. Asher winced but fought to maintain control, his vision clouding as the power from the remaining gems surged unevenly through him.

Savio's eyes widened, sensing his advantage. "Without all the stones, your ring is nothing!" he spat, lunging for Asher's ring and gripping it tightly. Asher felt the icy pull of defeat as the ring edged off his finger, scraping painfully against his skin. The world around him spun; the once vibrant sounds of the room faded, now distant and hollow. His vision blurred, and his strength drained, leaving him paralyzed under Savio's relentless assault. But as the ring slipped past his knuckle, Asher shut his eyes, focusing every ounce of willpower into a single, desperate thought: Fight. Hold on.

The master ring vibrated faintly, responding to his mental plea. Savio growled in frustration, yanking harder, but the ring resisted, glowing fiercely.

Suddenly, the room erupted in the brightest light Asher had ever seen. Even with his eyes shut, he squeezed them tighter in response. His body instantaneously felt rejuvenated, his soul invigorated. A sharp crack reverberated through the room, echoing in his chest. Just as quickly as the light had come, it vanished, and the weight of Savio lifted from him.

Asher cracked open his eyes to see Annabel and Emily kneeling beside him, their trembling hands resting on his, the master ring pulsing like a strong, rhythmic heartbeat. "What just happened?" Emily muttered, her voice tinged with confusion. Annabel glanced around, her heartbeat pounding in her ears, trying to match her rapid breathing.

Asher sat up cautiously, their hands still resting on his. Glancing to his right, he saw Savio lying motionless, face-up, arms stretched out on either side. His lifeless figure seemed faded like an old flannel shirt washed too many times; its vibrancy drained away.

With his free hand, Asher gently squeezed the hands resting on his. Catching Annabel's gaze, he leaned in and pressed his lips to hers in a delicate kiss, embracing the depth of his love for her. He then turned to Emily, offering a soft smile before closing his eyes and bowing his head in silent gratitude for her help.

"Can someone explain what just happened? I'm a little lost," Emily said, her brow furrowed. "One minute, Annabel and I were racing over to stop Savio from pulling your ring off, and the next thing I know, he's lying over there, and we're here, kneeling beside you, all our rings touching." She lifted her hand, inspecting her ring.

In unison, Annabel and Asher brought their hands closer to their eyes, joining Emily in examining their rings. "Looks the same as before," Annabel remarked.

"Mine too," Emily added, holding her hand higher to catch the light from the window.

Asher grasped his ring with his opposite hand and slowly rotated it, inspecting each stone. "Mine is decidedly different," he said in a hushed tone.

Both Annabel and Emily dropped their hands, their eyes locking onto Asher's ring.

"Look," Asher said, rolling the ring around his finger for them to see. "Notice anything different?"

His onlookers were silent, unsure of what to say.

"It's restored. All the gems have reunited. The master ring is whole once again," Asher said, twisting the ring. Its enchanted gems flickered majestically, casting vibrant colors across his hand. Both Annabel and Emily stared at the ring, captivated by the glowing gems pulsing with life.

"It must have happened when all of our rings touched Savio's one-gemmed ring," Asher added instinctively.

Just then, something caught Annabel's eye. "Look!" she shouted, pointing toward the motionless Savio lying nearby.

Asher and Emily turned just in time to witness Savio's body fade, becoming more translucent before vanishing completely in swirling dust. His precious gold ring dropped to the floor, spinning to a halt.

"Did I just see what I think I saw?" Carlos asked, stepping out from the back of the room rubbing the back of his head. "I must have really taken a hit," he muttered, rubbing his head again. His eyes widened as he pointed behind them. "Who are all these people, and where did they come from?"

The trio turned to find nine men standing in a semicircle behind them, each dressed in robes from different eras. To the far right stood a slender man in a scarlet robe, a sparse white beard framing his face. He held a shepherd's cane intricately carved with designs that mirrored those on Asher's ring. Beside him stood a short, stocky man in leather sandals and a dark green tunic that fell to his knees. His thick black beard was streaked with silver. Each man to the left wore attire from a time long past, but it was the two men at the far left who caught Asher's attention: Kristoff and Corbit Hayes, dressed in an early 1900s Santa suit.

This gathering of Santas, all who had once held the title, now stood united before them, surrounded by an aura of magical energy. They gazed down at the small Santa Order in front of them with admiration and approval.

"It's a rare sight to see us all together, Joseph Amesbury," Kristoff said, addressing Asher by his true name. "This night was long prophesied— a vision showed me someone you knew would try to take your ring. This is the prophecy I speak of, known since the gem was lost from the master ring." The Santas exchanged knowing glances, nodding in agreement. "Emily was under an evil curse," Kristoff said, his voice somber. "Someone you had known in the past; she was the one mentioned in the prophecy. Yet, her being controlled by evil through Savio's influence wasn't clear, making the prophecy difficult to interpret."

Kristoff's voice trailed off, the weight of his words lingering in the air

"So, was it the rings touching that vanquished Savio?" Asher asked, his question hanging in the air.

Corbit Hayes spoke next, his voice deep and scratchy yet calm and piercing. His kind eyes, a mix of cool blue and shades of gray, met Asher's. "It wasn't just the rings touching that created the magic," Corbit explained. "It was the love within Annabel's ring, her love for you, that overpowered the evil, weakening Savio and his magic. Once Emily's hand joined hers, the three rings—united in friendship and the Santa order—formed a portal that allowed us to enter."

"At that moment, unseen to you, we rushed to your side and placed our hands on the master ring," added the short, stocky man on the right.

"The magic in all of us, combined with your rings touching the lost gem, reminded it of its true loyalty, and it returned to its rightful place in the master ring—like the prodigal son coming home," said the 17th-century Santa in the center, his long white beard braided and tied with a golden string.

Kristoff stepped away from the semicircle of men, bent down, gathered up the crumpled spectacles, wadded up the remaining strings of Mr. Baggins, and then retrieved Savio's gold band, which was left behind. "Nothing but earth's precious ore in this band of gold," he said, holding it up for all to see. "Something should be done about that." He gestured toward Asher. "You three, please stand."

Pointing to Asher, he continued, "Open your hand." Asher did so, and Kristoff placed the ring inside, folding Asher's fingers over it, encapsulating the ring inside. "Now, both of you," he addressed Annabel and Emily, "place your hands with your mortality rings on his."

Annabel and Emily followed his instructions, placing their hands gently over Asher's. "Very good, now repeat after me," Kristoff instructed. In unison, the three repeated:

"Three rings of gold, both powerful and old,

Your magic is needed now.

Our desire is pure, and he's a friend for sure,

Will you grant immortality for one more?"

Inside Asher's hand, the gold band vibrated excitedly, tickling his palm. He turned his hand over and opened it, revealing a polished gold ring adorned with intricate carvings that matched the rings of the Santa Order.

"Carlos, you look to be about a size ten, if I'm not mistaken?" Asher asked, a smile stretching across his face.

"I am, Asher. How did you know?" Carlos replied, standing up and approaching his friends.

"Let's see how we did. Hold out your finger for sizing," Asher said.

As he slipped the ring over Carlos's knuckle, he spoke, "With this ring of immortality, we welcome you to the Santa Order, with the blessing of sustained life upon the earth—until the day you choose to remove it."

Carlos felt a surge of energy course through his veins, the pain from his altercation with Savio dissipating instantly. For the first time in his life, Carlos was part of something special—a group of friends, a family. "So this is what it feels like," he said, his voice cracking. "To be wanted, to be loved, to be part of a family." He wiped a tear with his sleeve.

Emily wrapped her arm around his waist and pulled him close. "You are wanted Carlos, and you are needed," she said, her cheeks flushing.

The nine Santa-robed men reformed their semicircle, smiling at the group of four embracing one another. Kristoff stepped forward, holding the lifeless Guinevere, Savio's Heka ring, and the wadded ball of string that had once been the magical Mr. Baggins. He approached Asher slowly.

"Hold out your hands," Kristoff said reverently.

The moment Kristoff laid Guinevere and Mr. Baggins in Asher's palms, the Santas gathered in closer, encircling them both. The room lit up with a brilliant green hue as sparks of gold and yellow swirled around the bent brass glasses and the unraveled ball of string. With a loud crack, the light faded, and Asher found himself holding a soft velvet bag and a shiny pair of brass spectacles with crystal-clear lenses.

"Well, it's about time I got a facelift! All these years with foggy lenses and worn brass frames, and it took all nine of you to do it! What can I say more than—it's about time!" Guinevere chimed in, vibrating in Asher's hand, her tone full of sass.

The velvet bag stirred to life floated up, and performed an aerial loop before bowing in gratitude to the nine men. Kristoff stepped forward, holding the Heka ring up to the bag's opening. "Why don't you hold onto this and keep it safe?" he said, gently placing the ring inside. With a renewed sense of purpose, the soft, confident bag floated down and tucked itself securely beneath Asher's belt.

"We have witnessed friends restored and a new bond forged in the rings of the Santa Order," Kristoff said as the nine men slowly faded from view.

29

Beautiful Magic

C an you believe it's been almost four months since Savio's attack?" Asher remarked as Carlos adjusted his bowtie.

"I know, it's hard to believe it's been that long. So much has happened in such a short time. There, how's that?" Carlos said, snugging the tie close to Asher's neck.

Asher glanced in the mirror and tilted the black bowtie slightly upward on the right side. "Perfect. Thanks, Carlos. I've never been able to figure out how to tie one of these. Where'd you learn?" Asher asked, combing his thick black hair for what felt like the twentieth time that morning.

"Well, working for Savio, he sent me on a few heists that required me to 'blend in' with the crowd, so to speak. Those assignments, plus a few YouTube tutorials, did the trick," Carlos chuckled. "Glad those days are far behind me now."

Asher turned and gave Carlos's bowtie a playful tug to the left. "You almost had it centered," he said with a grin, returning the favor.

"So, are you nervous?" Asher shook his head."No, I don't feel nervous. I'm more excited than nervous, to be honest." Asher tapped his ring finger, then locked eyes with Carlos. "Did you bring it?"

Carlos reached down and tapped his tuxedo pant pocket and gave a tap to the small box inside. "Yep, I have it, and I'm keeping it good and safe," Carlos said, beaming.

Since the time the master ring had been restored, Asher and Carlos had developed a deep friendship between them. Perhaps it was the long nights talking with him or the moment Carlos risked his life to stop Savio. Whatever the reason had been, Carlos and Asher had become close friends and enjoyed working together in the Santa Order. On an occasion when Annabel was unable to attend events with Asher, Carlos stepped in and found joy in visiting several children's hospitals and charity events with Asher. Providing service for others in need helped him recover from years of forced service to Savio.

"Do you ever wonder about..." Carlos stopped his question midsentence.

"Do I wonder about what?" Asher probed.

Carlos looked down at the floor, paused for a moment, then looked back at Carlos. Do you think back on the night you invited me to the Santa Order and wonder about those nine men? What are they doing now in the next life, and what were their experiences and adventures here in mortality?

"From what Kristoff told me, he, Lorelei, and the previous Santa Order are now in a place of rest, free from their responsibilities and cares. They've been reunited with family and friends in a realm without pain or affliction. He said it was more beautiful than words could describe."

"It sounds incredible," Carlos said softly, his voice tender as he reflected on the afterlife. "Comforting to know that life continues beyond this world."

"As for their time as Santas, their adventures are all recorded and bound in leather books, stored in the hidden room of the Santa Order house. I'm especially curious about Corbit Hayes. I was down there just last week and took a peek at his book. He served during the Civil War and World War I. You know how much I love history—this is going to be an exciting read." Asher's voice brimmed with excitement.

Carlos smiled wider, his eyes lighting up. "Your enthusiasm is contagious. Maybe I'll get a chance to read that book after you."

Asher chuckled and nodded. "Of course, after I'm done with it."

He stepped away from the mirror where he'd been adjusting his tie and walked over to a bouquet of twenty-four red roses interspersed with delicate baby's breath. Bending down, he inhaled their scent. "These are perfect," Asher said, his voice soft and affectionate. "Annabel deserves the best."

Asher had become even more devoted to Annabel since the day she was kidnapped by Savio. The moment she was taken from him, reality hit hard, and he knew he never wanted to be without her again. From that point on, everything he did for her was with the full purpose of heart. With every compliment, every bouquet of flowers, and every door he opened for her, he made sure she felt important and loved. He wanted her to never question his loyalty to their relationship, to always feel like royalty in his presence. As each day passed, their bond grew stronger, with Asher continually putting her needs before his own. In return, his affection was deeply appreciated and reciprocated, leaving him feeling both adored and needed.

Today was the long-awaited day—the day Annabel and Asher would finally become one in unity, bound by the blessing of marriage. Having led lives of secrecy within the Santa Order, both had been forced to sever any remaining ties with the outside world. With no extended family, the wedding would be small and simple. But for Asher and Annabel, it wasn't about the crowd—it was about making sacred promises to one another, sealed in matrimony.

Pipe organ music interrupted the conversation, signaling to Asher and Carlos that the moment had arrived.

"Well, my dear friend Carlos, this is the moment I've been looking forward to for a long time. Let's go meet the girls in the chapel." Asher said, grabbing the roses and opening the door to the hallway.

Stepping into the small white wooden chapel, the pews were devoid of friends or family. For today's event, Carlos and Emily would serve as those most dear to Annabel and Asher. Annabel had formed a tight bond with Emily and had asked her to be her maid of honor. As for Carlos, it was easy to choose him as his best man; the two men had become incredibly close and shared many attributes.

The two men walked down the aisle toward the chaplain standing behind a pew. A temporary vibrant white wooden arch had been set up for the day, trimmed with lively flowers. It wasn't until Asher and Carlos approached the front of the chapel that Asher noticed two of his faithful confidants sitting on the first pew.

"Looking very good today, Mr. Baggins," Asher said with a warm smile. Resting on top of the bag was the magnificent Guinevere. Her lenses were clear, and her polished brass arms reflected the sunlight streaming through the stained glass.

"Oh, Miss Guinevere, you look dazzling today. I couldn't be happier than to have you both with us," Asher said, reaching over to pat Mr. Baggins and his brass spectacles.

Turning to the pew in front of him, Asher's face flushed red when he noticed the chaplain staring at him, slightly perplexed.

"I guess it's not every day you see a man talking to a pair of glasses and a velvet bag," Asher admitted, his voice tinged with embarrassment.

The chaplain nodded his head. "No, I can't say I've ever seen that. Now, if they had talked back to you, that would have been something to discuss." Asher and Carlos shared a half-suppressed chuckle. The old chaplain had no idea how spot-on he was about talking glasses.

"Ah, there we are," the white-haired chaplain said, holding his hand outward and presenting Annabel.

Asher turned around, his eyes widening and his mouth gaping open. Her beauty was majestic in every way. Never before had he beheld such grace and charm. She was a princess from a fairy tale, a treasure that only a fortunate reader could discover. Her magnificent, glowing white gown, adorned with intricate embroidery, complemented her hourglass figure as she sashayed down the aisle, approaching the mesmerized Asher.

Emily, in a radiant blue gown, locked arms with her best friend, beaming with pride. Carlos stared at Emily before meeting her gaze, coupled with a warm smile. Emily's cheeks flushed as she returned Carlos's smile, her heart swelling with affection for him after three months of serious dating.

The captivating women made their way to the front, where Emily let go of Annabel, and Asher clasped her hand, pulling her close to his side. Facing one another, Asher tenderly grasped her veil, letting it fall gracefully over the back of her head. Her beauty was flawless, her expression warm and caring. Asher felt his heart race and his hands moisten as he looked deeply into her eyes.

"This is really it," Asher said in a soft, tender voice. Annabel beamed, her soft, glowing lips stretching into an innocent smile that reflected her inner soul. "It is happening, Asher, and I couldn't be happier than I am at this very moment." Her tone was gentle, the love in every word palpable.

"Emily, please stand to the right of Annabel. Carlos, please take your place to the left of Asher, just over there," the chaplain instructed. "Now, I will ask this lovely couple to turn and face me. Please take each other by the hand."

As Asher held her hand, he couldn't help but feel an overwhelming love and respect for the woman who had stood by his side for so many years. Her devotion, her laughter, her tender voice—all the ways she made him laugh and turned even his worst days into something bearable with her soft touch and gentle smile. Now, it was real. She was his forever.

"Asher, your response—a simple 'yes' or 'I do'—will suffice." Asher was so lost in his bride's beauty that his admiration caused his mind to wander. He knew his answer and understood what the chaplain was asking. "Yes, I do, and I would do it a million times over." His response made Annabel giggle, for she knew Asher had let his mind drift. This was the man she loved—the man she had worked with late into the night at the Gazette. A man, any father, would be proud to have his daughter marry.

"I do," came Annabel's words, filling Asher's chest with a warmth he couldn't explain. It felt good, it felt right, and he sensed divine hands were guiding their union in matrimony.

"With your words of affirmation sealed with his, I now pronounce you husband and wife. Asher, you may now kiss your lovely bride."

Asher leaned in and pressed his lips softly against hers, sealing their matrimony in a symbol of love. Emily stretched her hand forward with a small red pillow, which held both Annabel's and Asher's rings.

"Exchanging rings," the chaplain said. "Don't keep her waiting, son; you should really kiss her again." The group joined in with a hearty laugh as Asher stole another kiss while the organ music played once more.

As Asher began to escort Annabel back down the aisle, he paused, reaching over to grab Mr. Baggins, tucking him under his belt, and gently placing Guinevere on his nose. "I thought so," Asher said, beaming.

"What? What do you see?" Annabel asked, curious.

Asher slipped the brass glasses off his nose and handed them to Annabel. "Here, put them on and see for yourself."

"But these won't work for me," Annabel suggested.

"Just put them on," Asher instructed gently.

Slipping the brass handles over her ears, green and red magical vapors swirled in the lenses. Annabel gasped. "Where did they all come from? Look! It's Kristoff and the eight others that showed up that night we fought Savio."

"They were here the entire time. We were never alone," Asher said, his voice full of emotion.

"The entire chapel is packed! Who are all the others smiling at us?" Annabel asked, handing Guinevere back to Asher.

"They are all who have served in the Santa Order throughout Earth's history—our extended family, you might say." Asher's voice was filled with pride as he placed Guinevere back in his pocket.

"Why is it that I can see the magic through Guinevere's lenses now?" Annabel questioned, her eyes wide with wonder.

"It's because you are now Mrs. Claus," Asher replied, his tone brimming with love.

"Mrs. Claus... I think I do like the sound of that name," Annabel said, a twinkle in her eye.

As Asher and Annabel reached the back chapel doors, Asher halted and instructed Annabel to look back at the wooden arch they had just walked away from. She turned and watched as Carlos reached into his pocket and retrieved a small square box, then knelt on one knee before Emily. Though they couldn't hear the words spoken, Emily's reaction—falling into Carlos's arms, followed by a passionate kiss—was all the answer they needed.

"I think you once said it best, Asher," Annabel grinned. "There is beautiful magic in the rings of the Santa Order."

THE END

www.ingramcontent.com/pod-product-compliance
Lightning Source LLC
Chambersburg PA
CBHW050313110726
47899CB00007B/2223